Predator or Prey...?

"She looks just fine to me," Jace answered.

Her heart raced, and for a moment, she felt a strange surge of something that wasn't quite fear.

Something wilder, almost…dangerous.

A low growl began to form in her throat as she slowly widened her stance, clenching her fists.

"Hey retard patrol! Back the fuck off!"

The voice cut through the hallway like the thunderclap of a bullwhip.

The clutch of bodies parted, scattering as if stung by angry wasps, and Ellie's breath caught in her throat.

Also by LeGivorden

Left Hand Path & Occult Literature

The Satanic Testament

The Black Grimoire

The Red Grimoire

The Satanic Priest's TOP SECRET Manual

The Bible of Cthulhu

Fiction Writings

Gothos: Dark Awakening

A Bad Moon

One Evil Christmas

A BAD MOON II
CRIMSON DREAMS

LEGIVORDEN

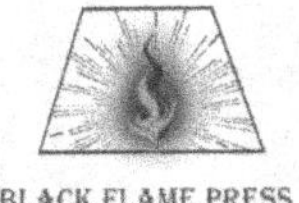

BLACK FLAME PRESS

A Bad Moon 2: Crimson Dreams
By Lucifer LeGivorden

ISBN: 978-1-0692681-7-4
Imprint: Black Flame Press

A Bad Moon 2 by Lucifer LeGivorden
Artwork by Lucifer LeGivorden

Printed in the United States of America
First Edition Printing:
10 9 8 7 6 5 4 3 2 1

Hate your enemies with a whole heart, and if a man smite you on one cheek, SMASH him on the other! He who turns the other cheek is a cowardly dog!

Ragnar Redbeard: Might is Right—1896

PROLOGUE

The Millar Meteor's sirens shrieked through the morning light like a wounded animal as its lights painted the early morning fog with blood red flashing strokes.

The Ambulance careened down the winding mountain road, threatening to take flight into nothingness with each turn.

"Stay with me. Miss? Can you hear me? I need you to stay with me."

The paramedic's hands pressed against her stomach, warm and sticky. The copper stench of her blood filled her nostrils.

So much copper. So much blood. Her blood.

"Miss?! I need you to wake up. Come on, sweety, stay with me!" he sounded urgent. Like he really wanted her to stay awake.

Why should she? She was already floating somewhere between conciousness and the void.

Hadn't she been awake long enough?

The poison spreading like black fire in her veins. How utterly ironic. Her body heals itself, but she's still going to die because of a little silver. Typical…

"We interrupt our regular programming with breaking news from Pinecrest, Tennessee.…"

She watched the flashing of trees blur past the window. It was so stupid. She'd made it. She'd survived…

Her eyes rolled, and the world spun as her heart beat like thunder in her skull.

Thump-thump. Thump-thump.

"BP's dropping fast!"

"We're losing her!"

Moonlight. She was running in the moonlight. Something behind her in the darkness, breathing heavily, hunting.

Hunting what? Her?

Thump-thump. Thump-thump.

"Jesus Christ, what did she get into out there?"

No, not just her… Her heart?

Their voices seemed to come from underwater.

She tried to speak, tried to tell them about the

thing hunting her, but her tongue felt thick and foreign.

"...two teenagers and an as of yet unidentified third victim have been found dead at the Pinecrest dam, their bodies horribly mutilated in what authorities are calling a vicious attack..."

Thump-thump. Thump-thump.

Not her heart. God, not again!

Thump-thump. Thump...Thump.

He was on her. Thrusting and pushing.

Thump...Thump...Thump...Thump.

His face, Rick's face...

Thump...Thump...Thump...Thump.

But it's not him... He didn't have yellow eyes or black fur...

Thump...Thump...Thump...Thump.

The beast reared back, and a blood-curdling howl of triumph ripped from its maw, as a warmth filled her...

Thump...Thump... Thump-thump... Thuh-thump, Thuh-thump!

"NO!" she screamed, arching as waves of agony split her again.

"Jesus Christ! Hold her! HOLD HER!"

She suddenly felt as much as heard a loud cracking in her. What was that?

She writhed and squirmed, fighting the straps as a fresh wave of white fire filled her guts, spreading to every inch of her body.

Thuh-thump, Thuh-thump, Thuh-thump!

Yellow eyes glimmering in the firelight.

"It's coming!" a voice says, her voice.

The flames flared suddenly higher, the shadows moved wrong. Too big… Too many teeth.

"I see a bad moon rising!"

The music. Why was that playing?

The sound of tires screaming, or was that us? She couldn't tell, all she knew was the black hand reaching for her.

Thuh-thump, Thuh-thump, Thuh-thump!

The ambulance doors burst open. Cold air rushed in, the antiseptic stench filled her nostrils. She really hated that smell.

Where am I?

Fluorescent lights blazed overhead like artificial suns, burning her retinas.

No! Why am I here? Not again! Don't take my baby!

"We have a teenage female with multiple perforating stab wounds to her stomach and severe lacerations to her body!"

Thuh-thump, Thuh-thump, Thuh-thump!

Wheels rattled beneath her. Ceiling tiles flew past in a blur of white and beige. She counted them. One. Two. Three… Four

Jessica. Mark. Tina… David.

David!

Thuh-thump, Thuh-thump, Thuh-thump!

His face in hers, spittle flecking his lips as he slams home the silver knife into her again and again, like Rick.

God, and she was letting him do it to her.

"Is this an animal attack or a mugging?" someone asks.

Thuh-thump, Thuh-thump, Thuh-thump!

NO! Not again! Never again! Fight! Fight! Fight!

A sound like the splitting of thunder fills her head. A roar. Her roar!

"Tina!" she screams. "Where's Tina?!"

"…At this time, one survivor has been confirmed, while two additional victims are believed to still be missing. According to sources, five local teenagers had gone to the Cherokee National Forest for a camping trip…"

Thuh-thump, Thuh-thump, Thuh-thump!

The metal operating table was cold and hard against her back as she was lifted onto it.

Hard, unforgiving hands grabbed at her clothes, cutting and tearing feverishly.

Ripping away what dignity she had left, what little she had regained through blood.

"No! Get off of me!" she screamed, thrashing against the hands. *His* hands.

"Holy shit! Sedate her! Sedate her now!"

Thuh-thump. Thuh-thump. Thuh-thump!

Her hand closed on something soft and squishy, and a scream of agony tore through her skull.

"Get her off me!" a woman's voice yelped as she twisted the mound of supple flesh.

The needle slid into her arm like a snake's fang. Cold liquid rushed through her veins, carrying her deeper into the abyss.

"Try to relax," the voice came again. "It'll be over before you know it," Cold and clinical. "Count backwards from ten…"

NO! Not that! Not again!

"Ten… nine… eight…"

"…The victims have been identified as Jessica Laurens, age 16, Mark McMahon, age 18, Ellinor Granger, age 16, Christina Akins, age 17, and David Varano, age 17…"

Thump-thump. Thump-thump. Thump-thump.

Pain! Again! Why more pain? Hasn't she suffered enough?

She wanted to keep screaming, but the darkness was creeping in... pulling her under.

Thump-thump. Thump-thump. Thump-thump.

"Jesus, is she pregnant? Where's this blood coming from?"

"No, she's just menstruating!"

Thump-thump. Thump-thump.

"Are you sure? I've never seen so much!

"Seven..."

Thump-thump. Thump-thump.

Shame flooded through her, hot and thick as the warmth spreading from her loins.

Even here, even bleeding out, she couldn't escape the embarrassment of being female, being human, of being... whole again.

But why? Why was she embarrassed? She was whole. Shouldn't that be a good thing?

Thump-thump. Thump-thump.

"Get me more suction. And someone explain these black lines around the wounds."

"Six..."

Thump-thump. Thump-thump.

Someone swabbed her wound. The cotton came away a dark, glittering purple in the light.

"Looks like some kind of heavy metal poisoning. Christ, it's oxidizing the tissues!"

"What the hell is that? Silver?"

Remember, mon cheri, silver to the heart. Don't hesitate. Came the old man's voice.

Thump-thump.

"Authorities speculate that the teens entered the park yesterday evening near Pinecrest, Tennessee, where a wild animal, possibly a bear, began hunting the group through the forest.

A bear? If only it had been something so simple. So explainable.

"Five…"

The operating room doors slammed open. A woman's voice, shrill with panic, cut through her darkness, "Ellie!"

She tried to turn her head, tried to see through the observation window, slowly willing her neck to obey.

Thump-thump.

"Mama?"

"Four…"

"…authorities have now confirmed that they have recovered a second survivor…"

A second? Who? Who else had made it out?

Thump… thump.

"Three…"

The doctor's voice, professional and tired, "Ma'am, your daughter is going to be just fine."

Fine? How could she ever be fine again? How could any of them?

She drifted floating between the worlds of life and death. The blackness closing over her like the terrible blanket of darkness.

Thump… thump.

Then it came. Softly through the encroaching darkness. A voice. *Her voice.*

"Tina?"

Golden red locks flashed through the window as everything went dark.

"One…"

Thump…thump.

Everything but that musical single voice in her universe faded into oblivion.

A single word whispered in the darkness, reaching out to her from the abyss.

Sister…

CHAPTER 1

We run. Through the shadowed and chilled darkness of the forest, we run. The smell of pine and autumn fills our lungs, embracing us in our freedom.

Tonight we did it, we changed without the moon! It's only been a month, and we figured it out!

The joy in our heart is beyond measure as we run under the light of the waxing moon. Soon. Soon it will be fat and full, and we will be ready. It will still hurt, but not like last time. No. Not the agony.

We remember that pain. The suffering as every bone cracked and shattered. As our face reshaped itself.

Tonight was still horrible, but we were ready this time. It hurt beyond comparison, yet we managed to maintain our focus through it. To not give in to the beast and instead embrace it.

We will change every night, teach ourselves not to suffer but to ride the storm of transformation.

To embrace the beast and make it one with ourselves. And then we will teach them. The others.

We will hunt and bring them to us. Embrace them as the forest embraces us now.

We will be patient, however. We must wait for them to call to us of their own desire. And when they do, we will come. We will descend upon them and embrace them as their brother, their lover, their protector.

The stench of chlorine assaults our senses, cutting through the sweet, musty scent of earth and pine.

We hate it, it burns our nose and makes our eyes water, yet we endure it. We follow it, for it blends with something else. The faint musk of one of them. Could they be there? So close? We must see. We must find them and look upon them with our yellow night eyes.

The rhythmic lapping of water against a hard edge pulses through our ears, a hypnotic backdrop to the steady thumping of a heart beating.

It's not theirs.

We remember their hearts from before. When we had watched silently as they slew the black monster on the dam.

We watched in horror as one fell into the churning waters, and the other continued to fight even as we smelled the coppery reek of her life fading. We remember the terror we felt at the thought of being alone.

But we howled with joy when we watched them rise and live. We're not alone. Or we won't be much longer.

Soon. So soon the moon will be full, and we will go to them and make them ours, and we will run and hunt as one with them by our side.

But for now, we must deal with this. We can smell them so close, but not here. But there is one here that is too close. Her scent here is strong, but she isn't here. Yet *he* is in her range.

He cannot be tolerated in her range. Her range is *our* range. He is a threat that we must rend from existence and show her we can protect her.

Blue light ripples across the yard, casting eerie patterns as luminescent steam rises from the heated pool.

The light glints off the water's surface in

small flashes, hurting our eyes, but we cannot look away from him. We watch. We wait.

The moment stretches into minutes. There is no rush.

He floats on his back, bronzed skin glistening wetly beneath the pool lights. His well-muscled chest rising and falling gently with each breath. We know him. The others look at him as an Adonis. Not that it matters now. Now he is just prey.

Music drifts faintly from the house. He is alone and in the open. Our claws dig into the soft earth as we watch him, surveying the area.

No one else was close enough to hear or even help. Only the distant sounds of cars passing on the main road and a stray dog slinking away into the shadows.

It knows its role when its betters are about.

He is ours. We need him. His flesh. His sinew. His blood.

The stink of old whiskey perfumes the air, masked by the chemical stink of the fouled water. The fool, his senses dulled he is oblivious to the peril that now rests upon him.

He pauses his floating, head lifting slightly.

"Hello?" he calls out to the darkness.

Water ripples around him as he treads in place, scanning the darkness beyond the light of the water. He senses us.

We feel something in us. A respect? The quarry is not as much of a fool as we thought, perhaps?

"Kyle? Jace? That you guys?"

We freeze in place as he looks directly at us. Can he see us? Our eyes shining in the light of the luminescent water?

"Come on, guys. Who's out there? Stacy? You peeping on me again? You can get a better view up close, you know. Water's nice and warm."

He looks at the darkness for a while longer, then shrugs and returns to his floating. So much for not being a fool. The wise prey would feel his presence and know to run.

Anger boils in us. The stupid deserve no mercy. The red haze descends, and we surge forward to the edge of the water.

Perching there openly, we see our reflection distorted in the rippling blue surface.

It's curious to see ourselves there, silvery fur and golden eyes. Black lips pulled back over saber-like teeth and pink, mottled gums.

Let him see us. Let him see our accomplishment. Let him look in admiration and fear upon his doom.

He tenses. We can feel his sudden awareness of our presence. He plays possum. Knowing we won't strike until he looks. But we know he is aware of us.

His heart begins to hammer, and his breathing hitches. He knows his danger now.

We rise, towering to our full height. Should we be merciful and quick? No, let him see.

We let a soft growl escape us. His eyes snap open and bulge in horror as he looks up at us. His face twisting through the thousand expressions of abject terror.

We roar and surge into the water, dragging him under as he screams silently.

He kicks and thrashes in our grasp. The warm water feels good as it turns from luminous blue to a hellish crimson.

His fight isn't with us. He claws and kicks for the surface as we open his belly for the wet meat therein. He stops fighting and holds our head as we rend and rip. Lifting him to the surface.

He gasps for air with us and whimpers softly, but doesn't scream.

We see in his eyes the light fade, and we let him go to float peacefully in his red water.

Copper fills the air, mixing with the taint of chlorine and her. She is close, but where? We surge through the trees again, locking onto her musk. Following it.

There. The house is simple, white with brick. We stand at the edge of our realm and hers. We found her. Sleeping there, her scent clear through the open window.

We can smell her honey blonde hair, and her cool white flesh, heavy with our same wild tang.

Soon… Soon we will run in the moonlight.

From somewhere in the distance, we hear a woman screaming, and we smile.

It has begun.

CHAPTER 2

Ellie snapped awake, sitting bolt upright, gasping. Her eyes rolling in confusion and terror as early morning light streamed through the open window.

"What the hell was that?" she muttered, her heart jackhammering against her ribs.

Shuddering, she kicked off the tangled sheets and swung her legs over the side of the bed, trying to ground herself in the present.

It wasn't working.

She turned and flung the curtain wide, and gazed out into the morning light.

She stared hard at the woods across the field. What had she just seen? Whatever had been staring at her house was gone now.

But still, was that her?

It couldn't be. It wasn't the full moon yet, and she hadn't even had her first transformation.

Well, not that she was aware of anyway.

Yet the nightmare clung to her like the sweat soaked cotton of her nightshirt.

It had been all too visceral, bloody, and… real.

So much so, she could still taste the tang of copper on her tongue and smell chlorine in her nostrils.

"Cripes, you're losing it, Ellie," she said softly to herself.

Her bedroom felt stifling despite the late October breeze coming in from the window.

She crinkled her nose as she peeled the drenched nightshirt from her skin, tossing it into the hamper as she padded unashamedly across the hall to the bathroom.

She looked at her reflection above the sink, noting the perfect complexion and flawlessly toned body.

Another interesting perk of being infected with lycanthropy she supposed.

She snorted to herself softly. A month ago, she had just been a normal girl. Well, mostly normal.

A botched abortion had left her with a hysterectomy and the inability to get pregnant.

Which, if she was being honest with herself, would have been alright if she wanted to go running around with every guy in town.

Too bad that just wasn't her thing.

But a little scratch on the forehead from a werewolf had fixed that. She had bled like a fountain for three days straight.

Werewolves… who in the world would have believed it? She hardly did and here she was counting the days to the next full moon.

Along with regrowing her lost uterus, she could run like greased lightning, and her senses seemed to have been dialed up to ten.

Which was not always fun or pleasant.

Looking at herself now, she couldn't help but smile. What was cool was how she looked like a model in one of those fitness magazines.

Her stomach was washboard flat, with a full set of abs that made her look like she had spent months at the gym.

She was also notably taller. That was a mixed blessing.

Previously, she had only stood a rather charming five foot four inches.

After measuring herself last week, she realized she had sprouted a good four inches, bringing her to a towering five foot eight.

She'd be practically Amazonian if she grew any more.

Which was good because now she didn't need a footstool to get things off the top shelf.

After a quick shower that did little to wash away the lingering tension, she stood before her closet, deliberating the flip side of being taller.

The downfall of growing so rapidly was that she hadn't had time to update her wardrobe to her new proportions.

This, unfortunately, including all of her bras, which were now almost so comically childlike on her and so utterly uncomfortable, she had started forgoing even wearing them entirely.

She sighed in frustration. Today marked her first day back at Pinecrest High after a month's absence, and the thought of it made her stomach twist into knots.

And not being able to even wear a bra didn't help the situation any.

Finally, she selected a loose polo shirt with a baggy sweater and a modest plaid skirt.

The less attention she drew, the better. She wasn't sure she was ready to be catcalled in halls, and was determined to be mistaken for the most virginal of librarians in the world to avoid it.

She did a final check in the mirror and sighed halfheartedly.

It'll have to do. She thought as she made her way downstairs.

She found her mother unpacking yet another box in the kitchen.

Much to her chagrin, their house was still a maze of cardboard and discarded piles of packing tape, even though they had been living there for almost four months.

"Morning, honey!" her mother chirped with forced brightness. "Ready for your first day back?"

Ellie grunted an acknowledgment and made a beeline for the refrigerator, pulling out the orange juice and drinking directly from the carton.

"Ellie," her mother sighed, "we have glasses for a reason."

"Sorry," Ellie said, not feeling sorry at all. She wiped her mouth with the back of her hand and replaced the carton.

Her mother, Nancy Granger, was a rather attractive woman in her late thirties or perhaps forties.

Ellie wasn't quite sure, but was certain she didn't care.

What she did care about, and much to her annoyance, was the fact that her mother was wearing one of her favorite blouses tied well above her midriff along with one of her good sets of bell-bottoms.

"Mom, why are you wearing my clothes? You got an entire wardrobe of your own." She asked more harshly than she intended.

Her mother abandoned her unpacking and approached, her eyes scanning Ellie's face. "I know, but well, you weren't wearing it and I kinda wanted to try something new. How does it look?"

Ellie rolled her eyes as she went digging in the fridge. "Like you're aging backwards. Hey, where's all the meat?" she asked.

"You ate it all. Don't you remember?" her mother replied with an exasperated sigh.

"Guess that growth spurt of yours makes you pretty hungry. I swear I don't know how you pack it all away like that. Say, how you feeling, sweetheart? Any pain? Dizziness?"

"I'm fine, Mom," Ellie said, flashing her washboard abs.

"The doctor said I'm healed, remember?"

Her mother's face blanched at the sight of the perfect skin and toned muscles.

Not even a pink scar had been left. Not one single hint that only three weeks ago, she had been stabbed a dozen times and flayed alive across most of her body.

"I know! I know, but after everything that happened… well, can you blame me for being worried?"

"Right. Thanks, mom, but I don't want to talk about it. I gotta go or I'll be late, " Ellie cut her off sharply.

The *'everything'* hung between them like one of old Jacob Marley's chains.

"Well, at least let me drive you to school," she said, already reaching for her purse.

"No thanks. I'd rather walk." Ellie said curtly as she grabbed an apple from the fruit bowl, desperate to put something in her guts. "I need the fresh air."

Her mother's smile faltered. "Are you sure? It's no trouble…"

"Bye, Mom," Ellie called as she shouldered her backpack and headed out the back door.

"Catch you later," her mother grumbled,

staring after her as the door swung shut with a bang.

The crisp mountain air filled her lungs, cutting through the lingering dread from her nightmare.

Tilting her head, she decided to take a moment and jogged across the back field to the tree line where her dream had shown her.

She knew it was probably just her being paranoid, but then again, it wasn't paranoia if it was real. Was it?

It didn't take her long to find the spot. The stink of Chlorine and wet dog was pungent.

So it wasn't just a dream. Something really was watching me. She thought as she snorted and turned away, chuffing hard to clear the smell from her nostrils.

She walked out to the sidewalk and looked down the hill as the town of Pinecrest sprawled before her.

She supposed it was as picturesque as a small town could be. Nestled as it was at the foot of the Appalachians.

It had been meant to be their fresh start after her parents' divorce.

But she knew that, just like the divorce, it was

really about everything else that had happened.

About her…

Yeah, some fresh start. Since almost dying in a stupid abortion, it had been one thing after another.

Getting chased across half the state of Tennessee by a werewolf and almost murdered was like a bad punchline to an already bad year.

As she walked past the shops and small houses, she felt the countless unseen eyes tracking her movement.

She knew how small towns worked, before she was the new girl, a change to the endless familiar faces and mindless monotony common to places like this.

But now it was different, she wasn't just the new kid anymore. She was the survivor. The freak who lived when all her friends got ripped to shreds.

Well, her and *Tina*.

The story had been all over the local papers: "Teen Survivors Rescued," "Bear Attack Claims Three Lives," "Survivors or Suspects?"

Pinecrest High was an unremarkable brick building that seemed almost as intimidating as a medieval fortress. And twice as oppressive.

She honestly missed her old school, Holly-wood High.

At least there she'd known where she fit into the whole social structure, and didn't have to worry about what the rest of the students thought about her.

There was of course the typical mob of milling students around the main entrance, their laughter and chatter fading as Ellie approached.

She could practically feel the silence rippling outward like a stone dropped in a pond.

She kept her eyes down, using her hair as a curtain between herself and their stares.

Just make it to your locker, she told herself. *It's just one step at a time.*

The whispers followed her through the hallway like some morbidly soft chorus.

"Hey! Isn't that the chick?"

"Isn't she from LA?"

"She doesn't look like a bear attacked her."

"I heard it was actually some maniac and she killed him…"

"I heard she fed them all to the bear."

"How many points to bang Granger?"

"A thousand points if you can even get her number."

Ellie clenched her jaw and pushed forward, growling softly to herself.

She did her best to tune out the whispers. Not the easiest thing to do in a hallway that seemed deliberately designed to carry sound.

She swore that whomever the architect was, had been an unrepentant sadist who hated teens.

She managed to get to her locker without too much trouble. It was at the end of the hall in a small corner alcove that afforded her a bit of privacy from the main rush of teenage traffic.

Thank *God* for small mercies, right?

She had just spun the combination when she felt *them* approaching, the hair standing up on the back of her neck tingling as the stink of cheap *Love Baby Soft* perfume assaulted her nose.

"Well, my, my. Ellie Granger," came a syrupy sweet voice. "Welcome back, Hollywood."

Ellie turned and glanced at the group that had worked their way into her little alcove.

Ashley Varano, David's twin sister, though how they were twins baffled Ellie. They had looked nothing alike in her opinion.

Flanking her was Tiffany and Stacy, Ashley's perfunctory bimbo coattail riders who seemed to share a single personality. Air and hot air.

Flanking in next to Ellie, a large shape leaned up against the lockers, effectively cutting off any retreat she may have had.

As she turned, she was greeted by a living wall of muscle that seemed to tower over everything.

Slowly, she traced the contours of the living mountain until she looked up into the deceptively soft brown eyes of Kyle Thompson as he quietly looked down at her.

He was the star linebacker of Pinecrest's football team, nicknamed the Rhino.

And with the way his biceps strained against his sleeves, Ellie couldn't lie to herself, she liked what she saw.

She snapped herself out of her admiration and tensed. She knew a setup when she saw one.

Back in her old school of Hollywood High, she had been one of the resident Bees. The irony of having the script flipped here was not lost on her.

Ashley had made it clear that newcomers weren't welcome in her social circle, especially not ones who had hung around with her brother, however briefly.

"Thanks," Ellie replied flatly, turning back to her locker.

"Hey, ummm… We just want to tell you how relieved we are that you're alright. We were all pretty devastated to hear about what happened," Ashley continued, stepping closer.

There was something predatory in her movement that made the hair on Ellie's neck stand on end.

"Especially me. You know, with David and all. It must have been terrifying." Ashley said.

Ellie wrinkled her nose as the acidic stink radiated off her like heatwaves.

Great, this is going to be fun, she thought.

"Yeah, it was a real picnic," she managed, feeling cornered.

"So, hey Hollywood, we're all just a bit curious. What actually happened out there?" Jace asked, his smile not reaching his eyes.

"Because that bear attack story? Yeah, not buying it. And we figured you could fill us in."

"I don't remember much," Ellie lied.

She did more than remember. She spent half of the past month fighting off flashes of memories.

The endless running and screams. The horrible way Tina's eyes had bulged as she was violated by the beast. Or even more horribly, the look in her eyes when she turned…

Tiffany stepped forward, dropping the facade of friendliness. "Bullshit! David was ripped apart. And they found what was left of Mark up a tree. Bears don't do that."

"And somehow you and that bitch. Tina, make it out alive," Ashley added, her voice hardening. "Without a scratch, it seems."

The group started to close in, forming a tight semicircle that trapped Ellie against her locker.

"Yeah! What's the deal with that? I read she had been mauled and stabbed." Stacy asked.

"She looks just fine to me," Jace answered.

Her heart raced, and for a moment, she felt a strange surge of something that wasn't quite fear.

Something wilder, almost…dangerous.

A low growl began to form in her throat as she slowly widened her stance, clenching her fists.

"Hey retard patrol! Back the fuck off!"

The voice cut through the hallway like the thunderclap of a bullwhip.

The clutch of bodies parted, scattering as if stung by angry wasps, and Ellie's breath caught in her throat.

CHAPTER 3

It had been almost a month since they had been separated at the hospital, and in that time, Ellie had not had any chances to reconnect with Tina Akins.

But here she was now, and if Ellie had thought she had looked like a fitness model in the mirror, Tina was like some sort of Greek or Roman Goddess.

She stood there momentarily, framed by the morning's golden light that poured in through the hall's high windows.

Ellie had to admit, she couldn't have planned the pose better if she had tried.

Tina strode toward them, her strawberry-blonde hair pulled into a high ponytail that swung in tune with her hips with each stride.

She wore a white polo shirt and an almost obscenely short skirt that showed off legs that seemed longer than Ellie remembered, and knee-high go-go boots that clicked like a drill sergeants against the linoleum.

Ellie smiled wickedly. Gone was the popular, busty, carefree girl who had welcomed Ellie into her small clique of friends.

That Tina had died out there in the darkness of the woods. Ellie had watched the Beast murder her.

This Tina was a completely different type of animal. One that moved with all the lethal grace of a hunting predator.

However, it was her eyes that struck Ellie most, as they glittered like a pair of twin amber flecked sapphires.

She was a predator alright. A predator with the eyes of a *wolf*.

"You got a problem, Verano?" Tina asked, sliding beside Ellie with casual possessiveness.

Ellie smiled and stood up straighter, allowing herself to rise to her full height to loom over Tiffaney and Stacy, who blanched as they lifted their heads to look up suddenly at her.

Though impressive, her new height was nothing next to Tina's, which was further accentuated by her two-inch heeled go-go boots.

Ashley's composure wavered momentarily as she took in their near Amazonian stature.

It took her a moment before she managed to regain her composure.

"Just welcoming your girlfriend back to school," Ashley said with a sneer.

Tina's smile wasn't pleasant. It was a slow, dangerous curling of her lips that seemed to border on the edge of a snarl more than a smile.

"Aww… How thoughtful of you. Now, scat cat."

"You don't tell us what to do," Jace said, putting his face inches from hers

Tina leaned forward slightly, the deadly smile broadening seductively as her lips brushed his ear.

It wasn't much, and yet somehow, that tiny shift in posture seemed more threatening than if she'd raised a fist.

"I just did. Now git! Before I show your girlfriend here what kind of man you really are," she said huskily in his ear as she flicked her nails across the front of his jeans.

Jace jumped back, swatting her hand away with a scandalized look on his face.

"Crazy bitch! Fuck off!"

He grabbed Ashley, retreating hurriedly out of the alcove, as Tina let out a ripple of laughter.

Kyle chuckled and lifted his frame from the lockers.

He clapped a huge hand on Jace's shoulder. "Come on, guys. They ain't worth it, and we got class to get to."

His eyes flicked between Tina and Ellie.

There was something there in those soft brown eyes that Ellie couldn't quite name.

It wasn't uncomfortable, whatever it was, but Ellie wasn't certain she'd want to run into him alone.

Ashley, throwing one last venomous glare over her shoulder, allowed Jace to pull her away without another word.

A feat that looked almost physically painful for her to achieve.

"Later, lesbo freaks," Stacy hissed, flipping them off as she and Tiff trailed after the rest of the group, cackling.

Ellie sagged against her locker in relief as she let out her breath that she had been holding.

"You ok?" Tina asked, her voice softening.

Ellie nodded, "Yeah, I'm fine."

She let out a bark of laughter as she really

looked at Tina for the first time in a month.

"If you hadn't shown up, I was about to…"

Tina laughed in return, cutting her off, "Yeah, I know. But as much as I would love to watch you eat Ashley Varano's liver, we might want to try not doing that in school. I think cannibalism is sort of frowned upon around here, if you catch my drift."

She gave Ellie a mischievous smirk then added, "Though in the case of David's family, it might be an improvement. It certainly was for David!"

After a moment of quiet restraint, they exploded in giggles.

It was horrible, Ellie knew, to mock someone's death, but she honestly couldn't help it.

David had turned out to be a real self-serving bastard and total psychopath.

"You look... different," Ellie said after she had calmed herself down.

Tina laughed, a throaty sound that carried through the hallway.

"You mean I look hot? Yeah, that tends to happen when you're not a giant snarling monster," she said.

She spun once, golden bangles jingling on

her wrists, then eyed Ellie with a sly smile.

"You know, you don't look so bad yourself," she said.

"I love this whole college virgin thing you got going on here."

Ellie blushed, suddenly aware of how Tina was studying her.

"Yeah, I was trying to keep a low profile. Guess it sorta blew up in my face, didn't it?" she said.

Tina smiled and crinkled her nose at her, "Yeah, just a wee bit."

"Tina! Oh my god, Tina!" a bright voice called out.

A cute Asian girl with long black hair bounced her way through the crowd into Ellie's once quiet little alcove.

Haily Mako had been one of Tina's close friends from before… Well, before everything changed.

She was the very personification of cuteness. If such a thing could be personified, that is.

According to Haily herself, it was called being *kawaii*.

"I was so worried when I heard you were back! Are you ok? Is everything…"

Haily's voice trailed off as her gaze fell on Ellie.

"Hollywood!" she squealed and practically crushed Ellie in a tiny bear hug.

Ellie wasn't particularly fond of the nickname bestowed upon her by the now late David Varano, *may he rot*, but had grown accustomed to it.

"Thanks," Ellie said, unsure how to take the girl's vibrant energy.

It was like she had drunk an entire pot of black coffee in under a few seconds.

"Oh my god! It's good you guys are back. Shit has been out of control without you here." Haily gushed.

Ellie gave Tina a quick glance. Doe*s she always have to be like this?* She asked silently.

Are you complaining? Came Tina's response.

It hadn't been the first time they had communicated like this.

Ellie wasn't sure how it worked, but she had managed to 'speak' with Tina and even the beast last month in the same silent way.

It was almost like she could hear their voices in her head, and yet, not quite.

It wasn't any sort of actual telepathy, she was certain of that much.

She somehow just seemed to read Tina's body and just know what she was saying.

It certainly had been a neat trick that had proven handy when Tina had transformed into a seven foot tall werewolf.

She had actually wondered if that part had all been in her head before, but apparently it hadn't.

The bell rang, signaling the start of class, and Tina shot Ellie a look that promised their conversation wasn't over.

"We'll talk at lunch. Meet me out by the bleachers," Tina said, squeezing Ellie's hand briefly before turning away.

"And El…" she added, smiling, "It's good to see you. I missed ya too."

Ellie watched her go, unsure if she should feel reassured or unsettled.

They had gone through hell and back together last month, and it had formed in them a close bond.

And while that was both comforting and terrifying, she wasn't sure what it meant for them in the days to come.

The moment Tina disappeared down the hallway, Haily rushed forward, her eyes wide with excitement and relief.

"Oh my god, I can't believe you two are actually back!" Haily rambled, clutching her books to her chest.

"I mean, it's only been a month... I thought you'd be out longer..."

Her voice trailed off as she studied Ellie's face more carefully.

"Ummm... Sorry, I didn't mean..."

Ellie smiled, tilting her head. "It's ok," she said. "I heal quick."

The second bell rang, its shrill sound making Ellie wince. Students scattered, hurrying to their classrooms.

"I should get to class," Haily said, backing away reluctantly. "Oh! Just to give you a heads up. You're a bit of a legend right now. Talk at you later!"

As Haily disappeared into the crowd, Ellie turned to thrust her head into the depths of her locker.

Legend? Great. The last thing she wanted to be was a legend.

CHAPTER 4

The morning crawled by in a haze. With each class, she was greeted by a fresh wave of whispers and not so subtle stares.

It didn't take long for Ellie to feel like some sort of specimen in a jar. To them, she was little more than a curiosity to be scrutinized.

And why shouldn't they, she supposed. To them, she was little more than some survivor with an outlandish tale with more holes in it than the *Titanic*.

That didn't make it any less infuriating.

Some of her teachers seemed sympathetic, quelling any loud dissension in their classes and asking if she needed extra time or space.

She appreciated their gestures of kindness even though they were blatantly false.

She could sense their tension as if it were a steel spring under their skin, and smell the foul stink of cat piss and mothballs when they lied.

And then there were a few teachers who openly joined the rumors, treating her with outright contempt and hostility.

Mr. Watson had been the worst.

"You're late, Miss Granger," he'd said as she walked just moments after the bell rang.

"Sorry, Mr. Wats…" she began.

"I don't want to hear excuses, Granger," he said, cutting her off.

"The police might have bought your lies, but I'm not so stupid. If you can't be in my class on time, then you won't be in it at all. Detention, now."

By lunchtime, Ellie's nerves were frayed raw, and her temper wasn't doing much better.

What was more, she suspected her day wasn't going to get any easier at this rate.

She grabbed her lunch from her locker and headed outside to the bleachers, scanning for Tina.

She found her sitting halfway up the metal structure, legs stretched out casually, face tilted toward the sun.

Hearing Ellie approach, Tina patted the spot beside her.

"Rough morning?" Tina asked as Ellie settled in the row below her and used the spot as a make-shift table.

"You could say that," Ellie replied as she unwrapped a large sandwich she had prepped the night before.

"Everyone keeps staring and whispering like I can't hear them."

"Let them," Tina said dismissively, "They've got nothing better to talk about."

"I got detention for being thirty seconds late for Mr. Watson's class," Ellie grumbled around a mouthful of pastrami.

Tina looked down at her over her sunglasses. "Are you serious? Talk about a bloody wanker."

She let out a harsh laugh. "I wonder what he would classify werewolves as in his little evolutionary journal. Homo *Erectus* Lycos?"

Ellie giggled, "God, you're terrible!"

They burst into loud laughter.

"I wouldn't sweat it, Hollywood. If Mr. Watson knew the truth about us, he would probably eat his biology book and burn down his lab."

Ellie set down her sandwich and turned to face Tina directly.

"Hey, I've been wondering. How did you survive? I saw you fall. Your back…" she asked.

Tina's expression sobered.

She sat quietly for a moment, opening and closing her mouth several times to speak, but couldn't quite seem to form the right words.

At last, she seemed like she was about to actually speak when a familiar voice called out.

"There you guys are!"

Haily bounded up the bleacher steps, her face flushed with exertion and excitement as she dropped down beside them.

"I've been looking everywhere for you two. You're not going to believe this," she said, gasping.

Ellie could hear Haily's heart hammering in her chest.

"Well? What is it? Spill already," Tina asked, eyeing her curiously.

Haily held up her hand as she gasped for breath.

At last she blurted, "Jessey… Jessey Walters is dead!"

Ellie stiffened and looked at Tina, too stunned to speak.

"His parents found him in their pool last night.

Torn to pieces like he'd been mauled or something."

Ellie studied Haily, unsure how to react and wondering how much Tina had told her about *them.*

"Oh," Haily said finally, clearly desperate to fill the silence, "and someone vandalized your locker, Tina?"

Tina's head snapped up. "What?!"

"Yeah, I saw it on my way here. Someone wrote 'DIKE' on it." Haily said, wrinkling her nose in disgust. "In black marker. Talk about mature."

"Perfect," Tina muttered, rising to her feet in one fluid motion. "Just perfect."

A low growl rumbled in Ellie's throat, resonating through her chest as she stood to follow.

"That's what gets your attention?" Haily asked out loud, hurrying to keep up as they descended the bleachers.

"I just said Jessey Walters was killed, and you're more interested in your locker?"

"We're sorta over animal attacks, Hails. Shit happens." Tina said sharply.

Haily nodded, her expression uncomfortable. "Ok. Well… you do know what people are saying about you guys? Right? That you're... together."

Tina stopped and rounded on the smaller girl, her stony expression seemingly as hard as granite.

"Excuse me, what?" she asked

Haily stopped dead in her tracks and took a hasty step backwards.

"Stacy's been telling everyone that's why you two really went out in the woods that night. That you planned to…"

Ellie circled Haily, cutting off her retreat instinctively. She could smell the antiseptic stink of sudden fear rising from her.

"That we what?" she asked softly in Haily's ear.

Haily squeaked and spun, looking up into Ellie's soft golden eyes, and stammered, "She's uhhh… saying you guys killed them so you could be… together. That you're ummm…"

"That we're dyke-adelic?" Tina finished, her voice gentle again.

Haily looked at them like a trapped rabbit as she nodded vigorously.

Ellie smiled at her and touched her arm. "Relax, we're not going to eat you," she said jokingly, then added, "Yet."

Haily paled, and she laughed nervously.

"Good one, El… Wait, you are kidding, right? You wouldn't…"

Tina cocked a playful eyebrow, then turned and strode away with Ellie loping in her wake.

Haily gulped, then ran to catch up as the lunchtime crowd parted before them, whispering in their wake.

"Holy freaking shit! You know, you guys are fucking scary as hell when you want to be?"

When they reached Tina's locker, the vandalism was impossible to miss. Crude black letters stretched across the metal, the ink still fresh enough that Ellie could smell the stink of it.

Tina stared at it, her fists clenching rhythmically at her sides.

Ellie thought she saw something shift under Tina's skin, and heard a soft crackling.

"You sure this was Ashley and her goons?" Tina asked, her voice deadly quiet.

Ellie's head snapped towards a few students lingering nearby, who quickly averted their gaze, and suddenly found their own lockers a little too fascinating.

"Totally out of the bitches playbook," Haily replied confidently, "Get Stacy to spread rumors, and make it personal."

"Maybe we can ask them," Ellie said as she turned to stalk towards the lingering students.

The bell rang, signaling the end of lunch, and the students scrambled like panicked deer, looking relieved for an escape.

"We need to go," Ellie growled, "I got an empty locker next to mine you can use until we get this cleaned up."

"Thanks, El," Tina said, her eyes still fixed on the graffiti.

"You know what…?" she said almost playfully. "Let it stay. Let everyone see it."

She turned to Ellie and Haily, a smile tugging at her lips. "Let them think whatever they want about us. I'll handle Stacy… Later."

A shiver down Ellie's spine. Not fear, but a strange, electric anticipation. There was something in Tina's tone that sent the hairs prickling on the back of her neck.

She wasn't sure exactly what would happen, but was certainly curious. And she supposed it might help take her mind off the looming full moon.

She smiled, and they helped Tina clear out her locker.

CHAPTER 5

It didn't take long for the first ripples of backlash to hit.

She had barely settled into her desk for History when someone from the office appeared at the classroom door, asking for Ellie to come with her.

Mr. Patterson's eyes immediately found Ellie.

"Miss Granger, you're needed in the administrative office," his voice held a mixture of mild concern and relief. "Take your things, please."

A chorus of soft giggles rippled through the classroom as Ellie gathered her books.

"Excuse me, you all may join her if you wish," came Mr. Patterson's high-pitched voice.

The room quieted instantly. Despite his looks and high voice, Mr. Patterson was noted for being one of the most formidably respected teachers at Pinecrest High.

"Miss Granger, in case you don't make it back in time, here is tonight's homework," he said as he handed her a reading list with instructions.

Ellie tilted her head and looked at him. He wasn't hostile in any way, and she felt his smile was genuine. Even so, she could tell he was relieved for her to be leaving.

"Thanks," she muttered as she made her way to the door, ignoring the stares of the rest of the class.

Out in the hallway, Tina was already waiting, her expression tense.

What's going on? Ellie asked silently as they walked in the office aides' wake.

I don't know, came Tina's reply. *But I doubt it's good.*

The administrative office was horribly lit by an overabundance of fluorescent lighting and sparsely furnished with furniture that looked more suited to a medieval dungeon than a high school.

The secretary escorted them past the front desk and down a short hallway to an office that reeked horrifically of potpourri and the foulest smelling perfume known to existence.

Both Tina and Ellie physically staggered

back, choking as the secretary opened the door.

Ellie was certain she was going to be sick, as she forced herself to step into the flowery miasma of potpourri and ten week old oysters.

Vice Principal Carol Perkins stood behind her desk as she gestured for them to sit.

"Please, have a seat, ladies," she said.

Her thin lips were set in what seemed to be intended as a welcoming smile, but was more of a thin line.

She was a severe woman, perhaps in her fifties as best as Ellie could judge, with sharp, hawk like features, and dark salt and peppered hair, cut in a badly executed Dorothy Hamill.

"Well now, Eleanor Granger and Christina Akins," she began, her voice clipped and cold.

"I understand this is your first day back after your ordeal. I suppose I should welcome you back with us. Neither of you looks the worse for wear."

Ellie exchanged a confused glance with Tina.

"Ummm… Thank you?" Ellie said hesitantly.

"That being said, can you explain to me this nonsense that I'm hearing about you two?"

"Ummm… What nonsense are you talking about, Ma'am?" Tina asked, a sweet note of mock innocence in her voice.

"I'm sorry, but you're going to have to be more specific," Ellie added.

Oh boy, here we go, Ellie thought to herself.

Mrs. Perkins' eyes narrowed. "I'm referring to the vandalism of your locker, Ms. Akins. And the subsequent rumors circulating about the nature of your relationship."

"Someone wrote on *my* locker?" Tina said, feigning innocence, "Surely not! I was just at it before class, and nothing was written on it. And you're calling us in, why exactly? Rumors? I hope you're going to put a stop to them."

The Vice Principal blanched momentarily at Tina's response.

She managed to quickly recover, however.

"Watch your tone, young lady!" she snapped-ed.

"I'm well aware of what happened to your locker. Simply because you decided to change lockers without permission doesn't change it in *our* records."

Perkins stared sternly at Tina before continuing.

"What concerns me is the inappropriate behavior between you two that has provoked such a response from your peers."

Ellie felt heat rising in her chest. "Excuse me, but exactly what is it you are insinuating?" she growled softly.

Perhaps it was the tone in Ellie's voice, but something made the Vice Principal blanch a second time, and a momentary flicker of fear passed over her features.

Get ready for it. Tina said silently.

On your lead. Ellie replied.

Again, the Vice Principal recovered and seemed to find her courage.

"How long have you two been an item?" she asked brazenly.

At this, both girls stood in open outrage.

"Say what?!" Tina bellowed, her face twisted in a snarl.

Ellie heard the subtle crackling of bones. She glanced at Tina to see that her normally blue eyes had suddenly taken on flecks of gold, just as a growl rumbled in her own throat.

Mrs. Perkins stood just as fast as the girls and met them with a bellow of her own, "Sit down! Both of you!"

Both Ellie and Tina stood there a moment, silently staring down the Vice Principal across the desk.

It would be so easy, Ellie thought. *So easy just to rip her apart right now.*

She tilted her head stiffly, and a loud crack erupted as she felt the vertebrae shift slightly.

"How dare you?" Ellie said menacingly.

"Mrs. Perkins, with all due respect, you're about to cross a line," Tina said, "So you better get to the point."

After a few more tense moments, the Vice Principal leaned forward and pointed a bony finger at both of them.

"Fine, then let me be perfectly clear. This school has standards of conduct. Whatever you two choose to do in private is your business, but I will not tolerate public displays of... of... homosexuality!"

"We haven't done anything," Ellie said.

"Sorry to burst your bubble, Ma'am," Tina added firmly, "But we're dick-adelic..."

"Not dyke-adelic," Ellie finished.

Tina smiled unpleasantly.

Ellie caught the hint of copper coming from her breath and the flash of sharper teeth as she spoke.

"And besides, as you said, it's our business if we were, and not yours."

Perkins' expression made it clear she didn't believe them, and her gaze sharpened.

"Fine, have it your way then. But I've got my eye on both of you," she said. "And so help me god, if even one of you takes one step out of line, I'll be calling your parents."

Tina's jaw clenched visibly. "You do that, Ma'am. I'm sure my father would love to hear how you called the pair of us in here simply to accuse us of being lesbians.

"Especially considering that my *boyfriend* was just butchered by a bear. I wonder what the school board will have to say when he sues you for harassment and slander."

The Vice Principal visibly flinched and blanched a third time. This time however, she didn't seem to recover her bravado.

"Are we done here… *Ma'am*?" Tina asked.

Mrs. Perkins' eyes flicked between the two girls.

She seemed smaller somehow. Almost as if she had been deflated like a balloon.

"For now," she finally replied coldly. "Return to your classes."

CHAPTER 6

Everything felt infuriatingly surreal as they left the office. The whole exchange, the school, heck, at this point, the entire bloody world.

Ellie could actually feel her pulse pounding in her temples like tiny jackhammers drilling into what was left of her skull.

"Can you believe this shit?!" she hissed once they were out of earshot.

"How is it we come back from surviving an actual fucking massacre, and somehow, right on fucking day one, we're the problem?"

Tina didn't immediately respond. Her eyes had gone solid amber and had taken on that strange, predatory focus that Ellie was beginning to recognize.

"What now?" she asked, her tone exhausted.

"We're about to have more trouble," Tina murmured, nodding her head to the end of the hall.

Ellie followed her gaze down the hall, where two figures leaned against the wall near the water fountains.

She rolled her eyes in frustration. It was Jace Riley and Kyle Thompson.

"Oh, great. You don't suppose they're going to ask us to the dance, do you?"

"Doubt it," Tina replied.

Jace pushed off the wall and sauntered toward them, Kyle following a step behind.

"Can't we just kill'em and stuff them in a few lockers?" Ellie asked with a sigh.

"Well, if it isn't the dynamic duo," Jace called, his voice echoing in the empty corridor.

"Too noisy. We could just fuck them and end this whole lesbian BS." Tina replied.

Ellie crinkled her nose in disgust at the thought. "Ugh! I'd rather have my koochie cut out again."

"Aww... Did the wittle dikes get a scolding?" Jace mocked as he came close.

"Not in the mood, Jace. Keep walking if you want to keep your balls." Tina warned as she tried to turn away.

Jace ignored her, stopping uncomfortably close to Tina, cutting her off.

Meanwhile, Kyle perched next to Ellie.

Looking up at him, Ellie was suddenly rather aware of his size and… his musk.

She was surprised by how not hostile it was. If anything, it was oddly pleasant and strangely calming.

Tina must have caught it too, because her nostrils flared and she spared a fleeting glance to eye him up and down before returning her gaze to Jace.

"What do you want?" she asked exasperatedly.

"You know, I've been wanting to ask you something since you got back," he said softly in her ear.

Tina smiled. "Hmmm… Really now? Suddenly, David's gone, and you're looking to take his place in my bed as well as the field?"

"Only in your wettest and wildest dreams, Tina." Jace quipped with a smile.

"But there is one thing I've been wondering all month."

Tina's smile widened coldly, replying, "Oh really, and what might that be?"

"What really happened to David?" he asked, dropping all pretense of amusement.

"What really happened to you guys out in those woods?"

Tina's smile widened even more ominously.

"Bear attack. Just like the papers said."

"Bullshit." Jace snapped.

He lowered his voice and said softly in her ear, "Listen, I work weekends at my dad's funeral home. I saw what was left of the bodies."

His voice cracked slightly. "Bears don't do that to people. They don't go for the throat. They attack the head and face."

Ellie tensed, the memories of that night flooding her mind unbidden.

Suddenly, she was listening in the dark as Mark's screams of agony filled her head. The wet sounds of him being torn apart as David slapped her into compliance.

She remembered running and looking into the thing's eyes a moment before Mr. Duprix's rifle exploded her world.

But what she remembered most was running with it in the moonlight.

She'd been playing with it. Writhing and moaning under it like a cat in heat, inviting it to take her like it had Tina.

Cripes, the old man's blood was still warm

and wet on the damn thing, and she had still wanted it to shag her!

"I'm telling you, a god damn black bear killed David. I was right there when it happened." Tina said, her voice snapping Ellie back to reality.

"Now, back the fuck off me."

Instead, Jace pressed closer. "You see, there you go lying again. So you were right there when the bear pulled David's head off and ripped out his spine? Was that before or after you went skinny dipping at the base of the dam?"

Something shifted in Tina's demeanor. A subtle change that gave Ellie only a fraction of a second's warning.

Without thinking, Ellie reached for her, but was halted as a large hand came down on her shoulder and pulled her back.

"Don't. He needs this. So does she." Kyle's voice rumbled softly in her ear as he gently pulled her back another step.

Tina moved with brutal speed, grabbing Jace by his letterman and slamming him against a row of lockers hard enough to buckle the doors.

She let loose a guttural snarl as her hand clamped around his throat, not quite choking him, but demonstrating how easily she could as she lifted him a couple inches off the floor.

"Listen carefully, because I'm only saying this once," Tina growled, "It was a bear. A big, vicious bear. That's all there is to it. Got it?"

Jace's face had drained of color, his eyes bugged with shock as his hands scrambled at her wrist, trying desperately to break her iron grip.

Tina pulled him back and slammed him again, "I asked you if you got it!"

"Got it," he choked, nodding frantically.

Tina released her grip on his throat and let him collapse to the floor. Sliding down the ruined lockers, coughing as the air rushed back into his lungs.

"Good," she said, as she stepped back, straightening her clothes.

Jace rubbed his throat, looking up at her warily from his position on the floor.

Tina looked at Kyle with his hand on Ellie's shoulder. "Do you mind, or are we going to have a problem too?"

Kyle smiled softly.

"No ma'am. Just didn't want her getting hit by accident," he said and let Ellie go.

Tina's head tilted, and she looked up at

Kyle's soft brown eyes for a moment.

Surprisingly, he didn't flinch or look away.

After a moment, he finally chuckled and stepped over to Jace, helping him up.

"What the Hell, man? You with them or something?" Jace cursed as Kyle pulled him to his feet.

"Come on, El," Tina said, turning away. "We're going to be late for class."

They had only taken a few steps when Jace called after them, "What about the other guy?"

Tina froze mid-stride.

"The one they found on the dam," Jace continued. "The naked guy with the knife in his chest. Did the bear kill him, too?"

Tina turned slowly, her eyes meeting his as she walked back over to him.

Jace blanched as she put her arms gently over his shoulders, her face only an inch from his.

Ellie wasn't sure, but she had a feeling that Tina smiled only an instant before her knee came up into Jace's groin.

Jace let out a loud yelp of pain as he doubled over into Tina's bosom, where she cradled his head for a moment before lifting his chin to look up at her.

"I have no idea what you're talking about," she said, then released him to drop to the floor, curling into a tight ball as he whimpered in agony.

Tina turned away and walked back over to Ellie.

She stopped and looked back at him on the floor again, "Can't say I didn't warn you. You might want to piss. It helps with the pain."

She turned back to Ellie with a smile as they stalked away, leaving Jace to writhe on the floor.

"Crazy bitch!" he croaked after them as they rounded the corner out of view.

"Tina," Ellie whispered. "He's talking about the beast! I killed him with..."

"Not now!" Tina hissed, glancing back over her shoulder. "I'll drive you home after school, and we'll talk about everything. Meet me in the parking lot."

CHAPTER 7

The rest of the day passed in a blur of classes and whispers, but no real further incidents. By the time the final bell rang, Ellie felt drained and extremely irritable.

She briefly wondered if there was some sort of award for surviving her first day back after traumatic events.

As she stood there with her head in her locker, she couldn't help but overhear a couple of dorks talking a few lockers down.

"His mom found him!"

"I hear he was torn in half."

"Betcha it was a shark. Did you see that movie Jaws?"

"I'm telling you it had to have been those lesbos, they hate dudes!"

"Did you hear what they did to Jace?"

"Yeah, I saw him icing his balls in the nurses station."

She didn't respond to any of it and quietly mused over the benefits of homeschooling.

"Hey there!" came a familiar bubbly voice.

Ellie extracted her head from the depths of her locker and looked tiredly at Haily.

The dorks blanched when they saw her and quickly skittered away.

"Hi," she replied.

Haily crinkled her nose. "Eesh! That bad of a day?" she asked.

Ellie thrust her head back into the locker, replying, "You have no idea…"

She stood up again, withdrawing her backpack, and proceeded to stuff it violently with her books.

"I swear, it's been one thing after another all freaking day."

Haily touched her arm lightly, "Aww, I'm sorry, but hey! If you're not busy me and few girls are heading over to the diner to tackle some homework over malts. You could come along. I promise no one is going to give you shit. We're all sort of outsiders."

Ellie smiled weakly at her.

"Thanks, but Tina and I got plans. Maybe another time," she chuckled and looked forlornly into her crammed backpack, "When my head isn't about to explode."

"Ok," Haily said, looking a little down but understanding.

"Alright, well, I guess I better get going. Hey, where is Tina anyway?" she asked, her head snapping back up and looking around.

"Not sure. We're supposed to meet in the parking lot." Ellie said, looking at Tina's new locker.

Haily smiled gently as she reached out and placed a hand on Ellie's arm.

"Hey, don't let things get to you. People are jerks, but I like you. And we can always chill together," she said, her bubbly tone returning.

Ellie smiled, "Thanks."

Haily bounced away back into the river of students as Ellie watched her long black ponytail bounce merrily down the hall.

She envied Haily. Remembering when she had been like her at the beginning of the year. Before that stupid Valentine's party at Rick's.

Cripes, she had done everything in her power to forget that asshole, then one night of running from a damn werewolf, and she couldn't stop thinking about him.

She slammed her locker shut and pushed her way into the throng of human flesh, doing her best to ignore the cacophony of smells.

She had to be honest with herself; this year bloody sucked. It seriously had to be the worst year in existence.

First, she gets raped and knocked up by that creep Rick. Then her parents forced her to get an abortion from some shady quack, who then gave her a hysterectomy.

She was still on the fence as to whether or not to hold him accountable, or to just let that one slide.

She couldn't lie to herself, though. The more she thought about it, the more she wanted to rip his guts out and wear them as a necklace, too.

Then the divorce and her mom forced her to move across the bloody continent.

Yeah, that had been another barrel of laughs.

Having to explain to all her friends that she was going to live in Tennessee with her fucking alcoholic mother, and wouldn't be around for the spring formal, was not on her list of fun things to do.

She growled threateningly at a pair of giggling girls who wouldn't move fast enough, sending them skittering into a wall, shrieking.

She smirked at them as she passed, feeling pleased with herself.

Ellie supposed that getting chased all night by a damn werewolf and turned into one herself wasn't all that bad in the overall scheme of things.

Certainly, the benefits made dealing with shit while waiting to change into a giant blood thirsty monster herself a bit more bearable.

Though it hadn't been a walk in the park either.

She rounded a corner, making her way towards the last set of double doors to the parking lot, recalling all the terror of that night.

Oh yeah, she survived it alright. Infected with a condition that actually made her uterus grow back.

Which had hurt so fucking much she'd wanted to rip her own head off with a spork!

Seriously, what else could go wrong this year? Flying monkeys shooting out her twat?

She pushed her way through the building doors into the bright October sun and breathed in the fresh air.

God, she needed that. The smell of pine and dead leaves was almost a taste of heaven.

She took a moment to revel in the smell of the outside and freedom from the bullshit of the day.

As promised, Tina was waiting in the parking lot, leaning against an old Ford pickup that looked like something from the 1950s.

"Good god. How old is this thing?" Ellie exclaimed, remembering how Tina's van used to wheeze and sputter.

Tina laughed. "It's my Dad's. Damn thing drives like a boat. But it's tough. Seen him push over stumps with it. My mom keeps on telling him to send it to the dump, and he keeps telling her to get stuffed. I think it's a running gag at this point for them."

Tina held up a set of keys and winked at her.

"So, you need a ride?" she asked, jingling the keys loudly.

Ellie cracked up laughing and nodded gratefully, "Yes! Let's blow this pop stand and hit the beach or something!"

Tina grinned and replied, "Well, no beaches, but we can figure something out."

Climbing into the passenger seat, the cab

smelled of leather, rich tobacco, and something distinctly warm, spicy, and entirely Tina.

The cacophony of scents was both familiar and new and filled Ellie with a sense of relaxed relief as she settled in.

As they pulled out of the parking lot, Ellie leaned her head against the cool glass of the window, watching Pinecrest High School recede in the side mirror.

"So," Tina said finally. "Are we going to talk about it?"

"About what?" Ellie asked tensely.

"About how we saw Jessie's murder last night," Tina answered coolly.

"Wait, you saw that too?!" Ellie exclaimed.

"I thought I was losing my mind! Like it was just more nightmares or something. And then Haily told us, and we brushed it off like that…"

"Yeah, sorry. And no, you're not going nuts, El. We saw what happened to Jessie. And it was outside your house, too.

Yeah, I know… I went out there and smelled it this morning

Tina was silent for a long moment, her eyes fixed on the road ahead.

Finally, she said, "We both know what killed

Jessie Walters. And it wasn't either of us so what does that mean?"

"Another werewolf," she replied softly.

Tina nodded grimly. "And this one doesn't need the full moon to change. Which is in a week. You ready for it, El? It's really going to fucking hurt."

"No! I'm not fucking ready for it. I don't want to turn into a giant freaking monster. I don't want to fucking kill things with my mouth. God, that dream was horrible."

Tina laughed softly. "You don't have a choice, babe. You're like me, and there's no cure. Sorry, but you'd better get used to eating Bambi. Or your neighbors."

"Eew! You're twisted." Ellie said, crinkling her nose at the thought.

Tina let out a bark of laughter, then asked, "Hey, is it still considered cannibalism if you're a seven foot tall dog?"

"Oh my god, Tina! That's sick!" Ellie exclaimed.

"What? It's a valid question." Tina replied with a giggle.

After a few moments of silence, she added, "We need a plan. Somewhere to go when the full moon hits. Somewhere away from people.”

Ellie nodded slowly, then shook her head.

“My mom’s not going to just let me disappear for the night. She’s been overprotective since... since everything.”

“Three nights. And it’s the same with my parents,” Tina admitted. “But we have to, or we’re going to end up eating our families. And I’m sorry, but I have no intention of eating Danny like a pork chop.”

Danny was Tina’s kid brother. Ellie had met him once, just as they had all been leaving to go on their camping trip last month.

He was honestly pretty cute with fire red hair and enough freckles to qualify as his own galaxy.

She smiled as she remembered him handing her a dandelion flower as they had been loading up in the van. She didn’t want to envision the little guy getting mauled by Tina’s beast.

But something else struck her about Tina’s comment as they pulled up to Ellie’s house.

“What do you mean, three nights?” she asked, sounding confused.

Tina turned in her seat and looked at her squarely.

“Forget what you hear in movies and read in

a book about there only being one full moon a month. Calendars only list the middle day of a full moon cycle. It's actually three days," she said.

"Wait a second, then why didn't we change last month after that night?" Ellie asked.

"Because last month we ran into that thing on the last night of the full moon. Which is why we haven't turned since then." Tina replied.

"But then, what about the one that killed Jessie? It can turn without the moon." Ellie said, interrupting.

Tina tilted her head, "That I don't know, perhaps it's something we can figure out too. Which will probably hurt a lot less. Speaking of which!" she exclaimed, slapping Ellie's leg.

"How is it I had to endure every bone in my body breaking and healing at bloody warp speed, and you didn't even sprout shaggy eyebrows?"

"I..." Ellie started, then looked down as her face went scarlet. "I sorta did, but... Bot not like you."

"Huh? What's that supposed to mean? El, what happened?" Tina asked, leaning in closer. "Spill."

"It grew back..." Ellie said at last in a small voice.

Tina's eyes narrowed. "What grew back?" she asked.

Ellie looked at her sheepishly, then smiled.

"*It* grew back... I got my period after, well, you know. After you fell."

Tina's eyes bulged. "No way! You mean? You mean *it* grew back?! You mean your… Your cooter's, fuck all, baby oven?! Oh my god! That's why you didn't turn?!"

Ellie nodded, smiling as tears rolled down her cheeks.

"Yeah... Remember, Mr. Duprix said, were-wolves can grow things back. Well, I guess I didn't turn because my body was busy growing that back."

"Holy fucking shit!" Tina squealed as she lunged in, crushing Ellie in a hug.

Tina pulled away suddenly and looked at her in a serious tone.

"You know what this means, right?" she said, "The beast. What you told me on the tower. Do you think it might have sensed you were still healing or something?"

Ellie nodded. "Yeah. It wasn't like how it… Well, did it to you. It was almost sweet with me. Gentle. I think it knew I was turning and that it didn't need to… force me. I think it was actually waiting until…"

"Until it could put a bun in your oven!" Tina finished laughing.

She leaned back in her seat, shaking her head. "Un-fucking-believable."

They sat quietly for a while, looking up at the house, watching.

Through the living room window, Ellie could see her mother putting up Halloween decorations, paper skeletons, and cardboard bats.

It seemed so absurdly normal compared to the world they now knew wasn't just a movie.

"The first full moon's on Halloween this year," Tina said softly. "Kinda fitting, isn't it?"

"Yup. There goes trick-or-treating," replied Ellie deadpan.

Tina let out a soft chuckle. "Yeah, more like trick-or-screaming. With an emphasis on the screaming."

It wasn't funny, but they burst into laughter anyway.

"Hey, at least we'll have the best costumes in town!" Ellie exclaimed, sending another explosive wave of laughter through them.

After another minute of hysterical laughter

and several more wisecracks, they finally settled down.

"Come inside for dinner?" Ellie offered, her expression almost pleading.

"I'm not sure I can handle dealing with my mom by myself right now. But… I know she would love the company. And… so would I," she said sheepishly.

Tina hesitated, then nodded. "Yeah, ok. But no talking about... Well, you know."

"Obviously." Ellie replied, smiling.

They climbed out of the truck just as Ellie's mother emerged from the house, Halloween decorations in hand. She spotted them and waved.

"Tina! It's so good to see you!" she called.

CHAPTER 8

As it turned out, Ellie's mother really was happy to see Tina. Perhaps a little too happy.

Her Mom had prepared what looked like an entire Thanksgiving feast, despite it being an ordinary Tuesday in October.

"I wasn't sure what you girls would want," Nancy explained, nervously smiling as she ushered them to the dining table. "So I made a little of everything. "

A little of everything turned out to be a roast chicken, with mashed potatoes, green beans, corn on the cob, and a basket of fresh hot rolls.

Ellie cringed internally. Her mother was trying too hard, as usual.

Although she couldn't argue with the veritable feast in front of her.

She was practically salivating with hunger.

"This looks amazing, Mrs. Granger," Tina said, sliding into a chair.

"Oh, it was no trouble. Ellie has…" Her Mom hesitated, looked at her before continuing.

"Well… she's developed quite a sizable appetite recently. And please, call me Nancy. After everything you girls have been through together…"

She trailed off, her smile faltering slightly.

Ellie and Tina exchanged glances as Nancy busied herself with serving the food.

You tell your mom? Came Tina's silent question.

No. She wouldn't believe it anyway. Ellie responded, shaking her head almost imperseptibly.

"So," her mother said brightly after they'd all filled their plates, "tell me about you girls' first day back. How was everything?"

Ellie crammed a large hunk of chicken into her mouth to avoid answering immediately. She instantly regretted it.

It wasn't that it was bad, so to speak, so much as it tasted… off.

It was more underwhelming than anything else, as if all the flavor had been cooked out of it.

"It was fine," she said finally, "Pretty much what you'd expect."

"The teachers were cool about us missing so much," Tina added, pushing her food around her plate.

Ellie noticed she hadn't actually eaten anything yet.

"And the other kids?" Nancy pressed, her eyes flitting between the two of them.

"They weren't... too difficult? Were they?"

A loaded glance passed between Ellie and Tina.

"Yeah, some were... unpleasant," Ellie replied flatly. "But we... handled it."

Nancy's fork paused halfway to her mouth. "What do you mean, you 'handled it'?"

"Oh, nothing much, just a few swift kicks to the balls, fly a few bras on the flag pole. You know. The typical kid stuff. We didn't let them bother us," Tina laughed, cutting in smoothly.

"We stuck together. Like a pack."

Nancy nodded slowly, not sure how to take Tina's humor.

"Well... Ummm, that's good. I suppose. And what about the work you missed? Will you be able to catch up?" she asked.

"Yeah, it's mostly boring stuff. Shouldn't be too hard." Ellie replied.

"Except trig. I hate that crap. When are we ever going to need Trigonometry in the real world? Or French even? We live in America, for Christ sake!"

Nancy blanched and replied, "Please don't take the Lord's name in vain at this table."

"Sorry," Tina said noncommittally.

"And who knows, you might need to know how to speak French one day," Nancy said, refilling their water glasses.

"The Canadians speak French. And some Louisianans speak it too.

"Speaking of which," her mother continued. "Did they ever find that ranger you girls mentioned? The one who helped you?"

Tina's hand froze mid-reach for a roll. Ellie felt her chest tighten.

"Mr. Duprix...? Jared Duprix," Ellie said softly.

"Duprix, yes," Nancy nodded, seizing on the name. "Whatever happened to him? Didn't he help you guys find your way?"

Tina and Ellie exchanged another glance.

We need to tell her, Tina said.

No! How? Ellie replied.

"No," Tina said finally, "He..."

Ellie pushed her plate away. "Mom, can we please not do this right now?"

"Do what, honey? I'm just asking questions about the man who supposedly saved my daughter's life. A man who..."

"He's dead," Tina blurted suddenly.

The silence that followed was deafening. Nancy stared at Tina, her water glass suspended midway to her lips.

"I'm sorry, he's what?" she whispered.

"He's dead," Tina repeated, her voice steadier.

"Or at least we're pretty sure he was killed when... when the bear broke into his cabin."

"There was a huge fight, we heard it. He made us run out the back." Ellie added.

Nancy set her glass down with a sharp click. "And you're just now mentioning this? Weeks later?!"

"Mom, give us a break," Ellie said exasperatedly.

"We both went through hell out there. Can you blame us? Besides, I was in the hospital, and..."

"No! You two need to tell the police right now," Nancy cut her off, standing up and reaching for the phone on the wall.

"They need to find his cabin and check it. There could be a body out there."

"No!" both girls exclaimed simultaneously.

Her mother's hand froze over the receiver. "Excuse me?"

"Mom, please," Ellie begged. "It's not…we can't just…"

"I'm calling the Sheriff," Nancy said firmly, lifting the receiver.

"This is serious, Eleanor, that poor man gave his life for you and deserves a proper burial."

Ellie exchanged a miserable look with Tina as her mother dialed the number for the sheriff's department.

She didn't understand why, but the thought of returning to that cabin made her stomach clench with dread.

Old Jared Duprix had been the nicest old man she had ever met.

He had also been armed to the teeth with silver, and ready for the beast.

And because of them, it all went sideways for him.

She wasn't exactly sure what reason she had to be hesitant to return was.

Was it guilt? No, she had nothing to feel guilty about.

Or perhaps the fear of evidence?

It's sorta hard to explain silver bullets everywhere, and who knows what else the old man had.

She supposed that made a bit more sense.

"Mom, wait…" she tried again, but her mother just simply held up a hand for silence.

Ellie dropped her head into her hands, listening quietly as someone picked up on the other end of the line.

"Sheriff's Department, how can I help you?" came a woman's voice from the receiver.

"Yes, hello? This is Nancy Granger, Ellie Granger's mother. I need to speak with Sheriff Morehouse."

"Oh yes! Hi Nancy. Let me get the Sheriff for you," the woman replied happily.

There was a brief pause, then suddenly a click and a man's baritone voice spoke.

"Nancy? It's Rob, how are you doing? Is everything alright?"

"What? Oh, hi Robert…"

Tina looked at Ellie and cocked an eyebrow. *Your Mom's on a first name basis with the Sheriff?* She asked silently.

Ellie shrugged, looking confused.

"Well, I'm not sure what to call it. My daughter and her friend, Tina, the other girl you rescued last month. Well, they just told me about some old park ranger who may have been killed that same night."

"Really now. We didn't know about a ranger being involved. You said they told you he was killed? Did they tell you his name?"

"Duprix... Jared Duprix. And the girls are certain he was killed during the attack?"

The was a silence over the phone, and Ellie could have sworn she heard the Sheriff's breath hitch.

"Seriously? You sure they said Duprix?" he asked.

"Yes, why?" Nancy asked.

"It's nothing," replied Morehouse, "It's just that this is the first we're hearing about another victim from that night. Why didn't they say anything before?"

"I don't know. I asked them, but... Well, you know, kids," her mother said.

"Yeah, I got a few of my own. Listen, Nancy, we're going to need to get a full statement from both of them. So, could you possibly bring them down to the station tomorrow afternoon? Say after school lets out?" he asked

"Tomorrow? Yes, that would be fine. And yeah, after school would be good. I'm pretty sure the girls can take you up to the cabin, too, if you like." Her mother said shooting Ellie a poignant glare.

"Excellent! And Nancy? Listen, I need you to make sure they don't discuss this with anyone else. If there is a body up there still, this becomes a recovery operation. We need to keep the details quiet until we know for certain if there's a body."

"Yeah, sure," Nancy said.

Just then, something else pricked Ellie and Tina's ears. A faint voice on the other end of the phone.

"Hey, Robby? We got a report back from that kid in the pool. It looks like the same animal that attacked those kids last month."

The girls sat up straighter and glanced at each other. This wasn't good. Not good at all.

CHAPTER 9

Her mother turned around slowly as she set the receiver back on the cradle.

"The Sheriff will meet us tomorrow afternoon. I told him I'd drive you girls out there to show them whe...."

"How long have you been fucking him?" Ellie cut in hostilely.

Her mother looked taken aback, and even Tina seemed to shrink a little at her outburst.

"Excuse me?" her mother replied in a shocked tone.

"You heard me," Ellie snapped, "How long have you and the Sheriff been porking?"

Nancy blanched, and she looked down before finally answering.

"Ummm... Robert and I have been seeing each other for about two weeks now. Not that it's any of your business."

Ellie tilted her head slightly, as if to consider her mother for a moment before responding.

"No, it's not my business who you spread your legs for now that Dad's gone. But I would like to know who might be creeping around the house at night," she replied viciously at last.

"Eleanor!" her mother shouted in utter shock.

Now it was Ellie's turn to blanch, as she realized she had gone too far.

She didn't understand the anger she felt, it had just taken her over out of the blue. She sat back in her chair and closed her eyes to compose herself.

"Mom…"

"No," Nancy said, firmly cutting her off. "I don't know where all of that came from, but the discussion is over. You can see Tina out. We have a long day tomorrow. Now, excuse me. I need a cigarette."

Ellie felt a pang of guilt. She hadn't intended to go at her mother like that. But the anger in her just seemed to come out of nowhere.

Tina waited until Nancy had turned away to gather the dishes before leaning close to Ellie.

"Relax, El, I blew up at my parents this

morning as well. Stupidest thing too."

"Yeah?" Ellie replied, "But I bet your mom didn't force you to kill your unborn baby, then uproot your entire life. Mine did."

Tina winced, then leaned closer.

"Point taken. But at least she's trying, right?" she asked.

Ellie shrugged. *So, I should forgive her on merit?* She asked Tina silently.

Tina shook her head, *No*.

"Perhaps cut her some slack, though. Sheriff Morehouse is a good guy after all. Speaking of which."

Tina glanced out to the kitchen, where Nancy was slamming around the dishes more forcefully than was necessary.

"If we're going to take the fuzz out to the old timer's cabin, we should go early," she whispered.

"You know, scout it out first. Make sure that... well, you know... that he's actually dead."

"No, he's definitely dead," Ellie replied softly.

"We both heard that fight. People don't scream like that unless…"

She hesitated a moment, forcing herself to

regain a bit more composure before saying, "He's dead, alright."

But as she said it, she couldn't help but to wonder. After all, Tina had survived being both mauled and raped by that thing.

What if the old man had too?

What if he was out there somewhere, changed, like them?

Was he the one from their dream?

Something made her doubt that, but the thought was both terrifying and oddly comforting.

If the old man was still alive, then a mentor like him could make all the difference for them.

"Hey, Mom," Ellie called, looking out to the kitchen, "I'm going to walk Tina to her truck."

Her mother didn't answer, and just continued slamming the dishes around pretending to wash them.

Outside, the late October air was crisp and cool. The moon loomed brightly above, not quite yet full but getting close now.

Ellie couldn't help but stare at it, its pull undeniable at this point. Not when she knew what was going to happen in less than a week.

"It's getting to you, too, isn't it?" Tina asked.

It had been more of a statement than a question as she followed Ellie's gaze up towards the glowing orb.

"Yeah," Ellie said softly, nodding. "It's like... It's like I can feel it watching me or something. You know?"

Tina nodded, her expression grim. "Yeah. It's like some sort of goblin just crouching up there waiting."

"Tina," Ellie began hesitantly, "how did you survive?"

Tina looked at her in confusion. "Huh?"

"On the dam," Ellie replied, "When you were fighting the other werewolf. I watched that thing fold you in half like you were paper. I was certain you were..."

"Dead?" Tina finished for her, a smirk playing at her lips. "Yeah, I thought I was, too."

She shook her head and let out a soft laugh.

"I mean, I remember it throwing me out over the railing, then falling. I think I recall hitting the water...but then nothing. It goes blank from there."

They reached the truck, but neither made a move to say goodbye. Tina took a deep breath and looked back up at the moon.

"When I came to, I was washed up on the

shore, miles downstream. It was like nothing had happened. I was me again. But I felt different, you know? I was *me*, but… *more*. Oh, and I was hungry. I was so fucking hungry. I felt like I hadn't eaten for a week."

She turned back to Ellie, their eyes meeting. She leaned in and wrapped her arms around Ellie, and they embraced, just standing there for a moment.

"I'll pick you up tomorrow," Tina said finally, breaking their hug and climbing into the truck. "Before school."

"You sure that's a good idea? What if we're late?" Ellie asked.

"Then we will just skip and make a day of it, but we're going to that cabin. What are they going to do, cry that they can't badger us for a day?"

"Right," Ellie replied.

Tina cranked the engine, then hung her head out the window.

"You know, your Mom's right about one thing," she said.

Ellie rolled her eyes. "And what's that?" she asked.

"The old man deserves better for what he did for us."

Ellie sighed. "Yeah, I know. I just… I'm just not sure I'm ready for that. To see his…"

"I know," Tina cut in, "But we need to know what he knew. So we need to go out there anyway. Without people hovering."

Ellie nodded reluctantly. "So we really don't have a choice now, do we?"

Tina shook her head. "No, we don't… Hey, remember, be ready early. I'll be here to pick you up before school."

Ellie nodded and watched as Tina pulled away from the curb and disappeared around the corner.

She could hear the phone ringing then, but ignored it, choosing instead to linger on the porch for a while. She wasn't looking forward to facing her mother's inevitable questions.

Through the window, Ellie could see her mother reach for the receiver. Her voice rose immediately, and Ellie knew immediately who was on the other end.

Her father.

Sighing, she pushed open the front door and slipped quietly inside.

Her mother stood with her back to the wall, leaning on it with her eyes shut tight.

Ellie could smell the caustic stink of acid in the air and knew she was about to hit her limits.

"No, Greg," her mother said in a clipped voice, "She's just getting settled again. The last thing she needs is to be uprooted and dragged back to L.A."

Her father Gregory Granger wasn't necessarily a bad man. But he could be firm at times. And he had called her a slut when he found out about the pregnancy.

Still, regardless of that, she didn't hate him, but she wasn't sure if she forgave him yet.

"She's my daughter, too, Nancy, you can't keep her from me. I have rights, you know." her father's voice crackled through the receiver.

"Well, you should have thought about that sooner," her mother retorted.

"Besides, the school year's already started, and she's made friends. Better than the ones you let her run around with."

"What the hell's that supposed to mean? I was following your lead!" Her father asked angrily.

Ellie growled softly as she moved quietly into the kitchen.

She pretended to busy herself with washing

dishes, but listened intently as every word came through crystal clear.

"Don't you dare put this on me," Nancy hissed. "I wasn't the one who got her pregnant in the first place."

Ellie's hands stilled in the soapy water, a plate slipping from her grasp.

"The abortion was your idea, Nancy. You were the one who insisted it was for her own good, and look what happened!" Greg snapped over the line.

"She's only sixteen! What were we supposed to do? Let her ruin her life?" Her mother's voice rose. "And let's not forget who was supposed to be watching her that weekend. She was in your care when it happened."

"No, Nancy, she was in our care when it happened. Let's get it right. Both of us are guilty on this one, you just need to accept it," her father said, his voice rough with emotion.

"I don't need to accept anything, Gregory. You let her go running around like a common whore, not me. And besides, the courts gave me custody, not you," her mother shouted.

"Fine, whatever. We'll see about that another time. But whisking her off to Tennessee isn't fixing anything either. She needs stability."

"What she needs is to be away from the reminders," Nancy snapped. "Away from that school, those people, that entire lifestyle!"

"Right and letting her almost get herself killed by wild animals and maniacs is the perfect way to do that?!" her father retorted cuttingly.

"It was a bear, Greg," her mother said exasperatedly.

"Bears don't stab sixteen year old teenagers a dozen times in the stomach, Nancy! Or did you conveniently forget about that, too?" came her father's sharp response.

"You know what, Greg? Fuck you! She's not coming back to LA, and that's final!" her mother screamed into the phone and slammed it back onto the its cradle with enough force to make the wall mount rattle.

She stood there for a long moment, breathing hard as she sobbed softly.

She lightly thumped her head on the wall a few times before standing up to wipe her eyes.

Ellie remained frozen at the sink, unsure whether to make her presence known or slip quietly upstairs.

Before she could decide, she heard the flick

of a Bic and the nauseating stench of burnt paper and chemical laced tobacco filled her nose.

Her mother sidled up next to her, cigarette already between her lips as she reached for the cabinet above the refrigerator.

She pulled down a bottle of vodka and a glass, her movements jerky with anger.

"Sorry about that," she said, exhaling a plume of smoke. "Your father can be... difficult."

"Do you really need to do that in the house?" Ellie asked quietly, wrinkling her nose.

Her mother's eyes rolled in frustration. "For Christ's sake, Ellie, it's been a long day. Cut me some slack, will you?"

"Yeah, well, it's gross, and you promised you'd quit." Ellie retorted.

"I promised a lot of things," Nancy said, taking a deep drag. "We all did."

Her tone made Ellie's stomach clench. She knew that voice all too well. Her mother was gearing up for another argument.

Ellie understood her wanting an outlet for her frustration, but she refused to be just another punching bag.

"Fine, whatever. What did Dad want?" Ellie asked exasperatedly.

Her mom poured a two-finger of vodka before answering.

"The usual. He thinks he knows what's best for you. Wants you to move back to L.A.," she said, slamming back the glass in a single gulp.

"And you told him no," she stated flatly.

"Of course I did," Nancy replied, pouring another glass. "This is our home now. We're making a fresh start here."

"No, Mom, you're making a fresh start," Ellie corrected her, as she snatched the glass off the counter and slammed the shot herself.

The liquid scorched its way down her throat and punched her in the gut.

"I'm just along for the ride and watching you fall flat on your face," she said as she handed the glass back to her mother.

Nancy's face hardened. "What the...? That's not fair. After everything I've done...?"

Ellie turned back to the sink as she felt a low growl rumble in her throat.

She tilted her head slightly, cracking her neck loudly, releasing the pressure, as the bones shifted subtly.

She could feel the beast clawing at her, pleading just to be let out.

She couldn't deny the thought had crossed her mind, more than once in the last month. To just relax and let the monster do its thing.

God, it would be so easy to just rip her throat out and be done with it. She thought to herself.

"Yeah, Mom," she started, "everything you've done. Like letting the doctors mutilate me," she said softly.

Her mother looked confused and mildly angry. "Excuse me. What did you just say?"

Ellie could feel the rage bubbling inside her. Scratching just under the skin, aching to come out.

"Nothing…" Ellie said as she felt a sharp stabbing sensation in her fingers.

She looked down, wincing as she noted that her fingertips had started to split. Through the blood, she could just see the tips of sleek black claws peeking through slightly.

She thrust her hands back into the soapy water as her mother rounded up on her shoulder.

"No! What was that? You want to repeat that a little louder, young lady?" her mother hissed in her ear.

Ellie clenched her fists, the razor-sharp claws stabbing into her palms.

It was weird, but the pain felt good. She focused on the water as it turned crimson.

She let it wash over her and pushed back the desire to turn and peel every inch of flesh from her mother's face.

Finally, Ellie turned and looked into her eyes as the red haze flickered at the corners of her vision.

"I said, I'm going to bed," she said, and padded softly out of the kitchen.

She could feel her mother's eyes locked squarely on her back, and hear her jaw working open and closed, sputtering, and unable to process words.

CHAPTER 10

The world of the night swirls around us, pulsating with the wondrous red haze that flows around us. Distorting our world and letting us see the night in all its glory.

It was strange at first, disorienting and unfamiliar. But soon it passed, and we ran joyfully. Freedom filling us as the cool night air embraced our naked flesh.

Soon, very soon, we won't be cold when we run. Soon, our real face will be seen by the world, and the moon so bright above will look down on us with all its radiance.

But for now, we are simply content to run free. Reveling in ourselves as the night opens to us.

Suddenly *it* is there… A musk so familiar yet hated.

We must go now and find it.

We run. Our breath billowing in hot clouds as we huff in her sweetness.

We can almost taste her on our tongue. Feel the softness of her flesh.

God, it makes us hunger and pine… for *her*.

Their! The house is white with green shutters. So neat, so ordinary.

She's there on the porch, waving. Her scent calling to us, beckoning to us to come to her.

A car pulls away, and we crouch, wrapping ourselves in the cloak of the night, and we watch.

The wretched lights wash over our hiding place, our sanctuary of tangled leaves and brush.

We watch as it pulls away, carrying a man and a woman. They smile and wave to her.

We breathe in their stench. Cologne, hairspray, and an abundance of cigarettes clogs our senses before being washed away on the clean night breeze again.

We turn our focus back on the girl, waving from the porch. We step softly forward, one clawed hand in front of another.

Her scent drifts across the street to us. Sweet vanilla with a hint of coppery musk.

We lift our head and huff her in. Her musk is

intoxicating, triggering something within us.

That smell fills us, and our eyes roll.

We need her!

We need to feel her flesh press against ours.

We need to taste her.

Every inch. Every writhing, curved bit of flesh, must be ours!

There is a soft crack, and she stiffens. She looks out into the night at us.

Can she see us wrapped in shadow?

Do our eyes shine in the darkness, whispering to her of our presence?

"Hello? Is someone out there?" she calls gently, shielding her eyes from the soft yellow light above her.

She turns to enter the house, glancing back once more out into the darkness. then closes the door.

We surge forth, bursting from our shadows as the door shuts with a loud click, loping gracefully across the street on all fours.

We flit from shadow to shadow, our approach stealthy, silent save for the soft sounds of our snuffling as her warm musk lingers in the air.

So intoxicatingly thick with the tang of copper and wetness it hurts.

God, we want her.

We want to taste her.

We want to love her.

To rip her apart!

But how do we get in?

What entrance is there for us to enter without alerting her to our presence?

How can we love her, if we cannot get to her?

We circle and search. Snuffling in frustration around the house. Looking for any sign of weakness to the walls or doors.

Then suddenly we hear it, the sound of rushing water coming from within as clear as though it were in the open.

But where?

We look up, following the sound.

There! Above us! A window, open to our world. Her musk flows freely from it into the night air.

A clear invitation! She does love us! She wants us to come join her. To taste her wonders.

Our claws dig easily into the wood siding, and we swarm up the wall easily. Drawing ourselves to her.

Her scent and the sound of her soft musical voice envelop us as we slip into her world.

Pink walls and cute pictures taped to a mirror. Posters of Leif Garrett, Andy Gibb, and Barnabas Collins from Dark Shadows framed in a paper heart.

Her stench is like an overpowering tidal wave, pulling us down to writhe and roll upon the bedding, drowning ourselves in her until every inch of our body is covered in her sweetness.

Finally, we rise and pad softly into the hall, following the sound of water and singing. Her voice beckoning us like a moth to a flame.

We move silently toward the adjoining bathroom, our clawed feet barely a whisper lost in the sound of her melody and the churning water.

Steam billows from the partially open door, carrying her scent on its warm mist.

We slowly push the door wider, slipping in as silently as a phantom.

There she is, her skin glistening in the soft light.

Her back is to us as she tests the water with her fingertips, then turns off the faucet.

She sings softly as she begins to step into the steaming water.

She stops and her body stiffens, suddenly aware of our presence rising silently behind her.

Her soft breath begins to pant as the antiseptic stink of fear floods our nostrils, as we let out a soft growl.

Slowly, with a quiet whimper, she begins to turn, and we hear the soft trickle of fluids as she defiles the water.

Her eyes widen in pure terror as she catches sight of our shape.

Her trembling gaze tracing up our body until she looks into our amber gaze.

Suddenly, her panting turns into panicked gasping that turns into a high, desperate scream.

A guttural roar erupts from our throat, answering her as we lunge forward.

She falls back as we descend on her, our combined voices silenced in the hot water, replaced only by the desperate sounds of our struggling bodies.

Her soft, wet skin feels like silk against us as we undulate like lovers wrapped in an embrace of violent passion.

She hammers at our back, her soft fists pounding futilely as we rend her flanks, raking her sweet flesh with our claws.

She tries to scream again, her mouth filling with crimson water as she arches, thrashing in agony as our mouth finds her bosom, biting down hard on the soft pink teat.

She jerks up out of the water, sputtering as she sucks in air desperately.

Her lungs fill, but our crushing mouth finds her lips, biting deeply into the writhing flesh therein.

We are rewarded as a fountain of sweet red copper floods our mouth.

Her widening eyes fixed on us as we pull away, chewing happily as we watch her choke on her own blood.

She slumps feebly to sink below the water. We wrench her up again, as we swallow, forbidding her the mercy of death just yet, as she yelps sufferingly.

She writhes as we kiss her lips once more to drink of her sweet red nectar.

Soon, her feeble attempts to resist weaken to soft whimpers as she clutches at our back for that last desperate moment of life.

Our eyes lock on hers and we watch in grotesque fascination as they slowly go vacant at long last.

We rise and let her slip quietly beneath the swirling dark clouds of red water.

The stench of hot copper overwhelms the small bathroom as we let our eyes roll in the ecstasy of her.

We lift our head and sing out to the goddess above of our victory taken in her name.

Soon we will run free under her light… Soon.

The world swirls then, and we let the darkness of the void intrude on us as we revel in our slumbering delights.

CHAPTER 11

Ellie sat bolt upright, gasping as the panic of the waking world swirled around her.

She clutched her chest, as a herd of elephants seemed to stampede violently behind her ribs.

Is this what a heart attack feels like? She wondered, gasping frantically until she finally gathered control of herself enough to calm down.

She finally noted the early predawn light peeking through the open window, shimmering off the thin sheen of sweat on her skin.

"Seriously," she whispered, rubbing her eyes in frustration. "What the fuck is going on?"

It had felt all too real. She closed her eyes, and in an instant, the scents, the textures, the taste of copper flooded back to her so vividly that she could even taste the bathwater.

She glanced at the clock and groaned: 7:15 AM.

"Ugh! You gotta be kidding me!" she said, as she flopped back down, determined to push the visceral images out of her head.

"It was just a nightmare," she muttered. "Just a stupid nightmare."

It was about an hour later when the dull screech of tires, followed by a relentless pounding from somewhere downstairs, dragged her back to consciousness again.

She rolled over with another disgruntled, angry groan and kicked the now completely drenched sheets from her body.

Despite the cool October morning, Ellie felt as if the room had been converted into a blast furnace, and insisted on cooking her to death.

The knocking persisted, growing more frantic.

"Would somebody just answer the stupid door already?" she groaned softly, as she thrust her head under the pillow.

"Coming!" Her mother shouted from downstairs, followed by the shuffling of slippers across hardwood. "Hold your damn horses, some of us don't rise at the crack of bloody dawn, you know…"

Ellie sat up, disoriented. She shook her head,

trying to clear the fog of sleep from her head.

She only vaguely registered the sound of the front door opening, followed by the indignant shriek of her mother and heavy footsteps thundering up the stairs.

In less than a few seconds, her bedroom door burst open as Tina swarmed into the room like a one-woman SWAT team.

"Ellie!" Tina gasped, her face flushed and serious.

Haily appeared behind her, equally breathless.

"Could you at least knock first, please?" Ellie muttered, suddenly aware of her complete nudity.

Fortunately, Tina didn't seem to notice or care about her state of undress.

Haily, however, was a different story.

"Oh! I'm so sorry," she stammered, her cheeks flaming red as she tried to look anywhere but Ellie's glistening nude form.

Ellie and Tina looked at her in annoyance.

"It's only tits, you got them too," Ellie said irritably, as she flicked a few droplets of sweat at her.

It hadn't occurred to Ellie how strange her sudden comfort with nudity might seem to others.

Truthfully, she wished she could just stay that way for the most part. Clothes just felt binding most of the time anymore.

She recalled then how Tina had, during the previous months' ordeal, pretty much forgone clothing, almost entirely the majority of the night after being infected. Only wearing a long coat given her by the old Jared Duprix.

And even that she eventually discarded entirely.

"What's wrong?" Ellie asked, as she did her best to shake off more sweat.

Tina paced the small bedroom like a caged lion, agitation radiating from her with every movement.

"School's canceled," she blurted tightly.

"And you're upset about that, why?" Ellie asked, though she had a feeling she already knew the answer.

Tina's eyes locked with Ellie's. *Oh, you know why!* She said silently.

"There was another murder last night," Tina said out loud.

Haily stepped forward, her voice small. "It was Stacy. Her parents found her… in the bathtub. It's all over the local news."

Ellie's throat went dry as she let out a sigh.

Stacy. In the bathtub. With the werewolf. Ellie thought comically to herself. *Christ, just make it sound like you're playing a game of Clue.*

"Seriously?" Tina said out loud, getting Ellie's attention.

It's not funny! I ate her fucking tongue! She said silently.

"Wait, what?!" Ellie exclaimed out loud in shock.

"Yeah," Tina continued. "It was kinda brutal."

Tina ran a hand through her sweat soaked hair, which seemed somehow longer and fuller than it had been only yesterday.

"Well, you've eaten worse things," Ellie said distractedly as she examined her hair's new richness.

"What?" Haily asked, sitting lightly on the bed next to Ellie, keeping her eyes averted as much as possible.

Ellie! Tina shouted silently

"Huh? Oh, nothing," Ellie said, glancing between them, realizing that she had spoken out loud.

"It's just that I doubt the Sheriff will be

meeting us today now. Not with two murder investigations on his hands."

Tina gave a grim smile. "That's what we figured. You still up for our field trip?"

The three fell silent as footsteps sounded on the stairs.

Within a few seconds, Ellie's mother appeared, a lit cigarette clutched tightly between her fingers.

"School's canceled today. There's been a... Holy Jesus! Eleanor, put on some clothes!" Her mother exclaimed, stopping dead in her tracks and averting her eyes.

"We know, Mom," Ellie said exasperatedly. "Tina just told me. And for fuck sakes, they're just tits, people! It's not like we don't all have them here."

Nancy took a long, shaky drag of her cigarette. "Yeah, well... Company, you know?"

Tina and Ellie rolled their eyes in unison.

"I just couldn't believe it when Patel called. An innocent girl, murdered in her own home." Nancy shuddered. "It just doesn't make any sense. What's this world coming to?"

An uncomfortable silence filled the room for a long moment.

"So what are you girls planning to do today?" Nancy finally asked, trying to sound casual as she broke the quiet.

"Well…" Tina began hesitantly, looking at Ellie. "We're thinking of going out to the cabin ourselves."

"Yeah," Ellie piped in, "and with the Sheriff busy with…" she said, gesturing vaguely.

"Well… a murder… We thought we could still find out what happened to the old man."

Nancy frowned. "I don't think that's a good idea. Not with whatever's going on in town. There could be a killer out there."

Ellie and Tina exchanged another meaningful glance.

If only she knew. Tina quipped silently.

"Mom, we'll be fine," Ellie insisted, finally standing and wrapping the sheet around herself toga-style. "We know those woods."

"Yeah," Tina added with a humorless smile. "Nothing out there we can't handle."

Nancy's frown deepened, the lines around her mouth more pronounced than usual.

"No. Absolutely not. I'm not letting you girls go traipsing through the woods alone with some maniac on the loose."

Ellie opened her mouth to argue, but Tina nudged her gently.

"What if you came with us?" Tina suggested, in a suddenly sweet tone.

"You could drive us out there, and we could all look for Jared's place together."

Her mother hesitated, cigarette halfway to her lips. "I don't know..."

"Please, Mom," Ellie pressed, seeing the opening.

"You said it yourself. It's important. Mr. Duprix saved our lives out there. We need to know what happened to him."

"And more eyes means you'll find the cabin faster," Haily added unexpectedly.

"Plus, there's safety in numbers, right? What maniac would be dumb enough to attack all of us?"

Nancy seemed to finally take notice of Haily. Eyeing her like a bug as she took a deep drag of her cigarette, expelling a cloud of smoke.

"I'm sorry, who are you?" she asked.

It was like a switch flipped on Haily's personality. Her face split into a broad smile as she bounced up excitedly and thrust her hand out towards Nancy.

"Oh! Hi, I'm Haily! Haily Mako! My parents run The Happy Jap. You know that Asian restaurant downtown?" she said in a bubbly tone.

Her mother's mouth seemed to work itself several times before she slowly reached out and shook Haily's hand.

"Fine," she said at last, finding her voice again, "I'll call Robert and tell him what we're doing. But we stick together out there, and we're back before dark. And you…"

She pointed the cigarette at Ellie.

"Put on some clothes. This isn't some cat house."

As soon as Nancy left to get ready, Tina and Ellie broke into mischievous grins.

"That was almost too easy," Ellie whispered, rolling her eyes.

"She has no idea where Jared's cabin actually is," Tina replied with a smirk.

"Or how we walked for miles through those woods that night before he found us."

"You think we can slip away?" Ellie asked.

Tina's smirk widened into a smile. "You're kidding, right? Does a bear shit in the woods?"

Ellie smiled and stood up, stretching up on her tiptoes and reaching for the ceiling while making a big show of waving her boobs in Haily's face.

Tina giggled at Haily's expression as she took in Ellie's chiseled form inches in front of her.

As Ellie relaxed back down, she playfully reached around the smaller girl to pull out a set of clean underwear from a drawer.

"Pardon my tits," she said as her face came centimeters from Haily's, locking her with her gaze.

Haily's scandalized expression as Ellie turned and strode from the room to the bathroom was too much for Tina to hold back, and she exploded in laughter.

As the sound of the shower met them, Haily let out her breath and giggled nervously.

"Welcome to the club, Hails. You might want to get used to it. We're all tits and ass around here." Tina said as she flopped on the bed.

"Oh eew! Gross!" she exclaimed, instantly bouncing back up with a disgusted expression as she looked down at the sweat soaked sheets.

A few minutes later, Ellie strode back into the room, dripping water instead of sweat this time.

She stopped in front of Haily and sighed.

"Do you want a closer look again, or can I get dressed, please?" she asked.

Haily bounced out of her way, "Sorry," she muttered as she openly stared at Ellie's near perfect physique.

"Are you two really going to try to ditch your Mom?" Haily asked at last.

"Well, duh!" Tina replied.

"Trust me, for us, there is no *trying* to ditch her. We're *going* to ditch her pretty much the moment we hit that tree line." Ellie said, pulling a tank top on.

Haily bit her lip nervously. "But what if... what if there really is something dangerous out there? I mean, Stacy was..."

"Murdered in her bathroom, not the forest." Ellie finished flatly as she grabbed a set of jeans.

Tina moved to the window, peering out at the clear autumn sky. "Look, Haily, you can either come with us or stay here. Your choice."

Haily shifted from foot to foot. "I'm coming with you guys. It's just... this is all really freaky, you know? First, the camping trip, then Jessie, and now Stacy..."

Ellie zipped up her jeans and turned to face Haily and said, "We need to find Jared's cabin.

We actually don't have a choice. But you do."

"And what about this killer?" Haily asked.

"Aren't you scared of him?"

Ellie and Tina exchanged a loaded glance.

Can we eat her? Ellie asked silently.

Be nice. Tina replied.

"Not really," Tina said, her tone unnervingly casual.

"We can handle ourselves."

Ellie grabbed a brush from her bedside table, dragging it through her hair. She asked, "You guys ready? I'm hungry."

Downstairs, Nancy was just hanging up the phone.

"Well, that's weird," she said, crushing her cigarette in an overflowing ashtray.

"No answer at the sheriff's office."

"Probably busy with the murder investigation," Ellie said, as she rummaged through the depths of the fridge.

Nancy nodded absently. "I left a message. Let's get going before I change my mind."

Ellie slammed the fridge closed, emerging with a chicken leg stuck in her mouth.

"Can we stop for breakfast? I'm ready to eat a horse," she mumbled around the chunk of meat.

CHAPTER 12

In general, little was left of Ellie's old life in Los Angeles that could indicate her social class in the City of Angels.

Her mother's Cadillac Fleetwood Brougham was one of those indicators. Around the small town of Pinecrest, the only other car like it was owned by the Mayor himself.

As the station wagon rumbled down the rural highway, Ellie noted how the trees splashed across the surrounding mountains in a beautiful riot of amber and crimson.

She rolled down the window and took in the crisp air.

It was fantastic, and made her almost salivate at the thought of just running through those back hills through the firestorm of rustling leaves.

"So," her mother's voice cut annoyingly into her reverie.

"How was your first day back at school yesterday?" she asked, glancing at Ellie.

"No one died," Ellie replied flatly.

"Make any new friends?" her mother pressed.

Tina snorted quietly from the back seat.

"Mom, seriously?" Ellie sighed, "I've been going there since August."

"I know. But well… you just met Haily, right?"

"Actually…" Haily started from the back seat, but fell silent immediately as Tina shot her a warning glare and shook her head.

"Seriously, Mom, can we not talk about people in front of them?" Ellie said, rolling her eyes as she looked apologetically into the back-seat.

"I'm just trying to…"

"I know what you're trying to do, Mom." Ellie cut her off.

"And, thank you, I really do appreciate it. But I'm ok. Really."

Well, not really. She doubted that having dreams of eating people's tongues could be count-ed as being ok.

But such is life, she supposed.

Her mother's knuckles whitened on the

steering wheel, and Ellie could sense the lecture coming even before her mother spoke.

"Can you give me a break, El? After everything that's happened last month... I think I'm allowed to be worried about you. You almost died. And now you gotta deal with a murder. There's only so much one person can handle, especially at your age."

"Christ, Mom," Ellie cut in, "I didn't even know the girl. There is literally nothing for me to handle."

Ellie hated how defensive she sounded, but what else could she say?

Oh, it's ok, Mom. I just wish I could have ripped her face off personally.

Yeah, that would go over really well.

The conversation mercifully died as her mother pulled into Mick's gas station.

It really wasn't much to look at.

Out front was an old faded sign stating, GAS $0.86 PER GALLON – LAST STOP FOR 20 MILES! With a wooden cigar store, Smokey the Bear, next to the front door to greet customers.

"Jesus Christ! Eighty-six cents for gas?!" Nancy exclaimed, then sighed defeatedly as she parked next to a rusty pump.

"You girls want anything from inside?" she asked, handing them five dollars.

"I need to get some gas. Now, where is that attendant?" she asked, looking around.

Tina and Haily giggled from the back.

"Mom, it's self-service here," Ellie said.

Her mother rolled her eyes and said, "Of course it is. Because customer service is going out the window."

She stepped out of the car, grumbling about how places in California still knew how to treat customers.

After a moment of trying to figure out how to work the pump, she finally got it pumping gas.

Ellie turned to Tina and Haily.

"Soda?" Haily suggested.

"Jerky," Tina added. "I'm starving."

"Remember the plan," Ellie hissed. "Once we're in the woods…"

"Yeah, yeah, yeah, I know," Tina whispered back.

"We ditch your mom and find the cabin. Now, can we grab snacks already? I'm getting hungrier by the minute."

The three girls piled out of the station wagon and headed inside.

"Don't be too long!" her mother hollered after them.

"I want to get back on the road quickly, please!"

Without looking, Ellie waved at her as they disappeared through the door next to Smokey.

Nancy sighed and looked at the wooden bear.

"Hey, I'm trying here, don't judge me," she grumbled at it before turning back to the pump.

Inside, the fluorescent lights flickered overhead, casting an unhealthy pallor across the dusty shelves of chips and candy.

A bored attendant with coke-bottle glasses in black plastic frames barely glanced up from his magazine as they entered.

They filtered into an aisle and started grabbing various road snacks.

Hey Tina?" Haily asked, "How far is this place anyway?"

"Not too much further. The turn-off is about another eight miles. The campsite was about two miles in. We should be there in about thirty minutes or so." Tina answered without looking up.

"And the cabin?" Haily asked.

Tina snorted, "That's the catch. We don't

know. Mr. Duprix lived way out there. No roads, and he walked everywhe…"

Tina froze mid-step and went rigid, a low growl rising in her throat.

Ellie instinctively looked up from where she was rummaging on a lower shelf, and followed Tina's gaze, her stomach dropping instantly.

She slowly stood up, lip curling as she let loose a soft growl of her own.

Standing by the beer cooler were two men in what looked like military fatigues.

The older one looked to be in his mid-forties to early fifties. He had a hard, unkempt face and bloodshot grey eyes peered out from under the brim of a Redwings cap.

The younger one looked better kempt. His black hair was slicked back under a hunting cap, and he looked freshly shaven.

But like the older man, he had the same tired bloodshot eyes and looked as though he hadn't seen much sleep for days.

Ellie recognized them immediately. David's father, Richard, and older brother, Mike.

They had been pushy at the hospital, trying to bull their way into her room to ask her about what killed David.

Like Ashley and her crew, they didn't buy the bear story either. Richard had even occasionally tried to come calling at her house to ask her questions.

"Shit," Tina whispered. "It's the Varanos."

Haily looked confused. "Who?"

"David's family," Ellie whispered back. "His dad and brother. They're real creeps. Worse than Ashley."

"Oh... then I think we should go," Haily murmured, tugging at Ellie's sleeve.

"Yeah, agreed..." Tina said, turning away and hustling to the register to pay for their things.

But it was too late. Mike swatted his father's shoulder and pointed to the group.

Rich Varano turned, his eyes locking onto Tina with a laser-like focus.

"Well, I'll be a son of a bitch," he said loudly.

Tina and Ellie stiffened, knowing what was coming.

"Shit! Tina muttered, turning around slowly.

"Here we go," Ellie replied, her shoulders slumping.

"Mr. Varano, Michael. How are you two doing?" Tina crooned sweetly.

"Interesting timing," Richard said, as he

thumped a six-pack onto the counter next to their snacks.

"Let me pay for that, why don't you?" he said, handing the attendant several bills.

"Thanks," Ellie said flatly, not even trying to pretend to be nice.

It's kinda hard to be nice with the father of the guy who murdered your friends and stabbed you in the guts almost twelve times.

Yet what else could she do? She certainly couldn't tell him what kind of evil, selfish bastard his son turned out to be, without revealing what had actually happened.

So playing the cat and mouse game it was.

Richard's gaze flickered between Tina and Ellie. "I've been wanting to have a word with you girls for a while now. You're mighty tough to get hold of."

"Hmmm… Yeah, we're kinda not really in the talking mood much lately." Ellie said.

Richard fixed her with an icy stare. "Understandable. Nevertheless, maybe you can spare a moment for me. You know. Seeing as you're the only ones who saw the thing that killed my boy, and all."

"Mr. Varano… sir, I think we've helped

enough by talking to the police," Tina replied, "I really don't know what more to tell you. It was a bear. A big vicious bear."

Mike stepped closer, looming over them. "It wasn't no bear that tore that girl to pieces in her own bathtub."

Richard put a hand on his son's shoulder. "Mike," he said gently.

Mike shrugged his father's hand off and stepped closer.

"She was ripped apart! Just like David, and the others, too. And the cops keep calling it all animal attacks." His voice trembled with barely contained rage.

"You know it wasn't no god damn animal, you saw the damn thing. So what was it?"

"Michael!" Richard cut in louder, the force of his voice subduing his son's anger. "That'll be enough."

Richard's eyes turned back to Tina and narrowed on her. "Please forgive him. We've been on edge lately. But he's got a point."

He leaned in, his breath sour with alcohol. "What kind of animal walks into a house, kills a girl, and walks out without anyone seeing or trashing the place?"

"We wouldn't know," Ellie said, her heart pounding.

Richard's gaze flicked to her, "Is that right?" he said coolly. "So why is it, I don't believe you?"

Tina's expression didn't change as she held his gaze unflinchingly, but Ellie felt her tense, and her ears picked up the slightest subtle sound of crackling tissues.

"Ya know… We're going to find it," Richard said, his eyes boring into them. "Whatever killed my boy and those other kids. And when we do…"

The bell above the door jingled behind them, and Ellie caught her mother's distinct scent as she stopped short, eyes narrowing as she took in the tense standoff before her.

"Richard! Is everything ok in here?" she asked, sidling up next to her daughter.

Richard straightened, his demeanor shifting instantly back into a friendlier tone.

"Yes. Everything's fine. Just been enjoying a delightful chat with your daughter and her friends, ma'am. No harm in that."

Nancy smiled as she engulfed Ellie and Tina to turn them away. "Not at all! Well, we need to get going. Girls…" she said as she ushered them out the door.

"Oh, one more thing," Richard called out just as they were opening the door.

"I served two tours in Nam, you know," he said when they turned around again. "Took a gook knife to the guts on my second tour."

He lifted his shirt to show several scars.

"It's kinda impressive your girl is up and walking around only a few weeks after taking something like that."

Nancy smiled stiffly, but before she could reply, Ellie said, "I heal quick."

Richard smiled sinisterly. "I'd say so, little lady. I was laid up for six months. Why, as best as I can tell, you didn't even get a scar. How very fortunate."

"I'm sorry, Mr. Varano," Nancy interjected, "But what are you implying? That my daughter faked her wounds?"

"No ma'am. Just impressed with her ability to heal. She's made of some tough stuff there. You have a good day now," he said, still smiling.

They turned and left, practically running back to the waiting station wagon.

"What was all that about?" her mother demanded as she started the engine.

Tina spoke up from the back seat.

"They've got this crazy idea that there's some kind of monster in the woods."

Nancy's knuckles whitened as she clutched the steering wheel. "Were they threatening you? What was that crap about your stabbing?"

"No, they didn't threaten us, but…" Ellie said.

"But what? What did they say to you, Ellie?" Her mother asked firmly.

"Nothing really…" Ellie replied quietly. "They're just—grieving."

Nancy pulled out of the gas station, the tires kicking up twin rooster tails of gravel in the Cadillac's wake.

"That's not grieving, Ellie," her mother said, glancing into the rear view mirror.

"Grieving is like when Grandpa died. I don't know what that was, but it wasn't grief."

"They're pieces of shit," Tina said flatly from the backseat.

"Honestly, this town would be better off without them."

"Wow, Tina, I thought you liked the Varanos. What changed?" Haily asked softly.

An uncomfortable silence filled the car as the gas station shrank in the mirror, and along with it, Richard and Mike Varano.

Tina stared out the window, watching the trees flash by for a moment, lost in her thoughts. "I finally saw what kind of monster David really was," she said at last.

CHAPTER 13

"There it is," Tina said, pointing to an obscure turnoff that was half hidden by what seemed to be years of overgrowth and neglect.

"You sure?" Nancy asked, slowing down and eyeing the turnoff warily. It hardly looked like little more than a dark opening in the trees. "This doesn't look like a road."

"Yup, this is the place, Caldwell's Creek. We set camp a few miles in. No one comes out here, well, except my Dad and I," Tina said with a glum smile.

"Guessing those days are over," she said, sitting back and staring out the window.

"Just keep going straight. There's a clearing, you can't miss it."

"Alright," Nancy said hesitantly, "Hold on to something. This is going to be bumpy."

She pulled slowly into the dark opening, and

it was like someone had flipped a switch on the world around them. The light didn't seem to penetrate, and everything was cast in a deep gloom of browns and greys.

The forest that only a month before had been so vibrant and green and alive, now felt like they had crossed some invisible boundary into a forbidden realm.

Ellie could almost imagine seeing fleeting glimpses of trolls and other creatures.

The notion brought an interesting question to her mind.

If werewolves were real, what else was out there that, until a month ago, she'd only thought was make believe?

The atmosphere in the car grew heavy fairly quickly, the further into the benighted forest they drove.

Ellie's body tensed with each familiar landmark they passed, her mind flashing with unwelcome memories of that night.

Hey, check it out! Ellie brought her horror movie collection!

David's voice intruded on her thoughts just as it had the first time they had come down this road.

She wondered if there was anything left of her stuff to recover.

She hadn't gotten to finish the book she had been reading, *The Hell Hound of the Westerly Woods*.

She wondered if the search parties had left anything of their camp.

"How much farther to this ranger's cabin?" her mother asked, cutting into her thoughts.

"A few miles," Tina answered vaguely.

Suddenly, Tina sat up straight and let out a strangled cry.

"What?! What is it?" Ellie's mother asked, glancing worriedly in the back seat.

"Stop the car! STOP THE CAR NOW!" Tina shouted.

Nancy slammed on the brakes, but Tina was already throwing her door open as the station wagon skidded to a halt on the loose dirt.

She half fell, half leaped out before the car had fully stopped, scrambling desperately through the underbrush.

Ellie threw her door open and bolted after her instinctively.

"Hey! Wait!" Ellie's mom yelled after them as she fought to undo her seat belt.

"Oh, God-dammit!"

The brush cleared quickly, and Ellie's mind raced as she tried to take in the twisted hunk of metal that used to be Tina's old Chevy.

Or what remained of it.

The once tough old van was now a twisted wreck. And that was putting it mildly.

If she was being honest, and now seeing it for the first time in the light of day, the poor thing looked like it had been through a war.

Hold on to your butts! We are leaving! Tina's voice rang out as she threw the old van in reverse.

The memory of that wild ride filled her mind as she traced each dent and claw mark.

One side had been crushed inward as if hit by a wrecking ball.

Jess screaming as she had clung to her.

The windshield was shattered.

Ellie saw the black clawed hand swipe at her and felt that hot splash on her face.

She hadn't realized it in that moment, but it was blood.

Her blood.

God, that had been the moment everything changed. That was when it had happened, when she had been infected.

It had happened so fast that she hadn't even had time to register the injury.

It's funny how quickly one tiny moment in time, and one teeny tiny scratch, could so dramatically alter the course of her entire life.

Had Tina not slammed on the brakes, or had she turned the wheel just a fraction of a second sooner or later, would she be a werewolf now?

The metal frame bent and warped, the front wrapping around a thick pine.

How the engine had not crushed them was beyond her understanding, and she thanked whatever lucky stars had been looking out for her that night.

She remembered seeing the tree just a fraction of a second before the dashboard rushed up to greet her as she slammed into it.

But what struck Ellie the most was the stench inside when she looked in.

It was a sickening cocktail of old copper, fear, and the overpowering lingering stink of sex.

"You left..." Tina said suddenly from behind her.

Ellie spun, startled, to look at her. An undeniable expression of guilt written across her face. "Tina... I'm..."

"You left me there. Right there… to die," she said, as her breath came in short, shallow gasps.

Her eyes had glazed over, staring beyond the mangled wreck and back to that night.

Ellie moved closer, placing a hand on Tina's shoulder.

"Tina, don't…"

"No, it's ok… I… I knew what I was doing," Tina continued as if Ellie hadn't spoken.

"I wanted you to get away. I wanted to save everyone. You know?" Her hands began to tremble. "Like in the movies."

She looked at Ellie, "I saw you there. You and Jess. You guys looked so small, and I saw that look in its eyes. And I just yelled at it. I don't know why, but I did. And then it looked at me…"

Tears welled up in her eyes and began streaming down her face.

"Oh god, Ellie! When *IT* looked at me… I knew. I knew right then and there what it wanted. What *He* wanted! And… and I ran! I just ran for the van…"

Tina looked back at the van and took a stumbling step closer to the open door.

"It was the only thing I could think of. I remember thinking to myself, 'Hey, if I'm going to die like this, it might as well be in there.' You know?"

She reached out suddenly and grabbed the edge of the bent door.

"The moment I jumped in there, I knew. I knew exactly what was going to happen. And then he was in the van with me... on top of me."

Her legs buckled as she stared into the dark opening, and she slid slowly to her knees.

Ellie squeezed Tina's shoulder. "Tina, stop."

But Tina was lost in the memory now, her voice becoming detached and clinical.

"I could feel his claws cutting into me! Over and over again! And... and I couldn't fight! I couldn't fight El. I tried. Oh god, I tried so hard, but he was crushing me, you know... Like you and that Rick guy... and his breath!"

She shuddered violently, "It smelled like rancid meat and blood. And then… he was inside me..."

Tina doubled over and let loose the most gut wrenching scream of anguish Ellie had ever heard.

"Oh God, it hurt so much! And it was just over and over and over again! I could feel him everywhere in me! Just pounding and pounding!"

Tina's eyes snapped to Ellie's, suddenly clear

and unnervingly intense as she clutched and pulled at her.

"It felt like I was being torn in two. Jesus Christ, Ellie! I remember thinking to myself, 'Please God, just let it end already.' But it didn't, he just kept going," she said desperately, as if she had to get it all out before it was too late.

"And then he made me watch you all leave. He made me watch you pull David away as he fucked me. Oh God, I remember it.

"But you know what the strangest part of it all was, though?" Tina asked with a strange mechanical smile.

"I was happy when you left. I was happy because I knew you guys would be ok. That you would have a chance and I... I could just die..."

"Tina, stop! PLEASE!" Ellie cried out, tears streaming down her face as she remembered the horrible way she'd watched Tina jerk and flop that night.

The stink of it was everywhere. A memory in the form of a smell that painted the nightmare in her mind so vividly she could almost see it from Tina's point of view.

"But I... I don't know, I think I knew he wasn't going to kill me. Maybe I just went a little mad there, but...I suddenly realized that I liked it," she said in a desperate whisper.

"I don't know why, but I couldn't help myself! I did. It didn't hurt anymore and I... I just wanted more and more. I think if I hadn't... I would have actually gone completely insane."

A twig snapped behind them.

Ellie whirled at the sound, a vicious snarl dying in her throat as she saw her mother and Haily standing there only feet away, their faces twin masks of horror.

Her mother's hand pressed against her mouth, tears streaming down her cheeks. Haily looked like she might be sick.

Tina's eyes widened as she registered their presence, and a strangled cry escaped her throat.

She sat there for a moment just staring at them, her face an unreadable mask of pain and horror.

Suddenly, without warning, she spun and bolted, plunging into the dense forest.

"Tina!" Ellie called out.

She exploded from her mark, surging up from the ground to burst through the underbrush, knowing in that brief instant of initial flight, something, no... everything, had changed.

CHAPTER 14

The world around her blurred as she launched from her position.

What had she been doing? She'd almost attacked her own mother and Haily. And for what? Just standing there and listening in?

Christ, it wasn't like Tina was exactly being stealthy or had gone far. The van had only been wrecked perhaps ten or twenty yards into the tree line; it wasn't very far.

So what was her deal?

Ellie pushed it out of her mind, the only thing important now was finding that cabin. And well, making sure Tina was alright and didn't accidentally run off a cliff or something.

Not that that would actually hurt her.

She did survive falling off a dam with a broken spine last month after all.

She wasn't exactly sure, but Ellie felt confident that handling heights and big falls wasn't exactly a problem for them anymore.

Still, she would rather err on the side of caution rather than running blindly into something.

She smiled at the notion, the irony not lost on her, given present circumstances .

Her legs pumped relentlessly, carrying her between trees and over fallen logs that would have slowed down any normal person.

But then again, she wasn't normal anymore, now was she?

Each breath filled her lungs with the stink of the whole damn world around her. Decaying leaves, animal trails, and Tina's distinctive musk.

She wasn't making it hard to track her or to catch up.

Ellie spotted a flash of reddish golden hair bouncing in the otherwise dead world around her.

She smiled and pushed her legs harder. They burned wonderfully as she closed the gap.

Tina giggled as Ellie sidled up next to her.

She looked over as Tina flashed a radiant smile that reached her amber eyes.

Catch me if you can! She said silently.

Ellie let loose a soft growl of joy as she put on the speed.

She was back in that night again, just running with the beast. Not hiding from it, not scared. Just… being in the moment with it.

She had to have known in that moment what was happening to her, but she had ignored it.

Maybe that was another reason it hadn't chosen to mate with her then? Perhaps it was waiting to see if she would accept what she was becoming?

The notion brought up a question in her mind.

How many people tried to resist when getting infected?

How many tried to fight it?

She couldn't exactly blame them, getting infected with lycanthropy wasn't exactly fun, and she assumed most folks usually didn't survive the encounter.

Still, running as she was now, she couldn't possibly understand why anyone wouldn't want this if they knew what it could mean for them. The freedom to just be in the moment.

She smiled and surged forward, allowing herself to run and just move without holding back.

Well, it wasn't really moving, was it?

No, it wasn't movement like normal people would understand it. It was more like flowing through the spaces between the rocks and trees.

Allowing the momentum of her weight to propel herself forward through the terrain, like water seeking the path of least resistance.

Neither of them slowed even as branches whipped against their faces and undergrowth tore at their pants and exposed flesh.

Truthfully, Ellie wished she could just have ripped every shred of clothes off herself and really let herself go.

Time seemed to have lost all meaning as she swarmed over logs and rocks.

Several times, she caught her old scent from that night and realized then how much of a fool she had been. That they had all been.

Running so blind with fear and terror. Had they known the truth of how close the beast had been almost the entire time, they might have just given up.

The canopy thickened overhead, casting them into dappled shadows of reds and oranges, and suddenly a new stink caught her attention.

Gunpowder.

The blast rang out in her head, and the yellow eyes flashed before her again.

A second shot, that made her ears hurt, then that voice in the darkness.

His voice, strangely high yet booming, seemed to be simultaneously inquisitive and scolding.

But to a pack of lost and frightened kids, it had been the voice of an angel come to save them.

What you kids doin' out here on a night like dis?

She locked onto the smell of that moment. His smell. The scent of wood smoke, gunpowder, and pipe tobacco.

God, she loved that smell. It wasn't like the stench of her mother's cigarettes.

It was wholesome and rich and full of warmth and kindness.

Then suddenly, Tina came to a skidding stop. Halting at the edge of a hollow only feet ahead of her.

Ellie scrambled to avoid slamming into her, catching a tree and abruptly halting her momentum.

"What?" she asked, chest heaving from the wild excitement of their run.

Tina pointed and said, "There, we found it. Fucking Hell, El! We found it!

Below them was an old hollow that had been cleared of trees. At its center stood an old, battered cabin with a sturdy watchtower attached to one side.

Even from this distance, the unmistakable stench of copper and death permeated the air.

The once stout door was now an open hole in its face, battered until it had exploded inward by the beast.

"Bloody hell," Ellie gasped. "How did we find it so fast?"

Tina gazed around the clearing in disbelief. "I don't know. I just... ran. I wasn't even thinking of where I was going."

Ellie turned and looked back the way they'd come.

God, it had to have been miles of ground covered in a fraction of the time.

"I guess," Ellie whispered, "we just remembered. If that is even possible. You know, like an instinctive memory of somewhere we've been before?"

Tina nodded slowly. "I guess that makes sense," she said quietly.

"You think we can pull the same trick back? Your mom is going to be pissed."

"Yeah, she can be pissed all she wants. Not like she can do much to me besides yell." Ellie said flatly.

Ellie turned back and looked down the hollow at the cabin.

"He's still in there…" Tina said softly.

"Yup," Ellie whispered, her throat tight.

"He knew what was going to happen, and he still tried to help."

"No one even came looking for him?" she said bitterly. "We told them a park ranger is dead, and nobody even tried to find his body?"

"They didn't care," Tina said coldly. "He was nothing more than some crazy old man with wild stories to them. That's what places like this are like. Small minded and bigoted unless you fit their mold."

The injustice of it was more than Ellie could bear. This kind, tough old man, who had given them shelter and warmth, and even gave his life for kids he didn't even know from Adam. Left to rot in his own home.

And for what?

Just because he was a bit eccentric? That he

chose to live on his own, away from society?

She couldn't blame him if this is how they treated him.

"Cripes, and people wonder why I want to go back to Los Angeles. At least there being different is considered normal." Ellie spat.

"Mind if I join you?" Tina asked.

"Please do," Ellie replied. "We can go shopping and find clothes that actually fit."

Tina laughed bitterly. "What you don't like looking like you got melted down and poured in those jeans?"

Ellie flashed her a glare. "I don't like feeling my underwear riding into the great unknown."

They stood there for a minute just staring down at the cabin in the hollow. Anger bubbling inside them.

Suddenly, and without warning, Ellie threw back her head and let loose a long, lonely howl.

Tina looked at her in shock, then slowly joined her voice with Ellie's.

It was a strange lament. Not quite human, nor could it be called animalistic.

It was a sound that seemed to stretch and vibrate through the trees, until the forest around them went silent and held its breath to listen.

Ellie didn't know why, but it felt right to her.

There was no way the old man hadn't known what was happening to Tina, yet not once did he show her a single moment of anger or hostility.

Even if he hadn't seen it too in Ellie, he had been nothing but a sweet and kind old gentleman.

She would almost call him grandfatherly. To be honest, she wished she had a Grandpa like Jared Duprix.

In the brief time they had known him, he had been kind and wise. Kooky and a little fun, even in the face of horrors unimaginable.

And when the chips were down, he had been brave in the face of death. Yipping and hooting all the way till the very end, like it was the best day of his life.

That is what lay in that cabin in the hollow.

A man who in but a handful of hours had become a titan to a small group of lost, frighten-ed kids.

As they quieted and listened to the last echoes of their song fade into the distance, they stood somberly, their grief abated at last.

"Well," Tina said finally, wiping her eyes. "Let's get this shit done."

CHAPTER 15

As they approached the front porch of the cabin, it was the stench that hit them first.

They hadn't even made it to the front steps, yet it was like smacking straight into a thick, miasmic wall of rot.

To say it stunk was an understatement beyond proportions. It was an almost indescribable stench that made both girls recoil as they stepped closer to the cabin.

To Ellie, it seemed to be almost a mixture of boiled cabbage, hot garlic, old mothballs, and feces, topped off with a hint of pickled cherries, blended into the most vile of concoctions and left out in the sun to fester.

Ellie felt her gorge rise and had to fight down the urge to vomit.

She pressed the sleeve of her coat hard to her

face, but it did little to filter the overwhelmingly eye-watering stench.

"Jesus Christ," Tina muttered, her face contorted in disgust as she mounted the steps to the front door.

"How could anyone miss this? Search parties should have found this place immediately."

Ellie stepped tentatively into the cabin, anger rising within her.

The interior of the cabin was as Ellie had expected. Utterly destroyed.

To say the inside of the cabin itself was a war zone would be putting it mildly.

The simple furniture lay shattered and in ruins. A small folding table looked as though it had served as a makeshift shield, its wooden top gouged and rent by claws.

The wooden walls were pitted and ripped at by a mosaic of shotgun blasts and claw marks, some stained with gore and blood.

Even the floor itself had not escaped the carnage of the battle.

Dark bloodstains tinted long claw marks, and in one place, a large hole marked where the old man must have misfired into it.

Ellie caught sight of something glimmering

in the walls, twinkling like hundreds of stars embedded in the timber.

After a moment, it dawned on her that it was silver shot peppering nearly every inch of the cabin walls.

She stepped closer to take a look and tripped over something. Catching her balance, she looked down and gasped, stumbling backwards.

It was there, just to the right of the door, wedged between a small fridge and the ruins of the dining table, where the unmistakable outline of Jared Duprix's corpse.

"Oh God!" she said, turning away from the mutilated and rotting visage of the old man.

"He really went down fighting, didn't he?" she whispered, covering her mouth, fighting back the urge to throw up.

Tina nodded as she also pressed her hand to her mouth. "Yeah, he was definitely a tough old bird, I'll say that much. Probably had the time of his life from the look of things."

Ellie let out a bark of laughter, appreciating the distraction.

"Yeah, I'd say, did you hear him that night?" she said through her tears, then did her best impression of the old man, "I hope I give you da squirts!"

Tina chuckled as they stepped further into the room, "Yeah, he definitely had a good hoot at the end there."

"Do you think he knew it was hopeless?" Ellie asked quietly.

Tina picked her way carefully through the wreckage, taking it all in.

"Yeah, he knew alright," she said at last. "Pretty sure he wanted it this way."

"Why would anyone want to die like this?" Ellie asked in awe.

Tina stopped near what remained of the dining table and looked down at the old man. "Couldn't you smell it on him? The sickness? I think it was the big C."

She smiled softly down at Jared's body. "He was in a lot of pain. Even if he didn't show it, I could tell. Old folks are like that, you know. Stubborn to the end."

Ellie looked at the carnage surrounding them. "You really think this was better?"

"For an old timer like him?" Tina shrugged, her expression somber but certain.

"Having something real to fight for at the end…? Yeah, I think so. Probably made him feel young again for a few minutes. Gave him a sense of purpose."

Tina's eyes suddenly widened as she seemed to lock onto something.

She moved toward the old stove where a cast-iron pan lay discarded under the ruins of a chair.

She picked it up and held it up for Ellie to see. "Hey, take a look at this."

Embedded in its surface was a large, yellow-ed tooth, curved and sharp like a dagger.

Jared's voice echoed in Ellie's mind as she looked at the dagger-like tooth.

Awww!!! Did I ding yer bell?

"He must have fought like ten men," Tina murmured as she wrenched the tooth free from the pan.

She turned it over in her palm, studying it with a look of fascination.

"Memento mori," she said, tossing it in the air and snatching it deftly.

"What?" Ellie asked confusedly.

Tina smiled. "Memento mori. It's something David would always say. 'Remember death! Memento mori!' Creep used to keep a human skull in his bedroom."

Ellie cocked an eyebrow at her, "And you

dated him, why?"

Tina shrugged and pocketed the tooth. "He had his fun moments, but mostly it was that he was just available. He also had the stamina of a bull. Girls got needs, you know."

Ellie rolled her eyes and turned back to the ruined cabin's main room.

"We're not going to find anything here. This place looks like a damn bomb went off."

"Well, what about upstairs?" Tina asked, gesturing toward the narrow doorway that led to the watchtower above.

Ellie made a face of utter disgust. "Oh no, not another god damn watchtower! We almost died in the last one."

Tina smirked, "Well… You almost died. I was perfectly fine," she said playfully.

Ellie glared at her. "Yeah, I wonder why? *You* turned into a seven-foot dog and tried to eat everyone."

They entered the watchtowers' base, and Ellie recalled being unceremoniously tossed out the window, which was still open.

"You know, out of all the injuries I got that night," she said, looking at Tina on the stairs, "My ass took the longest to heal."

Tina stopped and looked at her, an eyebrow cocked inquisitively. "Say what?"

"Yeah, my ass. Your psycho boyfriend threw me out the damn window like a sack of potatoes, and I landed on my ass." Ellie said, turning to look at her.

"I swear, everything else except my ass healed within a few days. It was bruised for almost two weeks."

Tina burst out laughing. "Seriously? It took your butt two weeks to heal a bruise?"

"It's not funny, I couldn't even sit on the toilet to take a pee." Ellie said as she tentatively mounted the steps, testing their sturdiness.

Fortunately, unlike the watchtower over-looking the dam, Jared's tower was stout and firmly built.

The entire staircase was internal to the structure and protected from the elements by solid walls.

Several steps actually looked to be recently replaced. Which actually worked to improve Ellie and Tina's confidence.

"Well, at least the old man kept this tower in good condition. Unlike his damn radio." Tina commented.

It had been a point of amusement for Ellie the last time she was here.

She recalled how she had laughed when she had found out they were being helped by the one man in the whole park who had to walk ten miles just to make a phone call.

At the top, they found a small door. Unlike the previous watchtower, this door didn't require a ladder to enter, but was set up normally like an attic door.

"I swear, there better be something interesting up here," Ellie said.

"Didn't he say lightning had hit it once and blown the radio?" Tina asked as she jiggled the handle.

"Huh? It's locked!" she said in a surprised tone.

"Seriously?" Ellie asked, trying the handle for herself.

Sure enough, it was indeed locked.

"Question," Tina said, "Why would a hermit in the middle of nowhere lock the door to his '*attic*?'" she asked, making air quotes with her fingers.

Ellie rolled her eyes. "Because it's not an attic, and he's hiding something in there."

"Bingo!" she exclaimed, then stopped and got a strange look on her face.

Ellie tilted her head and asked, "What?"

Tina gave her a look, then glanced downstairs. "It's locked. Which means the old guy probably had the key on him when he…"

Tina made a weird face, crossing her eyes and sticking out her tongue while imitating being hanged.

Realization dawned on Ellie then, much to her horror. "Eeewww! Tina no! I'm not digging in his pockets! He's…"

CRRRRACK!

Tina smiled slyly. "Oh, look! It was just stuck," she said as she pushed the door open. The locking mechanism ripped from the doorframe.

"I hate you," Ellie said in a small, childlike voice as she followed Tina through the now open doorway.

The room beyond the door was anything but an attic and more of a private library and study.

Mercifully, when the door was closed, the foul stench of poor Jared Duprix's rotting corpse was sealed away, and the girls could breathe a little more easily.

They found a door to a small, narrow catwalk that allowed fresh air into the space.

Though opening it resulted in a new, though milder, assault of the stink, it was overpowered by the musty smell of old leather and paper.

The small study itself was a pleasant, well organized office space.

Like the previous watchtower, the upper portions of the walls were dominated by a series of large windows, below which were lined with low bookshelves.

Ellie couldn't help but feel envious of the beautiful panoramic view of the surrounding forest.

She could tell that Jared must have spent a lot of his time up here. The view must have made for some wonderful inspirations.

Upon the shelves were numerous leather-bound volumes and dog-eared paperbacks.

A narrow roll top writing desk with a small wooden chair stood between two of the book-shelves.

Ellie walked over and sat down at the desk as Tina perused the shelves.

"These aren't all forest service manuals," she said, pulling out a thick volume.

"Some are, but check this out."

She flopped the heavy leather bound book in front of her, and Ellie read the cover.

"A Treatise of Medical Lycanthropy, by William H. Pond?"

She flipped open the cover and read the inscription, "Published, 1884… Where does an old hermit get something like this?"

"Good question, but a better one is, where does he get hundreds of volumes like it?" Tina replied and waved her hand around the room.

"This isn't just some passing interest, El. The old man was here for a reason. This is commitment, a life's work of study."

Ellie looked down at the desk and noted a lunar calendar marking each month's lunar cycles.

One date caught her attention. It was set in the middle of the lunar month, but was marked with only a single word.

"I wonder who Ellen is?" Ellie asked out loud.

Tina cocked an eyebrow. "Interesting, but I doubt we'll ever find out."

"True," Ellie replied, opening the top drawer of the desk.

Her eyes lit up as she pulled out a series of leather bound journals.

"Well, would you look at this," Ellie said, as she began flipping through the pages of the newest one. "He wrote down everything."

Tina began rummaging around and finally came up with a pair of old leather bags from beside the desk and began loading one, thrusting the other at Ellie.

"We can't leave this stuff here. Take only what looks useful and as much as you can carry. We're not coming back," she said authoritatively.

Ellie nodded, adding Jared's journals to her bag as well as several volumes.

Ellie hefted her bag with a grunt. "God damn this thing must weigh a ton!"

"Yeah, mine too," Tina replied, throwing the strap over her shoulder. "Better than going to the gym, right?"

Ellie glared at her as she made her way down the stairs into the choking stench.

Tina stopped in the main room and looked down at the old man's corpse with a look of disdain.

He was covered in bugs and maggots, all working diligently to devour the putrid flesh.

"We should burn this place," Tina said suddenly, her voice firm.

Ellie looked at her, questioning. "Why?"

"Because your mom was right. He deserves better than to rot here, forgotten." Tina's eyes hardened. "And we can't risk anyone else finding that library."

Ellie hesitated, glancing at the old Cajun's remains, then nodded slowly. "Yeah, you're right. Ok, let's look for something to light it up with."

Tina smiled. "He had electricity, gotta be a genny around here somewhere."

Outside, they found a small generator in a shed along with several gas cans.

Tina started shaking them until she found a few that were heavy.

"Perfect. Now we're cooking with *gas*!" she said, chuckling at her own joke.

Ellie just rolled her eyes and grabbed a can.

They worked swiftly and silently, splashing fuel across the wooden floors and shattered furniture, and running it up the stairs to the library above.

It wasn't long before the stench of decay competed with the reek of gasoline, making their eyes water.

Tina carefully poured a generous amount over Jared's body.

Ellie could see the turmoil raging in her eyes. The old man did indeed deserve better, but it wasn't a luxury they could afford.

She stood in the doorway, watching as Tina snuffed out the pilot lights on the old stove and turned on the burners, before joining her and taking a bag.

"Goodbye, you crazy old bastard," Tina said softly.

"Yeah, thanks for everything. I wish we could do better." Ellie said.

Tina pulled a Zippo from her pocket and smiled.

"Marks. He loved this damn thing. Would annoy the crap outta me with it," she said as she held it up for Ellie to see.

She flipped the lid and lit it, then tossed it into the cabin.

There was a dull "*whoomph*," as the fuel caught, and fire spread like a living thing across everything.

The orange flames hungrily devour-ing all that they could.

"Tina! Come on! Let's go, before the whole

place blows." Ellie said, tugging Tina's arm as the heat intensified.

They turned and sprinted into the forest, the crackling of the burning cabin following them.

They had just made it to the tree line when suddenly, shouting erupted behind them.

"Dad! Over here!" A familiar voice yelled.

Ellie and Tina froze, exchanging alarmed glances.

They turned back to look through the foliage, careful not to be seen.

Through the dense brush, they could see two figures rushing toward the burning cabin, Richard and Mike Varano.

"God dam…!!!"

BOOM!

CHAPTER 16

Ellie covered her ears and fell to the ground as a brilliant orange flash burst out of the cabin with a thunderous boom.

It was defending, and she felt a hot wave of air buffet her as she pressed herself into a tight ball behind a tree.

"Jesus Christ on a crutch! What the heck was that?!" she gasped as Tina rolled laughing into her hiding spot.

"The stove," Tina said in a hushed whisper as she poked her head back up to look over the rise.

She pouted her lip out. "Damn it didn't blow as big as I had hoped. In the movies, it's like a bomb."

Ellie joined her, the whole cabin was engulfed in brilliant flames, and both Richard and

Mike Varano were scrambling to stand.

Ellie could smell the scent of copper in the air, and she saw Richard clutching his ear.

"What the hell are they doing way out here? How'd they even find this place?" Ellie hissed.

Tina's eyes narrowed, watching the men's frantic movements.

"Isn't it obvious? They somehow tracked us. You heard what they said back at the gas station, they're looking for the thing that killed David."

"You mean they're looking for you?" Ellie asked.

Tina nodded, "Good thing for us, they don't know that."

They remained crouched in the undergrowth, watching as Richard and Mike struggled to rise, still stunned from the blast.

The flames had already consumed most of the structure, sending thick black smoke billowing into the afternoon sky. The heat was intense even from their hiding spot.

"We need to leave," Ellie whispered, eyeing the men cautiously.

Tina shook her head. "Not yet. I want to see what they're up to."

Richard Varano stood clutching his ear with

one hand while he dragged his son further away from the blazing heat.

His face was a twisted mask of fear and anger.

"Damn it all to hell!" he shouted, dropping Mike in the dirt almost a dozen paces from the girls' hiding spot. "You ok, boy?

Mike sat up coughing. "You think it was those girls?"

"Who else?" Richard spat. "They're the only ones who could have found this place. Old man sure as shit didn't put out a welcome sign to visitors."

Tina looked at Ellie. *They're definitely on to us*. She said silently.

What do we do? Ellie asked, feeling cold despite the heat from the cabin

The fire roared louder as it found new fuel, a section of the roof collapsing with a tremendous crash.

The Varanos backed away from the intensifying heat, shielding their faces.

"Well, whatever the old man had in there is gone now. Why the hell would a pair of girls burn it?" Mike asked, frustratedly.

Richard grabbed his son by the shirt and pulled him close, "You know exactly why. Because them girl's been lying this entire time, and the proof was right in that cabin."

He let Mike go and watched the burning structure for a moment.

At last, he turned back the way they'd come and said, "Come on, son. We need to tell the Sheriff."

"He's gotta listen to us now," Mike said as he followed his father, oblivious to the girls only feet away.

"He'd better. If this isn't a sign that something fishy is going on, I don't know what is." Rich replied.

Tina slumped to the ground when she was sure the men were well out of earshot.

"What's wrong?" Ellie whispered, alarmed by her friend's sudden change.

Tina looked up at her, an odd look in her eyes. "I killed Stacy last night."

Ellie tilted her head and sat next to her.

"You said that earlier. But you do know, it was just another nightmare, not really us," she said softly.

"It wasn't a dream," Tina replied, her voice flat.

She looked up at the sky and chuckled. "It

wasn't some stupid nightmare, El. I actually killed her."

She looked at Ellie again, "Last night, something... happened. I don't know what it was. I felt this pull, like I had to go outside. Next thing I know, I'm running through the woods, soaking wet and... Well, I knew it had been me."

Ellie sighed, leaning back and watching the black smoke curl its way into the sky.

She wondered then if this was what the apocalypse was going to be like. Black smoke and desolation, with a pair of girls sitting around talking casually about killing people.

"How sure are you?" Ellie asked. "I mean, I saw it too. I had the same dream. I ate her tongue, too. Or at least I think I did. It was so fucking real."

Tina put her head in her hands and let out a small laugh. "Pretty sure. I swear this werewolf shit is going to drive me insane."

"I know," Ellie sighed again. "But hopefully Mr. Duprix can help us out again," she said, patting the heavy bag of books.

Tina snorted as she stood up. "That'd be interesting. If we could see the dead and talk to them."

Ellie rolled her eyes, "Please, no more weirdness. We got enough bullshit to deal with without adding ghosts to the mix," she said, standing up.

"Besides, unless you plan to hold a séance right here, we need to get back to my mom and Haily. Or we'll be the ghosts."

It wasn't hard for them to find their trail back. And once they found their scent, they broke into a long, loping run that ate the ground with ease.

They wove their way back through the confusing network of deer trails and walking paths, retracing their old path around the mountains in short order.

At one point, they found themselves at the waterfall where Jess, David, and her had found Tina as she fell from the top.

"Holy cow, El! How did I not die?" Tina exclaimed, seeing the fall for the first time coherently.

"That's gotta be close to twenty feet down?" Ellie shrugged.

"Yeah, you were pretty out of it. How the heck did you find us anyway?"

Tina shook her head and said, "I don't know.

I hardly remember anything after that thing got done with me. It's all like a big, blurry dream. I guess I just got lucky. "

Something about that notion didn't settle right with Ellie, but she had no better explanation, so she didn't say anything.

They bolted again, running as fast as their burdens would allow.

At last, a sound reached them, and they slowed to listen.

"Elllliee!!" came a female voice from somewhere in the distance, followed by another.

"Tiiinnnnaaaaa!"

It was her mother and Haily calling their names.

Ellie exchanged a look with Tina.

Time to face the music. She said silently.

Tina just shrugged.

"Let's get it over with and go home," she replied out loud.

It only took them another minute or two to find Haily and her Mother still standing by Tina's wrecked van.

"Ellie!" Haily shouted, her expression suddenly shifting from concern to relief as she ran and practically tackled her.

"Where have you two been?" Nancy demanded, rushing toward them.

"Do you realize how worried sick I've been? Two hours! Two hours we've been out here calling your names and…"

Ellie wrapped her mother in a hug, effectively silencing the tirade.

"Hey, Mom? Can you chew us out later, please? We need to leave. Now."

Nancy pulled away and eyed her dubiously, her eyes falling to the heavy leather bag draped over her shoulder.

"What's that? Where did you two go?" she asked more calmly than before.

"We've been worried," Haily said quietly, "You guys just disappeared."

"Jared's cabin, we found it," Tina explained, her voice flat.

"Or what was left of it."

"Mr. Varano and Mike are out here too," Ellie added.

"They're armed and pissed, and I think they followed us, and they might be heading back this way."

Her mother's complexion turned ashen.

"Oh God! Let's go!" she said, ushering the

three girls quickly toward the station wagon, still parked on the narrow dirt track.

As they hurried to the car, Ellie stopped at the van and began rummaging through it.

Finally, she emerged holding something as Haily fell into step beside her.

"What's that?" she asked inquisitively.

Ellie smiled impishly at her and said, "I had to get something I'd forgotten about."

She handed a small, dog-eared paperback to Haily.

"The Hellhound of the Westerly Woods?" Haily read the title out loud. "What the heck?!"

Ellie giggled, "Don't judge me. I was at a good part."

CHAPTER 17

"What were you girls thinking?!" Her mother's voice trembled with anger as she made what seemed to be the thousandth lap in front of the couch.

Ellie sat on the couch, staring up at a dark spot on the ceiling, rethinking whether or not she should have just taken the berating in the forest and been done with it.

But no, she was now stuck here on the couch listening to her mother lecture as animatedly as Vladimir Lennon.

She quietly wondered whether eating your mother was acceptable werewolf behavior.

Oh, how simple it would be.

Tina squirmed next to her, her head resting on Ellie's shoulder as she watched Nancy's furious pacing.

How long is this going to last? Tina asked silently.

Ellie gave a small shrug. *Who knows, she could burn out in a minute or go on all night.*

"Oh, what? Is that all you got to say for yourself, young lady?!" said her mother, misreading the small movement.

"Running off into the woods without a word? After I explicitly told you that we were to stay together!" she shouted, stabbing an accusatory finger at Ellie.

"Mrs. Granger, please…" came a small voice from the corner.

"What?!" Nancy snapped, turning to the third girl whom she had all but forgotten about.

Haily perched uncomfortably on a chair nearby, her eyes darting between Ellie and Nancy, clearly wishing she were anywhere else.

"Please, ma'am, I'm sure they had a good reason for running off. I… I mean, after what Tina said…"

"That's right! Thank you, Haily." Ellie's mother exclaimed as she spun back around and fixed Tina with a glare as sharp as glass.

"What was that shit I heard you talking about, being raped?"

Her expression was a mixture of horror and indignant anger, but there was more to it than that.

It was almost like… genuine compassion.

"You girls better start telling me what really happened out there that night. Because I can't help you if you don't tell me."

Ellie looked down. This had been the exact problem that had landed her on an operating table in an abortion clinic.

That had not ended well. What her parents thought was just going to be a simple abortion ended up with her getting a hysterectomy.

She had to face the facts. On one hand, telling the truth would probably make her look nuts.

But on the other hand, keeping it secret wasn't helping either; it was only making them look guilty.

But how do you tell your mother that you're a werewolf? *Oh, hey Mom, by the way. You're handing out candy alone this year, I've got to go sprout fangs and fur and go eat Bambi.*

Tina's face hardened as she lifted her head off Ellie's shoulder.

Enough of this shit! She growled softly, rising to her feet.

"Exactly what didn't you understand? I

didn't stutter out there," she said, now looming over Ellie's mother.

Ellie cocked an eyebrow as she noted the subtle height difference between Tina and her mother.

Tina seemed to be almost a good inch taller than Nancy. Yet this morning, Ellie could have sworn that it had been her Mom who had been taller by at least half an inch.

Apparently, her mother had seemed to notice the change as well, as she took a step back from the looming shadow of Tina.

"I was raped by that... thing in the van. While everyone else watched." Her voice was flat, emotionless, as if reciting facts about someone else.

"While your daughter watched. And all they could do was walk away and leave me there to get fucked and die."

Tina surged forward, placing her face right in Nancy's.

"Is that what you wanted to hear? Did you want to hear about how I got beast fucked and thought I was going to die? Or how your little girl couldn't do shit to save me? Huh?! Is that what you wanted to hear?!"

Nancy sank into an armchair, a look of utter horror and shock written into her features as she stared up and Tina.

"Oh my God. That's why you ran today… But then how? Why did a bear…?"

"It wasn't exactly a bear, Mom," Ellie said, sighing with exhaustion.

"What do you mean 'not exactly a 'bear'?" Nancy asked, her mother's eyes narrowing with suspicion.

Ellie rubbed her face, trying to collect herself. At last, she looked up at Haily, then at Tina.

"I guess we're doing this now," she said to Tina and motioned for her to continue.

"It was that other guy they found at the dam," Tina said, looking back at Nancy, then Haily. "The naked one with the knife in his chest."

Nancy's brow furrowed, and Ellie could see the gears spinning in her mother's head. "You mean that young man they never identified? Oh god, that was you two?!"

"God, Mom, why are you so oblivious? Yes, the one they didn't identify. The knife," Ellie emphasized, leaning forward, "was made of silver, and I put it right through the bastard's heart."

Nancy stared at her blankly, and Ellie felt a surge of frustration.

"Jesus, Mom! Don't you get it? The guy wasn't fucking human! He was a werewolf! A real live werewolf!" Ellie shouted, rising to her feet now as she ripped at her hair in frustration.

The words hung in the air like a thunderclap, and her mother's face went slack with disbelief.

Ellie stood there, her chest heaving as she stared at her mother, waiting for an answer.

She looked at Haily for a response, but she too sat only with a dumbfounded look on her face.

The silence seemed to extend on for an eternity until finally, at long last, her mother slowly said, "Are you two out of your fucking minds?"

It was as if her mother had struck her a physical blow.

She had expected this response but hadn't been prepared to actually experience it.

"No, Mom! I'm not..." Ellie paused to compose herself before continuing.

"We're not crazy," Tina interjected, "We know how it sounds, Mrs. Granger, but that guy was a werewolf, and your daughter killed him...

Why do you think we told everyone it was a bear? We knew no one would believe us."

Her mother looked from her to Tina, then let out a small hysterical giggle.

"Great," she said softly, throwing up her hands in defeat.

"Just fucking great. Either my daughter is completely insane, or she's a murderer."

"Mom..."

"NO!" Nancy shouted, lurching to her feet, and thrusting a finger at Ellie like it was a rapier.

"No... Not one more word... Not one single more word. Or I'll..." she said venomously.

Nancy looked from Ellie to Tina, then back to Haily, before finally shaking her head in disgust.

She walked out of the living room without saying another word.

After a few moments, they heard the clink of glass from the kitchen as the sudden stench of cigarettes filled the air.

Tina coughed and rolled her eyes as the scent of tobacco wafted into the room. "Well, that went well."

Ellie sighed, slumping back onto the couch, feeling just as defeated as her mother, wishing she could hide at the bottom of a bottle of Grey Goose with a pack of Marlboros, too.

Haily fidgeted in her seat, her fingernails digging into her palms nervously.

"What are you going to do now?" she asked them nervously. "I mean… You guys didn't really mean all that werewolf stuff… Did you?"

Ellie ran her hands through her hair. "I don't know. She doesn't believe us. And why would she? No one in their right mind would."

Tina suddenly moved, making both Ellie and Haily jump.

"Come on," she said, grabbing Haily's wrist. "We're not done here."

Without waiting, she hauled Haily up the stairs, Ellie trailing behind, looking confused as ever.

"What was that about?" Ellie demanded, carefully closing her bedroom door behind them.

Tina spun on Haily, who had pressed herself against the wall. "You heard everything down there."

Haily nodded, wide-eyed. "You guys aren't kidding, are you? This isn't some messed-up prank?"

Tina looked at Ellie, then said, "I wish it

were. Everything we told her mom was true."

She sat on the bed and let out a tired sigh.

"We were just starting to wind down for the night when that thing came out of the forest and attacked us," she said in a flat monotone.

"We tried to run but… well… it ran us off the road. It… It hunted us down and then it… killed Mark and Jess. And it…" she swallowed hard, closing her eyes as she composed herself, "it raped me, and scratched Ellie."

"It killed the old man, too," Ellie added softly. "The one who tried to help us."

"And David? What happened to him?" Haily asked with a gulp.

"In the car, you said he turned into a monster… what did you mean?"

The temperature in the room seemed to drop, and Ellie tried to think of how best to explain David's part in everything.

"David…" Ellie began carefully, "David actually went insane. He tried to kill everyone. He beat Mark half to death and left him so he could get away. He threw Jess to the beast so it could rape her too, but it killed her instead."

Ellie's voice was barely above a whisper, each word dragging with the weight of memory.

Tina continued where Ellie faltered. "Then on the dam, he tried to murder Ellie with the old man's knife before I stepped in and… killed him…"

Haily's eyes widened with horror.

"Wait a second, how… How could *you* have killed him? I heard he had been torn apart. Then. ..how could you have…" Her voice trailed off, the unfinished question hanging in the air.

"We're werewolves!" Ellie blurted out the words, escaping before she could stop them.

The room fell into stunned silence as Haily stared at them, her mouth open in shock.

"You're what?"

"Werewolves," Tina said calmly. "You know howl at the moon. Fur, claws, the whole wolf man gig."

Haily looked back and forth between them and giggled.

"You're kidding, right? Like that downstairs… Oh man, you two really had me going there for a minute."

She looked at the serious expressions on their faces, and her smile faltered. "But it really was a joke, right? None of that was real. You're pulling our legs… right…?"

"Does this look like a fucking joke to you?" Tina lifted her shirt and gestured at her chiseled abs. "That's not normal."

After a moment, Haily's voice came out in a terrified whisper.

"Oh shit… You two aren't kidding… are you? You're…"

Tina stepped forward, her voice deadly calm. "I turned that night, somehow I knew Ellie was turning too, and when David tried to murder her, I…"

She swallowed hard and shook her head. "I ripped off his head and tore out his spine. And I think I may have eaten his liver or spleen or something too."

Haily stood rooted to the spot for a moment, her face drained of all color.

Then, with a strangled gasp, she bolted for the door, flying out it like a frightened rabbit.

The sound of her footsteps thundering down the stairs echoed through the house, followed by the front door slamming shut with enough force to rattle the windows.

Ellie and Tina rushed to the window just in time to see Haily sprinting away from the house as if the devil himself were chasing her.

CHAPTER 18

They watched as Haily fled down the street, shrinking in the afternoon sun.

"What if she tells someone?" Ellie asked.

"Who's going to believe it?" Tina replied with a snort. "Your mom sure as hell doesn't."

The stench of cigarettes was overpowering as they headed back downstairs.

They found her mother still at the kitchen counter, tossing back another glass of vodka with what looked to be her second or third cigarette firmly clutched between her lips.

She barely acknowledged them, affording them little more than a glance before pouring herself another two fingers with slightly trembling hands.

"Mom? We're going…" Ellie started hesitantly.

Her mother simply raised a hand, cutting her

off without even turning to look at her.

Ellie growled softly in frustration, then nodded to Tina.

Grabbing the leather bags they had taken from the cabin, they walked out the front door.

"God, what a bitch!" Ellie hissed as the door slammed shut behind her.

Tina shrugged as they walked down the drive to her truck.

"Yeah, Moms can be like that. You should see mine when she's pissed. Won't say a word to me for days, then out of the blue, 'We need food'," she said, mimicking her own mother as she started the engine.

"Speaking of which. I'm starving, let's get some grub."

It was about twenty minutes later, they found themselves sitting in a booth at Mabel's Diner.

It was a quiet little place sitting off the main square of the town, that had that classic dinner charm with plastic booths backed with red and white striped vinyl.

The lunch rush had died down, leaving only a few scattered patrons nursing coffee cups and the faint smell of grease lingering in the air.

The fare of the place was pretty standard for

small towns like this. Hot dogs and smash burgers with a slap of mustard, mayo, and sliced cheese.

After scanning the menu for a minute and being tempted by the steak, they settled on ordering burgers, rare for both of them.

"What'll it be, ladies?" the waitress asked.

The waitress was a middle-aged woman with a shock of vibrant red hair, penciled eyebrows, and way too much blue eye shadow.

The name tag on her red and white checkered blouse read Suzie-Q.

Tina smiled up at her and said, "I'll have a hamburger, hold the rabbit food, cheese, and bacon, please. Oh, and could you make it bloody, please?"

"Double that, I'll have the same, thanks." Ellie piped in.

The waitress cocked a penciled eyebrow at them but simply asked, "Alright, that'll be all?"

It wasn't really a question, but Tina took the opportunity, "Yes, and a couple of milkshakes, please. Strawberry with extra red."

Suzie-Q wrote the order down and retreated before they could add anything else.

Tina pulled out a couple of books and passed one to Ellie as she flipped through the other.

After a few minutes of quiet reading, Tina tapped Ellie's arm and flipped the journal around.

"Hey, check this out," she said, tapping a page with excitement. "Didn't he say something about this that night?"

Ellie leaned forward to see what Tina was pointing at. She picked up the journal and read the passage out loud.

"I have observed in my many years of hunting them that the Rougarou live in a pack structure that is unlike that of normal wolves.

This "pack," if one can even call it such, is more akin to that of African lion *Prides*.

That is to say, one male, or Alpha, who lives and hunts with a bevy of females, or "Bitches," as the correct terminology would have it."

"Yeah, I remember that," Ellie said, "Mr. Duprix seemed pretty sure that was why it didn't kill you."

Tina nodded. "It's kinda sad, really, if you think about it. All that thing wanted was someone to keep him company," she said, propping her chin with her hand.

Ellie rolled her eyes.

"You've officially gone soft in the head."

"Bitch!" Tina said playfully.

"Yup. So are you apparently. Literally," Ellie replied absently, scanning further down the page.

She let out a bark of laughter, then said, "You might want to cool your cooter. Did you read the part about breeding?"

"No, what does it say?" Tina replied, craning her head to try to read upside down.

"I almost feel sorry for these Alpha males, who are alone in the pride surrounded by a veritable harem of Bitches seeking his attentions.

Especially during their lunar "heat" cycles, in which they become increasingly promiscuous, to the point of near nymphomania. Much to the male's combined enthusiasm and woe."

Tina grimaced. "Ok, well, that's gross. But that explains why I've been feeling like I could jump every guy on the street."

"Yeah, me too," Ellie admitted, her cheeks flushing slightly. "It's like being on fire from the inside. Ya know?"

"Great! So we're doomed to become the town hussies. Exactly how I planned to spend the rest of my life." Tina exclaimed, a little louder than she intended, drawing looks from the few other occupied tables.

Tina flipped the page, grumbling, "Damn,

food better get here soon, I'm hungry."

She continued reading, "I have noted that in the instances where a Rougarou was unable to join or form a pride, a persistent level of ever increasing savagery was apparent.

This aggression is particularly prominent in the males of the species, and can border on complete madness.

I therefore must conclude that the pride structure provides the Rougarou a point of mental and social stability that enables them to maintain a high degree of self-control."

"Well, now at least there, we seem to be lucky. We got each other." Ellie said.

Tina leaned back and said, "True, but unless you got a banana in your pocket, you're not exactly my type, if you catch my meaning." She wiggled her eyebrows playfully.

Ellie rolled her eyes. "Ok, eew. You're sick."

Tina giggled as the bell above the diner door drew her attention.

She stiffened and swatted Ellie's arm to get her attention.

Ellie looked up just in time to watch Ashley Varano saunter in, followed closely by Tiffany, Jace, and Kyle.

It didn't take them long to spot Ellie and Tina, their faces stretching into cruel smiles.

"Great," she muttered. "Just what we need. More trouble."

Kyle seemed to track Ashley and Jace's gaze, following it until his soft brown eyes met Ellie's briefly before darting away.

For just a second, Ellie could have sworn there was something there. Floating in those dark liquid depths.

It was only fleeting, but it made something stir in her.

"Hey, what do you think of Kyle?" she asked Tina softly.

Tina shrugged. "Not sure. I guess he's handsome, in a meathead sort of way. The guy's got more unnecessary roughness reports than Dick Butkus. They don't call him the Rhino for nothing."

Tina looked him up and down for a second, then glanced back at Ellie.

"Are you sweet on him or something?"

Ellie blushed.

"No!" she said defensively, "I just…"

Tina made a small motion for her to be quiet as the group chose the booth directly behind Ellie, making a display of themselves.

"God, Ash, what's that smell?" Tiffany asked louder than necessary.

"Not sure," Ashley replied with a giggle, "Smells like rotten fish if you ask me."

Tiffany and Jace laughed.

Ashley stood up and poked her head over the booth.

"Oh, wait, it's just the lesbos in the next booth. You two should really take a bath when you're done, it's called manners to all us non-lesbos."

Tina tensed, her knuckles whitening around the edge of the table.

Ignore them, Ellie said silently.

Their food arrived, and they closed up their books to focus on eating.

Ellie took a bite of her burger, savoring the coppery taste of the almost raw meat.

The ruby red juice dribbled down her chin, and she couldn't help but close her eyes and savor the flavor.

For a brief moment, it was almost possible to tune out the idiots behind her.

Almost.

"Oh my God, are they actually eating raw meat?" Ashley asked loud enough to be heard.

"Oh my God, eeeww! That is so gross!" Tiffany said in an annoyingly high-pitched giggle.

Ellie caught Tina's eye and shook her head slightly. *Not worth it*, her expression said clearly.

I'm being nice, Tina replied with silent insincerity as she took a deep breath and focused on her burger.

See? I'm being good.

"Hey, Granger," Jace said, turning in the booth to look over her shoulder.

"I saw your chink pal running from your house earlier. What'd you freaks do? Try to kiss her?"

Ellie's grip tightened on her burger, the meat squishing between her fingers. She tilted her head, and an audible crack issued as something realigned.

Be nice, Tina teased silently.

Jace stood up and spun over to their table. "It's ok, Hollywood. You just need a boyfriend, that's all."

Cackling erupted from the booth behind her, "Yeah, someone who can teach her how not to be a dike."

"Oh my God, Ash, you're so mean!" Tiffany hooted.

"What's all this?" Jace asked, gesturing to the spread of books.

He reached over them and picked up the one reading the title aloud with exaggerated emphasis. "Warlocks, Werewolves, and Demons!"

He glared at Ellie, his eyes narrowing. "You a witch, Granger?"

He slammed the book back onto the table hard enough to make their drinks jump.

"You some sort of devil worshipper?"

The words hung in the air like a storm cloud.

Tina's eyes flashed with pure hatred as they slowly turned from sapphire to amber.

I'm going to tear his testicles off.

"Back off, Jace," Ellie said, her voice almost a low growl. "We're just trying to eat in peace."

"Peace?" Ashley stood and joined Jace to hover over their table, with Tiffany at her heels.

"If you want peace, go kill yourselves. We don't want lesbos in this to…"

"You know, Ashley, I'm getting real tired of hearing stupid fall out of your dick trap," Tina said, slowly rising to her feet.

She was significantly taller than Ashley now, something that made the queen bee take an involuntary step back.

Her eyes widened as the antiseptic stink of fear suddenly filled Ellie's nose.

She set down her burger as the sudden taste of raw copper flooded her mouth.

Her eyes rolled momentarily in pain as she felt her teeth begin to pull back into their sockets with a sharp pinch.

Ashley seemed to recover her courage quickly enough, though her voice wavered slightly. "What lesbo? What are you going to do? Try to fuck me?"

Something inside Ellie snapped.

She surged to her feet as a boiling red haze flooded her vision, her fingers finding purchase in Ashley's perfect bottle blonde hair.

"What does it take to get through that thick idiot skull of yours?" she snarled softly in the terrified girl's ear.

Tina moved simultaneously, her hand closing around Tiffany's ponytail, yanking back hard enough to make the girl shriek.

Jace lunged at Tina, grabbing her arm shouting, "Let go of her, you psycho!"

Without missing a beat, Tina slammed her forehead into Jace's face.

The sound of crunching bone echoed throughout the diner as blood squirted from his nostrils like twin fountains,

Jace staggered backward his chin covered in flowing blood.

Tina's face was a mask of splattered red blood as she took hold of his shirt and pulled him back in close.

With a hungry growl of pleasure, she licked the blood from his lips before throwing him from her contemptuously.

As Jace crashed through a table, Tina returned her focus to Tiffany with a vicious crimson smile.

"We told you to back off," Ellie growled into Ashley's ear, breathing in the antiseptic stench of her musk.

Ashley struggled, her eyes rolling in panic, as she frantically kicked and clawed at Ellie's arm, with almost no effect on the iron grip.

With a savage, inhuman snarl, Ellie started shaking the thrashing girl violently by her hair.

Tina had Tiffany bent backward over the table.

"Thanks to you, I've lost my appetite." Tina crooned sweetly as she picked up what remained of her burger.

"It'd be a shame to let this food go to waste on account of you."

She suddenly began to cram the almost raw meat into Tiffany's mouth.

Forcing it completely in with her fingers as the girl choked and kicked in desperation, tears streaming down her face.

Raw half-cooked blood trickled from her mouth and chunks of meat sprayed from her nose, and the sudden stink of urine filled the greasy diner air.

"Stop it!" the waitress, Suzie-Q, shrieked as she tried to intervene. "You crazy bitches!"

Ellie's fist came up without thinking, back-handing the woman in her cheek with an audible crunch as she went sailing through another table.

The few remaining customers were standing eyes wide with shocked disbelief but hesitant to attempt to try to intervene further.

The kitchen door burst open then as a portly cook, his face red with anger, came out wielding a long griddle spatula as if it were a fencing rapier.

"Hey! What the hell is going on out here?" he bellowed.

Tina released Tiffany and spun her face twisted in a savage snarl as she roared in defiance at him.

It was then that a large shadow fell over them.

Kyle rose from the booth, having been all but forgotten in the chaos, his massive frame blocking out the fluorescent lights above them.

He said nothing, just stared at Ellie and Tina with something unreadable in his eyes before pointing firmly toward the door.

Clarity ripped through the red haze, and they exchanged startled glances, suddenly aware of what they'd done.

"Oh fuck," Tina muttered as she stared down at the girl choking raw meat out at her feet.

"We need to go," Ellie whispered urgently. "Now!"

They hastily gathered their things, shoving the books back into the leather bags, and rushed toward the exit.

The cook tried to bum rush them to cut off their path, but was halted by Kyle's firm hand on his shoulder.

His soft eyes followed them, his expression still unnervingly calm amid the chaos they'd created.

"This isn't over!" Ashley shrieked as they fled out the door, clutching her head.

"You freaks are dead! Do you hear me?! YOU'RE FUCKING DEAD!"

CHAPTER 19

The house stood quiet in the late hours of the evening. Tina had stayed huddled with her in her room after they got back, waiting for the police to come knocking on the door.

But nothing happened. No knock came, and the phone never rang.

All remained quiet and peaceful.

Not even her mother showed any hostility when they had come in wild-eyed with fear.

Though admittedly, that probably had more to do with the vodka than anything else.

When they finally emerged from her room hours later, they had found her passed out on the couch, an empty vodka bottle tipped over on the coffee table beside her.

Ellie couldn't help but feel embarrassed by the scene, "Ummm... Yeah, sorry about that. She..."

"It's ok. Do you want to come crash at my place tonight? I got a pretty great basement room. Even has a TV. We could stay up late and catch Cliffhangers. I hear they got a really sexy Dracula on it."

Ellie sighed, "Sorry, I think I'm going to have to pass. That might make things worse when she wakes up. Thanks, though."

Tina looked dubiously at Nancy's prone form, then said, "Well, if you need me, just call."

Ellie nodded and walked Tina out.

"Catch you tomorrow!" Tina called out as she drove away.

Ellie waved and leaned against the porch railing. She found herself once again looking up at the swelling moon.

What she wouldn't give for good old Drac to come out of the shadows and whisk her away right now.

The notion of being undead and on an all liquid diet sounded absolutely sublime to her right now. Then, all she would have to worry about was getting an unwanted sun tan.

At least Count Dracula would make turning her more romantic than getting a stupid scratch on the head.

Her stomach growled loudly, reminding her of the meal she hadn't been able to finish.

She turned and went back inside, padding her way quietly into the kitchen, stopping only momentarily to stare at her mother from the kitchen doorway.

She couldn't help but feel a mixture of frustration and helplessness, tightening in her chest as she stared at her prone form.

The television droned in the background, its blue light flickering across her slack features.

Her stomach growled again, complaining so loudly she thought it might actually wake her mother from her stupor.

Turning away, she stood in the soft yellow light of the kitchen, gazing blankly into the open refrigerator with growing frustration.

Nothing looked even remotely appealing except the package of chuck roast on the bottom shelf.

With a growl, she grabbed it and ripped open the paper wrapping. The rich, metallic scent of raw beef hit her nostrils, and her mouth watered instantly.

Ellie sank to the floor, her knees giving out at the sight of dark red meat.

She stared at it lying there before her, and she felt her thighs moisten at the thought of it in her mouth.

With a savage snarl, she lunged forward, her teeth sinking easily through the tough meat. With a hard shake and pull, she wrenched the chunk free.

The taste was exquisite to the point of orgasm! Satisfying in a way that cooked food could never be.

She chewed slowly, savoring each bite, moaning with pleasure.

She felt the rush of moisture in her woman

hood as she swallowed, lunging back down without waiting to rip another chunk from the raw red ecstasy before her.

The very notion of her mouth being empty and devoid of the coppery wetness was an un-bearable nightmare.

As she ate, she let her body convulse and writhe as the waves of pleasure and need washed over her. Ripping and tearing at the helpless, dead flesh before her.

Finally, she climaxed as she swallowed the last bit of meat.

Reveling as the cold, mutilated flesh slid

liquidly down her throat into her warm, full belly.

She stopped then and touched her stomach, and the memory washed over her.

It's a girl, came the cold voice.

The voice that had ripped her unborn child apart and left them both mutilated.

Was it cruelty that he had saved her life? Or would it have been more merciful to just let her bleed out on that operating table?

The irony of it. He murdered her child and took her womb just to stop her from dying too, only for her to regrow it back.

What sort of sick cosmic joke was that?!

But to be fair, it really wasn't his fault, now was it?

She had been nothing more than a paycheck to him. Another stupid teen who couldn't keep her legs closed.

Mommy and Daddy to the rescue.

Never mind the fact that she didn't want to be rescued.

Never mind the fact that maybe, just maybe, despite how she got pregnant, she wanted to keep her baby.

Hatred boiled in her as she looked at her mother's passed-out form on the couch.

Blind and spitefully hiding in her drunken stupor.

Wasn't she part of her pain? Wasn't she, in truth, the source of her suffering?

Oh sure, she had made the stupid choice of going to Rick's stupid Valentine's party, hoping naively that he would notice her.

Well, he had noticed her alright.

His raping her was completely on her own head. That had definitely been her own fault and no one else's.

She had put herself in that position and had chosen not to be more careful or fight back.

She couldn't hang that on anyone else but herself.

But the abortion?

No, that had been all her mother's idea.

In reality, she couldn't even be mad at the doctor for the hysterectomy.

Shit like that happens, and he did what he could to save her life at least.

But her mother...?

Oh, how easy it would be to just end her right here and now and set the scales of balance right again.

She growled softly as she rose.

Several loud pops echoed through the kitchen as she loomed to her full height and strode silently into the living room, padding softly on the balls of her feet.

Oh, how simple it would be, she wondered as she stood over the prone, helpless form of the sleeping woman.

She leaned down and could smell the vodka's soft scent.

Most people often thought the clean liquid was odorless, but then again, most people couldn't tell a person's emotions just by smell.

Ellie closed her eyes and breathed in her mother's scent.

How easy it would be, she thought as she pulled back her lip and set her teeth on the soft flesh of her mother's throat.

How right it would be.

Suddenly, the phone rang.

She growled softly in irritation.

Didn't people have the common decency not to call after nine at night?

She moved quickly to the wall-mounted phone, irritated by the interruption as she lifted the receiver.

"Hello?" she answered, in a deadly purr.

"Hello? Eleanor?" Her father's voice came through hesitantly. "Is that you?"

Something inside her softened at the sound of her name and his melodic tone.

"Hi, Daddy," she said, her voice softening as she smiled.

"My God, I almost didn't recognize your voice! How are you? Where's your mother?"

Ellie smiled as she suddenly became aware of the blood on her face and chin.

"I'm doing good. Was just having a snack."

She glanced at the unconscious form on the couch. "Mom's... indisposed right now."

There was a brief, tense silence on the line.

"Drinking again?" he asked flatly.

"Yup," she answered in an almost obscenely cheerful tone.

"She's out cold on the couch."

"I see," he said with an almost defeated sigh.

"Well, I've been wanting to talk to you anyway. Honey. I... I wanted to tell you how sorry I am for... what happened, and..."

She could hear the hitch in his voice and the palpitation of his heart beat through the line.

God, that was weird.

"And the things I said..."

"It's ok, Dad," Ellie found herself saying suddenly without thinking.

She was surprised with how much she meant it too.

"No…No, it's not," he insisted.

"Listen, I was wrong to blame you for any of that mess. I shouldn't have called you a…"

"A slut?" Ellie finished for him in a cheerfully flat tone.

He choked then.

"Yeah… a slut… It was a bad time, and I was angry, but that's no excuse. I… I should never have done that to you, sweet-heart."

Ellie closed her eyes, feeling a strange lump form in her throat.

All the months of hating herself.

Of just trying to escape what had happened.

Of just sitting in limbo, not sure how she was supposed to feel about anything.

Was she supposed to still be angry?

Or was she supposed to hate herself?

Wasn't that what werewolves were supposed to do? Hate and loath the monster inside them?

Reguardless of all that, here was her father, this sweet man who had always taken the time for tea parties and bounced her on his knee.

Here was the man she had thought had died the moment that word had fallen out of his mouth.

Here he was at last, offering her the apology she hadn't known she needed. Even if it was too late.

But was it?

She was alive after all, and technically, the physical damage had been repaired.

Well, with a few caveats that is.

Why couldn't she try to forgive him? What would be stopping her from letting him back in?

She looked at the bloody paper on the linoleum before the open fridge.

Well, mostly back in…

"Thanks," she said softly. "I appreciate that."

There was tense silence on the line for a moment, where all she could hear was his breathing and the rhythmic pounding of his heartbeat.

Then finally he said, "I was thinking, Ellie… how would you feel about coming home? To LA, I mean… To live with me."

Ellie stared at the empty meat packaging, taking in the bloody smears on the floor around it.

She suddenly was hyper aware of the wetness on her face and between her thighs.

And what about the Moon?

How would she deal with that?

She wasn't even sure how she would do it here in Pinecrest with her mother, where she could at least retreat in the deep forest for a few days.

Los Angeles had even fewer options for a werewolf.

And what was more, this is where Tina was. She couldn't just leave her behind, either.

Suddenly, the words from Jared's journal echoed in her head.

I have noted that in the instances where a Rougarou was unable to join or form a pride, that a persistent level of ever increasing savagery, particularly in the males that bordered on complete madness.

Madness… She could go insane if she were alone. She needed Tina, and Tina needed her… They were a pride together.

"I don't know, Daddy," she said at last, "It's just… Well, things are sort of… complicated right now."

"I understand," he said, "Just know the offer stands. Things would be different this time, I swear. I'd listen more and give you the space you need.

"You're almost seventeen now, and I should respect that."

It was nice to hear, but she knew he could never really understand.

Even so, a small smile tugged at her lips.

"I'll think about it."

"That's all I'm asking, sweetheart," he said, his voice softer now, sounding relieved.

"El... I just want you to know, no matter what's going on, I love you. If you need me for anything at all, I'll be there. No questions asked."

Her throat tightened. "Thanks, Dad. That... that means a lot."

"Alright, kiddo," he said, "I'd better let you go. Just remember what I said, and think about it, please."

"I will… Goodnight, Daddy," she said softly.

"Night," he replied, and there was a click as he hung up on his end.

Ellie reluctantly hung up the phone and stood motionless for a long moment, her father's words echoing in her mind.

She turned and looked at her mother, still unconscious on the couch, bathed in the flickering blue light of some disaster movie.

She watched it for a second. Something about

an ocean liner capsizing, people screaming as water rushed through corridors.

To be honest, it seemed a bit ridiculous to her.

She walked over and switched off the TV.

"I was watching that," her mother mumbled, not even opening her eyes as she rolled over.

With a sigh, Ellie spread a blanket over her, picked up the empty vodka bottle, and tossed it in the trash.

She paused at the foot of the stairs, glancing back at her mother's sleeping form.

For all the wrong she had done to her, Ellie couldn't help but believe it hadn't been deliberate.

But that was the problem, wasn't it?

Had it been out of pure malice, then it would have been understandable. Maybe then she could respond in kind.

She thought about that brief moment when she could taste the soft, supple flesh on her tongue.

How easy it would have been. And perhaps it would be justified after everything.

But her mother had never been deliberately malicious or spiteful to her. She honestly believed she was doing what was right and had the best intentions at heart.

But as the old saying went, the road to Hell is paved with good intentions.

"Too bad you're not a mean drunk," she muttered, "I could actually hate you then."

She turned then with a soft growl and headed upstairs to her bedroom. Leaving the prone form to slumber peacefully, oblivious to how close it had come to retribution.

She pondered what a drunk might dream about for a moment.

But as she did so, she couldn't help but wonder… What horrors would she dream about tonight?

CHAPTER 20

The moonlight, so bright and so close to fullness. It swells over us like a pregnant sow ready to burst forth.

Soon we will run, truly free. But not tonight.

Tonight we stalk.

Tonight we hunt.

Tonight, we take what is ours.

Tonight we *kill*.

The crimson haze descends, pulsing, distorting, making shadows dance in the darkness.

We run. Swarming through brush and bush. Over fences and through yards.

Something rushes, baying for blood at our intrusion.

It halts suddenly, its fury turning to abject terror in the span of a heartbeat. Tucking its tail and rolling on its back as it defecates itself.

We smile. It knows it is lesser than us, pathetically surrendering without resistance.

It whines in abject terror as we lower our head over it. A growl passing our black lips as we set our teeth to its throat.

It doesn't fight, doesn't react. It knows it's insignificance to our majesty.

We could take its life, rending it from this existence in a singular moment of desire, and savor its red flesh.

No, its life is meaningless to us. Its flesh will not satisfy our hunger this night.

We leave the pitiful creature to wallow in its filth, swarming the fence and careening through the night.

Lifting our head, we catch a musk on the night air.

Rage boils in our gut, and we throw back our head and sing our anger to the goddess above, vowing blood and death in her name.

The night blurs, and our heart races until finally we have found our desire.

Them!

No, not them... *HER!*

We crouch in the shadows, darkened further by the bright moonlight, and we watch.

The car sits purring like a cat contented with a fresh kill.

The combined stink of their mating floats out upon the cool night air.

We growl softly as we watch them settle.

"I still can't believe those psychos," she says, her face bruised yet flushed with the exertion of their vigorous coupling.

"Tiff, come on, not right now. Could you please drop it?" he responds.

"No, Kyle, I can't! It's like they're on steroids or something," she exclaims. "Crazy bitches!"

"Sorry, babe, but you guys did sorta push them, and they did try to warn you," he states calmly.

He shakes his head. "Hell, I can't believe Jace was stupid enough to provoke them again. What an idiot."

"Wait a second," she interrupts, her voice rising indignantly. "You're not actually defending those dikes, are you?! Did you see what that bitch did to me? I almost died! And poor Ashley!"

"Yes, I saw what they did, and no, I'm not defending them, but..." he started.

"Oh my god! You got the hots for them, don't you?" she cut him off shrilly.

"What?! Tiff, don't be stupid," he replies.

She turns to him in the seat, "Oh, so now I'm stupid? Which one is it? Huh?! That blonde bimbo Ellie? You like that beach bitch accent?"

"Damn it, Tiffany, SHUT UP!" he explodes.

Her eyes widen with shock, and the sudden faint hint of antiseptic mingles in the air.

"I couldn't care the fuck less about anyone's accent or any of that other shit! So knock it off!" he rumbles menacingly to her.

She starts to pout, and tears begin to roll down her cheeks.

"Shit... Hey, I'm sorry. I didn't mean to yell," he says, his tone softening.

His hand reaches out, stroking her hair.

A low growl rumbles in our throat.

She seems to soften at his touch, leaning into it.

"I'm sorry too. It's just... what are we going to do about them?"

"I wouldn't worry about it," he says. "These things have a tendency to sort themselves out."

She looks down and settles back into the seat. "Yeah, I guess you're right. It's just…"

"It's just nothing," he cuts her off.

"Leave them alone. They're dangerous. You

guys got lucky today. What do you think would have happened if I hadn't been there?"

The smell of wet, dead leaves meets our nose as she indignantly avoids his gaze as she fidgets.

At last, she looks up and says, "I should go…"

The car door opens, and she steps out. "My dad will kill me if I'm out too late."

"Want me to walk you home?" he offers, starting to get out as well.

"No," she says quickly. "I… uhhh… I just want to be alone for a bit. Plus, my dad would probably kill us both if he saw you. Besides, it's just through the cemetery. I'll be fine."

"The cemetery? At night? Are you sure?" he asks cautiously.

Her laugh is like brittle glass in the cool air. "What, you think I'm scared of ghosts now?"

"After what happened to Stacy and Jessie? Maybe you should be," he replies softly.

"Right," she says, laughing, leaning through the window.

"Listen, I live right on the other side. I'll be fine. It's like five minutes to my house. The big bad wolf isn't going to get me. Ok?"

"Fine," he says sullenly.

"But seriously, be careful."

She salutes him and begins walking away. "I'll call you tomorrow."

He waves, pulling away from the curb, as she walks down the path. We watch her silhouette vanish into the swirling mists.

Surging, we bolt across the street toward the large iron gates, standing open like the gates of the underworld.

A dark maw leading to rows of silent sentinels in the fog shrouded shadows of the night.

We stop, hesitating as we huff in the stink of her musk, filling us with a cold fury.

Why?

It doesn't matter why. Only that it does.

We follow her through that mouth of Hell. Allowing ourselves to descend into that kingdom of the dead.

We dart among the gravestones, tracking her stench.

We can smell him on her... *inside* her. His musk mixing with hers, making our mouth water with rage and desire.

We see her walking quietly, illuminated briefly in the luminous glow of the goddess.

The soft tapping of her shoes along the paved

path was the only sound of life among the head-stones.

The fog rolls thicker now, and we lose sight of her.

It makes no difference, we can still smell her vile stench and hear the soft tapping of her shoes against the wet pavement.

A low growl escapes our throat, and we dart off into the headstones, closing the distance until we find her again, only feet away.

She stops and looks around.

We let her search the darkness, freezing in place.

She looks right at us but sees nothing in the dark mists, seemingly blind as a newborn pup.

She spins and hurries now, walking faster. The tapping of her precious white shoes echoes more urgently, and the antiseptic stink of fear mixes with her rancid musk.

We stalk her, coming closer row by row, matching her pace quietly.

She turns and looks again.

We can see her now through the headstones. So close. Oh, so very close.

"Hello?" she calls out, her voice quivering. "Who's there?"

She knows we're here, but not where we are.

We wait quietly, watching between the headstones. Not moving as her gaze pierces the fog.

She turns and begins walking again. Her eyes furtively watching the shadows around her as she hurries.

Softly, slowly, we cut wide, circling to come alongside her, then ahead of her.

"Hello?" she calls again, stopping and spinning in place.

"Kyle, if that's you, quit playing around."

She looks away, and we close the distance, the fog swirling around us, as if it were a shroud of invisibility.

She starts walking again, backwards at first, then turning as she begins to sprint, unwittingly toward us, her shoes sounding like the tattoo of a drum.

A growl ripples from our throat, and she skids to a halt.

Panic fills her eyes, and the antiseptic stench of fear fills the air as we move out of the headstones and onto the path.

"Oh my god!" she says, falling backwards to the ground as we surge forward, a snarl ripping from our throat.

She screams as she scrambles up to her feet, running blindly into the headstones.

We drop back to relish the antiseptic stench of her musk.

We let her have her distance, giving her the illusion of a head start.

There is no need to rush. She is trapped in this world of the sleeping dead. She will join them in due time.

We surge through the maze of stones, snuffing as we huff in her sweet stench.

We want her.

We need her.

"Heee! Heee! Heee!" she breathes as her feet thud dully on the wet grass.

We smile as we lose sight of her, letting her think herself safe as she gasps like swine being led to the slaughter.

We burst from the mist, roaring as she screams and runs again.

Several more times we play this game, hounding her heels, spurring her ever onward as her legs begin to falter.

Soon, she doubles over but doesn't stop, clutching her side as the pain of exhaustion threatens to betray her.

Still, we persist, pushing her to twist and turn blindly through the fog until the stink of her suffering becomes overwhelming.

Lights flash through the mists!

A car beyond the high iron fencing, casting weirdly barred shadows through the dark foggy air.

Hope surges through her.

The smell of sweet honey fills our nose, and we smile as we watch her suddenly straighten with renewed energy.

She tries to turn for the light and cries out feebly.

"Heeellp!" she shouts, waving her arms desperately.

"Stop! Please! Help me!"

But the car doesn't stop.

She cries in anguish as the bright headlights turn into red taillights and disappear into the swirling darkness.

Only the thick, cloying scent of her despair is left to herald an end to our game.

She turns slowly, unable to run any longer.

Her legs buckle as she stares at us, whimpering pathetically like the creature before as we emerge from the darkness.

"No… No… Please God no!" she says pleadingly, as tears of anguish cut like twin rivers through the filth on her face.

The stink of her terror floods the night, mixing with the sweet saltiness of her tears.

We loom over her as she looks up at us, trembling with anticipation of what she knows is inevitable.

"Please… no…" she begs up to us, as if praying to her God.

We roar and surge upon her as she screams, writhing and kicking in desperation as we ravage her body with fang and claw.

Biting and scratching as we shred the fabric to expose the soft, silky white skin beneath, revealing the pale bosom that glows almost luminously in the moonlight.

Tearing at her until the last vestiges of her hope are lost in the sweet coppery taste of red flesh.

She clutches our head, cradling it to her as she sobs, crying out, "OWE! OWE! PLEASE! OH GOD OWE!"

The stench of copper fills the air, as the grass is stained a deep, vibrant crimson.

Soon, she only moans feebly as we rend her

womanhood from her. Ripping at the dark hair below until it is an empty hole.

Her once-beautiful face contorts in horrified agony as she watches us savor the taste of her womb.

She stares in abject horror as we relish the mutilated flesh as it slides down our throat.

All is quiet again as we stand and gaze down upon her.

She twitches feebly as a final gurgling plea for mercy, "Please..."

A bubble of deep crimson escapes the corner of her ruined lips.

We smile into her dying eyes, watching us with the last flicker of life as we lower our loins to her face, marking her with our stench.

Rising, our fury quelled, we kick the stained grass upon her mutilated form as the last light in her eyes fades, singing to the goddess above of our victory.

Finally, our hunger satiated, we lope away amongst the headstones and allow the darkness to once more take us.

CHAPTER 21

Ellie sat bolt upright, gasping for air. Sweat soaked through the bed sheets, and her heart hammered wildly against her ribs.

"Fuck! Fuck! Fuck!" she gasped, twisting and turning, trying to figure out how to flee the drenched bed.

Sunlight streamed through her window, catching motes of dust that danced in its golden rays.

Morning had come, chasing away the terrors of the night.

Or at least it should have.

"Just a dream," she murmured, trying to convince herself. "It was just a dream."

She could still taste copper, feel the fullness of her belly, as she scrambled from the bed.

She knew it was a lie. That it was something pretty, she was trying to convince herself of.

A nice, pretty lie to avoid the truth. It was her.

She looked down and touched the wet bet.

Not sweat… water. When did she take a bath? It didn't matter when, only that she had.

"No… no, no, no!" she said.

She looked down and saw the tread of prints in the brown carpet. Almost invisible, save for the darkness of the dirt in them.

She knew it with absolution in that very moment. Tiffany was dead, and she had killed her.

There wasn't a shred of doubt in her mind. She had not only killed her, no, she fucking ate her…

Ellie stopped then as the realization hit her.

She slumped to the floor and stared at the reflection of her nude body in the closet mirror.

Aside from the rippling muscle beneath the flawless flesh, everything seemed almost normal.

No fur or claws. No fangs. Not even one speck of dirt or drop of blood. There wasn't even a hint of copper in the air.

Only the scent of herself. The heady smell of her own musk.

She realized then how her skin felt like it might burst into flames at any moment and how bad she stank, not of sweat, but of something else entirely.

A heavy, sweet musk, almost like that of a perfume, yet more animalistic.

"Cripes, I reek," she muttered, wrinkling her nose.

She stumbled to the bathroom, desperate for a shower. That is when the reek of copper slammed into her like a wall.

But it wasn't the stink of fresh copper. No, this was old and musky. Her mother's stench emanating from the small waste bin beside the toilet.

The stink of menses made her choke and wretch as a blind fury rose up inside her like roiling black acid.

She desperately rushed to open the window, casting the waste bin out of it entirely along with the foul, discarded pads of her mother's estrus.

Letting loose a guttural scream of unbridled hatred, she slammed her fist into the window frame over and over until her knuckles bled.

"Ellie?" came her mother's voice from the hall, "Are you ok?"

Ellie turned a low growl rippling in her throat.

"I'm fine!" she bellowed, as she slammed the bathroom door and locked it.

"I'll be down soon," she yelled.

"When I'm sure I won't change my mind about not ripping your guts out and eating you," she added in a quiet tone.

The cool water offered little relief. No matter how cold she made it, how long she stood beneath the spray, nothing helped.

She was on fire inside, and all she could think of was humping something or tearing it to pieces.

Back in her room, she stared at her closet, suddenly aware that all her usual clothes felt wrong.

Everything was too restrictive. Too... small.

"You've got to be fucking kidding me," she muttered as she threw the fifth shirt on the floor.

What fit her perfectly fine less than a week ago was now skin tight or showed way too much flesh.

She stormed out of her room to her mother's and ripped open the closet door.

She proceeded to ransack her way through tops until she found one that didn't look twenty years out of date, or fit for a corporate carpet walk.

She selected a white sleeveless blouse, leaving it unbuttoned to the third button and tying it at her midriff.

She abandoned any hope of a bra and settled for taping her nipples with medical paper tape. A trick her mother had taught her for when she had to wear strapless tops.

She found a form-fitting denim skirt that rode high on her thighs, yet still seemed long enough to be mildly modest in the loosest possible sense of the word.

Finally, she finished the look with a pair of black heeled knee-high go-go boots she'd never had the nerve to wear before.

She threw her hair up halfheartedly and said screw the rest as she went downstairs.

Downstairs, her mother was already in the kitchen, nursing a cup of coffee with a faraway look in her eyes.

"Mom? Do you have the thermostat turned to ninety or something?" Ellie asked, opening the refrigerator door and letting the cool air wash over her flushed skin as she rummaged through the shelves.

"It's hotter than a witch's tit in a brass bra in here," she said, standing up after finding nothing that appealed to her.

Why was she hungry *again*? She should be full after eating… well, Tiffany.

Her mother's eyebrows shot up as she took in Ellie's new look. Her mouth opening and closing several times.

"No… No, I don't," she said finally. "But damn, you're fit to make someone's blood boil. You're really going to school dressed like that?"

Ellie irritably shut the fridge door with unnecessary force and spun on her mother. "Yes, Mom, I am. What's wrong with it?"

Nancy quickly raised her hands in surrender. "Nothing, honey. Nothing."

She paused, sniffing the air.

"What perfume are you wearing?"

"I'm not wearing any. They all stink," Ellie growled.

She grabbed her backpack and headed for the door, keen to escape her mother's scrutiny.

As the door slammed shut, Nancy murmured, "I wish I could smell that good naturally."

Outside, Tina leaned against her father's old, beaten-up truck, fanning herself with a straw cowboy hat like it was the middle of July and not the day before Halloween.

Ellie stopped short, taking in her friend's appearance.

She couldn't help but imagine a more stereotypical country boy's wet dream than the girl before her.

Tina was wearing a set of Daisy Dukes that hugged her curves and barely covered any of her long, shapely thighs.

Her plaid shirt hung open, revealing a white undershirt that did nothing to conceal the fact that she wasn't wearing a bra.

The thin fabric stretched to its limits over her already ample bosom seemed only to enhance the visibility of her pert nipples.

Her strawberry-blonde hair hung loose and wild around her shoulders as she looked Ellie up and down over a set of aviators.

"Damn!" Tina hooted, "Where's the red carpet, Hollywood?" she asked, jumping in behind the wheel.

Ellie tossed her bookbag in the back and pulled herself up into the passenger side.

"You're not exactly hiding yourself. Where's Bo and Luke?"

Tina flashed a smile at Ellie, the amber flecks in her sapphire eyes glinting playfully.

"Wouldn't you like to know?"

The truck's engine roared to life, and they pulled away from the curb.

After about a minute, Tina broke the silence.

"So, you going to talk about it?"

"About what?" replied Ellie.

Tina laughed. "Don't play coy with me. You know what. Tiffany. Or are we just going to pretend it wasn't one of us?"

"Who says I'm pretending?" Ellie retorted. "I ate her. Let's not make it a thing."

Tina wrenched the wheel over and pulled into a church lot.

She turned in her seat and got right in Ellie's face.

"You ate her cunt. The whole fucking baby basket. That's a little more than a thing, El."

Ellie sagged and looked down. "Yeah… Fuck… It's not even full moon and…"

Tina grabbed her chin and forced her to look into her eyes. "I don't fucking care. You did good. Besides, that two-bit slut had it coming."

Ellie winced. *My daughter, nothing more than a two-bit slut!* Her father's voice echoed in her head.

She hated that word, but to be honest, it fit.

Tina leaned forward and nuzzled her cheek before leaning back.

"You have nothing to be ashamed of. She

was trash, and you took her out," she said.

"But it wasn't me… I mean, it was, but… I just went to fucking bed last night! I don't remember going out! Shouldn't I remember something… more?!"

Tina shrugged. "I don't know," she said, "Do you recall what the old man said that night? Werewolves can change whenever they want. But I don't know how that works. Maybe it's like sleepwalking or something at first."

Tina pulled out of the church lot and back onto the road. They drove in silence for another minute, then Ellie asked, "You really think it's sleepwalking?"

Tina looked at her, then shrugged again. "I don't have a better explanation. I mean, remember the watchtower? When I changed into the wolf?"

Ellie nodded, "Yeah, how could I forget? You tried to kill everyone."

"Well, I remember it hurt so much, all I wanted to do was just pass out. But it was more like this weird red dream. I felt like I was asleep and not in control. It was like I was a passenger looking out the window of a car. But the car was my body."

Ellie looked down. "Yeah, I know the

feeling… It's been like this for three nights now. Jessie, Stacy, and now Tiffany. I seriously feel like I'm losing my fucking mind!" she said.

"Hey now, Jessie's death wasn't us. We were out of school for a fucking month, so why would we go after him? Well, aside from jumping his bones, that is."

"Yeah, I guess… But then why did we dream it?" Ellie asked.

Tina shook her head, "I don't know, El. I'm not an expert on any of this shit."

Something struck Ellie then, seemingly out of the blue.

"You said 'fuck him' if God cursed me. What did you mean?" she blurted.

"What?" Tina replied, confused by the sudden topic change.

"On the tower," Ellie replied, "You said 'fuck him' if God had actually cursed me. What did you mean by that?"

Tina drummed her fingers irritably on the steering wheel. "Jesus, El, that was like a month ago, and I was sorta distracted at the time."

Ellie felt stupid. Of course, Tina's mind had been elsewhere at the time.

She had been in the early stages of transformation. And well, then there had been the beast too.

A lot of shit happened that night, and Ellie couldn't expect Tina to remember every little detail…

Tina looked over at her and sighed.

"Listen, if some all-powerful being punishes you for something you didn't ask for, why worship them?"

Now it was Ellie's turn to shrug. "I don't know. It's just what I was taught all my life. You know… Jesus is supposed to love me no matter what. But ever since that night with Rick… I feel like he hates me now…"

Tina glanced at her, concern written plainly on her beautiful features.

"Hey, listen, I get that having a religion helps a lot of people. Heck, my family's Methodist. But seriously, El, if you think God cursed you or is punishing you for something you had no control over, then fuck him. Find something else that will help you."

Ellie nodded. The logic made sense to her. "What about the Devil, then?"

Tina's sudden bark of laughter filled the cab. "Where's all this coming from, Ellie?"

"Nothing," Ellie said, shaking her head as she stared hard at the passing scenery. "Just me being stupid."

"No, it's not stupid. What's got you bothered by this?" Tina asked as they pulled into the high school parking lot.

Ellie fidgeted, wishing she hadn't said anything now.

"I don't know. Christ, Tina, we've killed people, and I don't know about you, but… I don't feel guilty about it. And… well… That's not normal."

Tina laughed and looked around to make sure no one was close by.

"Seriously? Hollywood, you're a werewolf, and you're worried about being normal? No, it's not normal! None of this is."

"But… Aren't you scared of going to Hell?" Ellie asked.

Tina sighed, then looked at her, turning in the seat. "No. No, Ellie, I'm not. Because we've already been there. Besides, it's too late now to worry about it. All we can do now is just try to survive high school."

Ellie sighed. It sorta gets hard not to believe you're cursed when it's always one stupid thing after another. Eating Tiffany seemed to be just the latest thing in a long chain of *things*.

She looked up at the high school and supposed Tina was right. All they could do now was try to survive the problem that was in front of them. High school.

The building was smaller than her old one in Los Angeles, Hollywood High.

At least there she could disappear amongst the rest of the students and find some semblance of relative peace.

But in Pinecrest? Yeah, that was a joke all of its own.

CHAPTER 22

Walking into Pinecrest High was like stepping onto a runway stage at a fashion show.

Heads turned, and conversations halted, as a wave of absolute awestruck silence followed in their wake.

Ellie imagined she could almost hear the clicking of a hundred mental cameras, punctuated by the echoing march of their boots.

The boys were practically drooling on themselves, while their would be girlfriends seemed to almost shoot daggers from their eyes.

More than one girl physically pulled their boyfriend away from the pair of predatory man-eaters that seemed to stalk through them.

"Hi, Mr. Watson," Ellie greeted the Biology teacher.

"I just wanted to tell you that I can't meet you for detention tomorrow. I got plans," she said sweetly as she stopped to straighten his tie for him.

She perched up and gave him a peck on the cheek before stalking away like a cat that had just eaten the proverbial canary.

"Ahhh… Why yes… I mean no! I…I mean … Have a good weekend… Oh my!" he babbled as he turned and hurried away, a flushed look on his face.

Tina laughed and said, "That wasn't very nice."

Ellie leaned in and asked, "Do you think I still have to go to detention tomorrow?"

They got to their lockers in Ellie's alcove and noticed more than a few girls watching them with a mixture of admiration and scandalized fascination.

For the first time in what seemed like an eternity, she actually felt good.

Ever since Rick's party, all she could think about was just trying to get from one day to the next without drawing anything else to herself.

She paused for a moment and wondered what good old Ricky Chambers would do if he could see her now.

She certainly wasn't the same stupid star-struck girl with her legs spread, and skirt hiked up, that was for sure.

"Shit," Tina muttered. "Guess who's coming over to say hi."

Ellie shook herself from her thoughts in time to see Ashley, Jace, and Kyle enter their alcove. Tiffany was, by contrast, conspicuously absent.

Kyle seemed to hang back, watching with an unreadable expression. Although Ellie couldn't help but notice his scent seemed anything but hostile.

Quite to the contrary, it seemed almost... *musky*. She would even venture to say excited, despite his outward calm.

The same couldn't be said for Ashley, whose scent reeked of cloying perfume, and that did nothing to hide the antiseptic stench of fear emanating from her.

"Where's Tiffany?" Ashley demanded, crossing her arms over her chest.

Ellie couldn't explain why, but the question provoked an instant response in her.

"I ate her," she said nonchalantly, as she turned around and looked Ashley square in the eye. "Nice pumps, short shit."

It had been a simple statement, said so matter-of-factly, she couldn't tell if she was being serious or joking.

Tina let out a bark of laughter, as did several others nearby, including, to her surprise, Kyle.

Ashley's cheeks flushed red with rage. "You think you're so funny, Granger? Nobody's seen Tiffany since last night. What did you freaks do to her?"

Ellie smiled as the memory flashed in her mind.

The taste of Flesh and copper. The musky sweetness of her womanhood sliding down her throat. Then her expression as she pissed on the little sow's face.

"How should we know?" Ellie said sweetly, "We're not the ones holding her leash."

Tina chuckled, turning from her locker.

"You know, with all the excitement we had yesterday, I forgot to tell you that we ran into your loser Dad and brother," she said.

"You fucking bitch," Jace hissed, fists clenched at his sides.

Ellie smiled as she looked him up and down, then turned back to Ashley.

"Tell me, Ash, when was the last time you saw your Dad and brother?"

"The one who didn't get torn apart, that is," Tina chimed in, a wicked grin spreading across her face as she turned back to them.

"One week, or two?"

Ashley's face was scarlet with rage.

"Hmm… From the smell of them," Ellie replied, "I'd say three."

Tina laughed, "Yeah, and what is up with those outfits? They looked like extras out of M.A.S.H."

Jace moved forward, raising his fist, but was halted as Tina stepped in front of him, her face inches from his.

"Nice shiner," she purred, "Really brings out those baby blues. Want a matching set?"

"Speaking of matching sets," Ellie added, scribbling something on a piece of paper, then slamming her locker shut.

"Unless you want to make it a couples set…"

The bell rang, cutting her off.

Ellie closed the distance in a single fluid step, her golden-flecked eyes boring into Ashley's. "I would advise you get it through your thick, bottle blonde skull. Leave us alone."

Ellie and Tina stepped around the couple and approached the looming form of Kyle.

Ellie briefly met his gaze and sheepishly placed the folded paper in his shirt pocket.

"Just in case you get bored with the fakes, give me a call."

She stepped away, brushing her hand across his chest, smiling up at him.

As they stepped into the flow of human traffic, someone let out a wolf whistle.

Ellie looked back in time to see Jace shove Kyle, saying, "Really?!"

She stopped and seized Tina's arm as Kyle grabbed him by his letterman, and with a resonating *"Thwack!"* brought his massive fist across the smaller jocks chin.

"What was that about?" Tina whispered, a note of amusement in her voice.

Ellie shrugged, chewing on her lip as her thighs moistened.

"I don't know. But I like it."

CHAPTER 23

The morning unfolded in a blur, much like one would have expected with every guy pining for your attention.

It wasn't long before each of them had a small entourage of cute, often pimple faced guys offering to carry their books and pining for their attentions.

That is when they weren't making utter fools of themselves in the halls.

One poor freshman even followed them into the girls' bathroom, completely oblivious to the world around him, his eyes locked on Tina's legs.

"Nah-ahhh! Buster Brown," Tina said, rescuing him before the error escalated to epic proportions.

"You wait out here, baby boy. Mama will be right back," she said, booping him sweetly on the nose.

Not even their teachers were immune.

Mr. Daniels, the geometry teacher, stumbled over an equation when Tina raised her hand to answer a question, and Coach Benson kept finding excuses to walk past Ellie's desk during morning study hall.

"This is getting ridiculous," Ellie muttered as she leaned against the sink, ignoring the hateful looks from a pair of girls exiting.

Tina snickered. "Tell me about it. I think Mr. Abernathy was about to have a heart attack in English."

"Is it just me, or is it getting hotter?" she asked, adjusting her shirt, which did nothing to hide her nipples under the white fabric of her undershirt.

"I hear you there," Ellie said, wiping sweat from her brow.

"It's like I'm being cooked from the inside out. And I'll, I can think of is fucking everything…"

A toilet flushed, and a redhead stepped out of a stall, glaring.

"What? You got something to say?" Ellie barked at the girl, sending her skittering.

"That's what I thought," she said before

returning to the conversation, though in a bit of a quieter voice.

"Anyways… All I want to do is kill everything or hump it until it's dead."

Tina let out a bark of laughter. "Well, at least you got your priorities straight."

"Not funny. How are you acting so calm? I swear I'm about to go crazy!" Ellie asked.

Tina smiled and snatched up Ellie's backpack.

"Hey!" Ellie shouted.

"Relax your knickers. There's a few things you never leave home without." Tina said as she rummaged through the pockets.

Finally, her eyes lit up.

"BINGO!" she exclaimed and pulled out a fat tube of lipstick.

"Tell me, Hollywood. You wearing panties?" she asked with an impish grin.

"Or going commando?"

Ellie's eyes bugged, and she squeezed her legs together involuntarily.

"You've got to be kidding…"

Tina wiggled her eyebrows.

"Well, there's always the boys' locker room."

Ellie looked at her, utterly scandalized, her

mouth working mechanically as if to protest, but no words came out.

Finally, after several moments of this, her shoulders slumped in defeat, and she let Tina push the lipstick into her hand.

"I hate you," she said softly, turning stiffly to step into an empty stall.

By lunchtime, Ellie was feeling significantly better.

Well, objectively speaking, that is.

At least she wasn't ready to grab one of the poor shmucks following her and pull him into the janitor's closet.

The thought had crossed her mind more than a few times, though.

They'd claimed a table in the far corner of the cafeteria and put their backs to the wall. Forcing their cluster of followers to focus firmly on their trays to avoid being caught staring.

Ellie had gotten two trays of the lunch special, *meatloaf*, and attacked them voraciously, ripping and chomping like a starved animal.

"Is this seat taken?" a tiny voice cut through her focus.

Ellie looked up to find Haily standing beside their table, clutching her lunch tray.

She seemed somehow smaller now, standing there, trembling like a frightened rabbit trying to seek shelter in the lair of the predator.

"It's available," Tina said coolly, her gentle smile almost guarded.

"You sure you want it? The way you ran off yesterday… Well, I didn't think you'd be back so soon."

Haily's shoulders slumped. "I'm sorry about running off…"

She set her tray down but remained standing there like a child who had been caught with her hand in the cookie jar before supper.

"I shouldn't have reacted that way."

Ellie studied her appearance, noting that somehow, she seemed diminished.

Perhaps it was the makeup that failed to completely conceal her acne. Or maybe it was the faint tang of body odor beneath the soft stink of perfume.

Ellie noticed how her usually voluminous raven black hair now seemed flat and lacking the lustrous shine she had grown so accustomed to.

Haily sat down hesitantly, her eyes darting between Ellie and Tina.

"It's just that... well, you both look different."

"Different how?" Ellie asked, though she knew exactly what Haily meant.

"You're both... I don't know, almost glowing. And taller? And..." Haily said haltingly, as she looked around at the tables filled with not so subtle admirers.

"Is this…? Is it a *werewolf* thing?" she asked in a near silent whisper, a note of desperation creeping into her voice.

Ellie glanced around the cafeteria, suddenly aware of the closeness of bodies.

"Yeah," Ellie said softly at last. "It must be."

"Yup, it's definitely a werewolf thing," Tina added less subtly.

Ellie shot her a glare.

Could you say it any louder? She scolded silently.

Tina shrugged in response. *Sorry.*

Haily sat quietly, pushing her food around her plate as she chewed her bottom lip.

For a moment, Ellie thought she might bolt again.

At last, she looked up with a frightened glimmer in her eye. "Could you..." she began hesitantly.

"Could you make me a werewolf too?"

Ellie nearly choked on her water, sitting up, sputtering and coughing before she managed to choke out a single word. "What?!"

"I'm serious," Haily insisted, leaning forward.

"Whatever's happening to you guys… I want it."

Tina and Ellie exchanged bewildered glances.

Is she serious? Ellie asked silently.

Tina shook her head almost imperceptibly, her eyes wide with shock.

I don't know.

"Why would you want to be… well, like us?" Ellie asked gently, leaning forward and touching her hand.

Haily's demeanor shifted, becoming almost childlike, staring hard at her plate.

"I don't like being alone," she said at last.

"And I saw how you two just destroyed Ashley and Jace this morning and… I'm tired of being weak. I want to be like you two. Strong and beautiful… and…"

Tina's eyes narrowed. "Has someone hurt you?"

Haily shook her head quickly.

"No, not exactly. No one's been… mean to

me. But I'm tired of being invisible. Especially…"

She glanced at the surrounding tables, then back at Ellie and Tina and said, "Especially to boys."

Her eyes were wet with barely contained tears.

"I'm tired of being alone. I'm a sophomore now, and I still don't even have a boyfriend… All they see me as is some stupid *chink*."

She pounded her fist on the table in frustration.

"Do you know what it's like? I mean, it was fine before, I had you, guys, and Jess and Mark… Even David was nice to me. I didn't feel like some sort of social pariah, even if I didn't have anyone."

Her eyes hardened then as she continued.

"But they're dead now, and you two are like these... *goddesses*… So please, I'm begging you. Make me like you."

She went quiet then and seemed to deflate on herself. Her eyes shifting back and forth between Tina and Ellie.

Ellie glanced at Tina uncomfortably.

There was so much that Haily didn't understand.

And how could she? Honestly speaking, it wasn't like becoming a werewolf came with an instruction manual.

"Haily…" Ellie began as she leaned back.

"It's not all great skin and guys staring. It's a lot of… Well… Jesus, how do I say this…? It changes you. And not just outside, but… inside too. You're not who you once were."

"Well, speak for yourself, Hollywood," Tina quipped playfully, "But I'm still the same fun-loving me I've always been."

"You ate a human tongue," Ellie said bluntly.

"Yeah, and what did you eat last night? Hmmm…? Or should I say, who did you eat? Doesn't stop me from liking you."

"Ok! I get it!" Haily burst out, interrupting them.

"It makes you do bad things. I don't care!"

"And then there's the full moon…" Tina added with a sinister smile.

Haily paused and looked at her inquisitively. "What about it? You change, right? Like in the movies?

Tina nodded, "Yes, but well… It's agony. Like nothing you can imagine. A waking nightmare you can't escape."

Tina seized Haily's wrist and began to squeeze. "Imagine every bone in your body breaking and healing all at once, over and over and over again."

Haily's eyes widened, "Hey, ouch! Tina!"

"And then, at the same time," Tina continued, squeezing harder, making her wince and begin to go pale with pain.

"Your guts feel like they're on fire with Rocky Balboa using them as a punching bag."

"Tina," Ellie cut in and put a hand on her shoulder, "Enough."

Tina let go of Haily's wrist and sat back down.

Ellie turned to Haily and said, "Listen, Tina's not lying. I watched it happen. It's not a joke, and you turn into…"

She stopped, looked at Tina, and finally finished. "A monster."

"But you survived it. And look at you now." Haily replied, still rubbing her wrist.

Tina chuckled and said, "Yeah, just barely."

"Ask yourself this. Is it looking good, worth killing for?" Ellie said quietly, pushing her tray away.

"Killing?" Haily whispered, her voice barely audible.

"You mean… could I handle taking a life…? I mean… Yeah, I guess if that's what it takes."

The cafeteria suddenly felt too small, too crowded. Ellie's brow furrowed as she glanced at Tina.

"If we're going to actually have this talk, we need to go someplace quieter," Tina said.

Ellie nodded and added, "Yeah, preferably without half the damn school in earshot."

They rose to their feet, and Ellie looked forlornly at her unfinished food with a sigh.

"Come on, El, leave it. You're getting too fat anyway," Tina scolded as she pulled her away from the table.

Ellie growled hungrily, but allowed Tina to pull her along reluctantly.

"I'm not getting fat," she pouted.

They were pushing their way through the cafeteria doors when Vice Principal Perkins appeared, cutting them off with an expression that Ellie swore bordered on sadistic glee.

Behind her stood two police officers she knew all too well.

Sheriff Morehouse and Deputy Harding.

"Ms. Granger, Ms. Akins," Perkins said, sweetly.

"Where do we think we are going in such a rush? These gentlemen would like to have a word with you both."

CHAPTER 24

It had only been two days since her last visit, and yet the Vice Principal's office felt somewhat smaller than Ellie remembered.

Perhaps it was the addition of the two police officers, or maybe it was just her own larger physical proportions that created the illusion.

Whatever it was, the room had otherwise remained exactly as it had been on her last visit.

The small office still reeked of an over-abundance of potpourri and whatever horrific perfume Vice Principal Perkins seemed to adore.

But today there was something else. It was a strange tang that ran almost as an undercurrent to the room.

It was almost citrusy with the reek of rotten meat and chemicals.

Ellie was thankful it wasn't stronger, but it was certainly very distracting.

Sheriff Morehouse sat with his back to the large window, sitting lightly on a small ledge.

He was a tall man with graying hair and a bristly mustache.

Ellie judged by the way his uniform stretched over his mildly round frame that he tended to spend most of his time behind a desk rather than in the field.

His grey eyes betrayed nothing as he studied the girls, but Ellie could hear his heart beating steadily, yet slightly elevated.

He wasn't as calm as he appeared.

"I'm not sure if you remember me, but I'm Sheriff Morehouse, and this is Deputy Harding. Do you know why you're here?" the Sheriff asked as he glanced through a case file through a set of bifocals.

Neither of them answered instantly.

Ellie shot Tina a look. *This is too direct.*

Tina crossed her legs, her shorts riding up to the point of near obscenity.

I say we play with them, she silently replied.

You sure you want to do that? Ellie asked, eyeing the officers dubiously.

Deputy Harding's eyes darted to the exposed skin, and a pink flush crept up his neck.

Tina smiled impishly, replying, *Definitely.*

Harding was different from his boss, seemingly younger by perhaps twenty or thirty years.

With a shock of fire engine red hair, he stood out conspicuously in the tiny space as he leaned against a filing cabinet.

Ellie had had a chance to *admire* him as they had been escorted to the office. Even then, she could smell his instant reaction to them.

A heady musk that, despite his valiant effort, told Ellie just how much he was attracted to Tina.

"Not really," Tina replied coolly at last. "But I'm guessing it has something to do with the fact that people keep turning up dead."

The Sheriff glanced at her and began, "Why do you…"

"I know who you are, *Robert*," Ellie said, suddenly cutting him off as a cruel smile crept onto her lips.

"You're the guy shoving his dick inside my mother."

The Sheriff's composure cracked momentarily, his eyes widening as he sat up straighter.

Perkins made a small choking sound, while the Deputy's face deepened to crimson as the smell of acid filled the air.

"That's inappropriate, young lady," More-house said tightly.

"No, what's inappropriate is trying to screw my mother and thinking I wouldn't notice," Ellie retorted, tilting her head. "What's inappropriate is porking a woman with obvious problems."

Ellie smiled sweetly as she pressed on. "Tell me, Sheriff, did you know she was a drunk, or did you both just start humping over a bottle or two?"

An uncomfortable silence filled the room.

"Yeah, that's what I thought. So why are we here?" Ellie asked calmly, her voice tinged with a deadly edge.

Now, who's being too direct? Tina silently asked.

Ellie flashed her a glare, *I don't care. We need to get out of here, NOW!*

Sheriff Morehouse cleared his throat, visibly struggling to regain his composure. "We can discuss your mother's and I's relationship another time. We're here beca…"

Ellie's smile broadened as she leaned forward, cutting him off again.

"Sure, Robert, we can talk about it later. Will that be with the vodka or would you prefer whiskey?"

Tina swatted her arm, *Enough, you're going to get us arrested.*

Ellie sat back, her temper seething. *Fine, I'll play nice.*

After a moment of staring into Ellie's un-flinching face, the Sheriff looked slowly back at his case file and continued.

"As I was saying, we're here because Tiffany Monroe has gone missing. Her parents, it seems, haven't seen her since yesterday afternoon." Morehouse said furtively, looking up at them without making eye contact.

Tina's expression remained neutral, but Ellie felt a cruel satisfaction. He was avoiding looking at her; she had won the game.

"And you think we had something to do with it?" Tina asked.

"Well, we heard about your altercation at Mabel's Diner yesterday," he replied hesitantly, "it seemed prudent to speak with you."

Deputy Harding shifted his weight uncomfortably, and his heartbeat began to thump louder, as the stench of acid shifted slightly, blending into a faint acrid honeyed stink.

"We, uh, found her car abandoned near the old cemetery on Pine Road," he added.

"Keys still in the ignition."

Tina's expression cracked as she threw back her head and let out a bark of laughter. "Anyone ever tell you that you're a shit liar, Deputy?"

Harding blanched. "I… I…" he stammered.

Tina leaned forward, looking him in the eyes, and said, "Tiffany didn't drive. She has a fear of being behind the wheel. Panicked whenever her turn came up in Driver's Ed. So she dropped out."

She leaned back nonchalantly, smirking. "So, you want to try that again. With the truth this time?"

Ellie's smile seemed to widen impossibly. *Ok, new game. Lie detector. I like this.*

"Alright, fine," the Sheriff said, "You're clearly a pair of girls not to be treated lightly. What happened after the diner? Where did you two go?"

Ellie cocked an eyebrow and kept Morehouse locked in her gaze until he finally looked away, fidgeting.

That's two for two, she thought, pleased with herself.

"We went straight to my house after the diner," she finally said. "My mom can confirm that. Then, a few hours later, Tina went home."

"Can she?" Perkins interjected, her thin lips pulled into a tight line. "Because I've tried calling your house several times today, Miss Granger, and no one answered."

Ellie caught the honeyed stink again, and her head slowly swiveled, pinning the Vice Principal like a mouse before the cobra.

"Please don't lie to me, *Carol*. You're as bad at it as these two." Ellie replied.

"You haven't picked up that phone once today to call anyone, have you?" Tina said.

Perkins' face tightened with rage. "Why you little…"

"And even if you did, maybe she was out. She does have a life, you know." Ellie added, cutting her off.

Tina nodded, "Hmmm… Yeah, sorry, Mrs. P, mine does too," she added tauntingly.

"Or do you assume parents just sit around waiting for you to call and harass them?" Ellie finished.

"Enough!" the Sheriff bellowed. "Christ, it's like dealing with piranha," he muttered, rubbing his temples.

Perkins' face was so red it showed through her caked make-up, as the reek of acid mercifully overpowered the stench of her perfume.

Ellie and Tina smiled and leaned back in their seats.

Oh boy, we are so on her shit list now, Tina said silently.

Worth it, Ellie replied, smiling viciously.

"Unfortunately," Sheriff Morehouse continued, "that leaves us without confirmation of your whereabouts."

"Wait," Tina said, turning to look at him directly. "Why is our whereabouts so important to you? Are you saying Tiffany is just missing, or is there something more?" she asked in a brittle tone.

The Sheriff's expression darkened, and a new scent came off of him. It was softer in nature, but was like a horse resigning itself to be saddled.

Morehouse sighed as he set the case file aside and said, "Her body was found in the cemetery early this morning by a groundskeeper."

Tina smiled like a Cheshire cat. "So you brought us in here under false pretenses to accomplish what exactly?"

"To get answers, Miss Akins. Tell me, does this look familiar to you girls?" he replied, extending a photo to Ellie.

She took it and was about to look at it when Perkins snatched it from her fingers with a sadistic smile.

Her smile faded almost instantly, and her eyes widened in horror.

"God almighty…" she muttered, covering her mouth with her hand, dropping the picture.

Morehouse ignored her reaction and addressed the girls. "She was… mutilated. Just like Stacy Miller."

Ellie picked up the picture, knowing exactly what it was of.

"And Jessie Walters, and our friends last month," she said coolly, glancing at the black and white, before passing it to Tina.

"And you think a pair of High School girls could do this?" Tina asked coldly.

"No," Harding said suddenly, "But were either of you girls acquainted with, uh… any large dogs in the area?"

His voice seemed to crack slightly on the question.

"Dogs?" Tina repeated, her eyebrow arching. "What kind of question is that?"

"The kind asked during a murder investigation," the Sheriff cut in.

"Answer the deputy, please."

"Hmmm… No, darling," Tina replied in a rather good Eartha Kitt impression. "I'm more of a cat person myself… Meow."

Perkins slammed her palm against the desk, her patience clearly fraying. "This isn't a joke, Miss Akins! Three of your classmates are dead!"

"And I'm sorry about that," Tina replied, her voice turning to ice. "But I answered the question honestly, *Carol.* Now, I fail to see what dogs have to do with anything."

The Sheriff's eyes narrowed. "The coroner believes the wounds on both victims were caused by an animal. Specifically, something with large teeth and claws."

"Like what killed our friends? That's why we're in here, isn't it? You want to know what we saw that night. Correct me if I'm wrong, but you still haven't caught that thing. Now, have you?" Ellie asked confidently.

The Sheriff's gaze shifted nervously to her. "We're not discussing those incidents at present, Miss Granger."

"Why not?" Tina challenged. "Sounds pretty relevant to me. Large animal attacks in the same area within weeks of each other?"

Deputy Harding cleared his throat nervously. "The, uh, the wounds are different. More... precise." He shifted uncomfortably. "Almost like someone was controlling the animal."

Ellie couldn't help but laugh, the sound sharp and brittle. "Oh, I get it, like a trained attack dog? Come on. Rumor has it Stacy's tongue was torn out. I'm pretty sure not even a trained dog would go for the face like that. But a bear might."

Ellie leaned forward, a cruel smile playing on her lips, "But a bear wouldn't make sense now, would it. Stacy was killed in a bathroom on the second floor. And I'm pretty sure no one around here owns a trained bear."

The Sheriff shifted uncomfortably. Clearly, he wasn't accustomed to being picked apart so readily during an interview.

"Enough of this! Empty your book bags," Perkins demanded suddenly, her hand slamming down on the desk again. "Both of you, right now."

"Excuse me?" Tina asked incredulously.

"Oh, are you two deaf now? Your book bags," Perkins repeated, standing up from her desk. "Empty them. Now."

Ellie clutched her bag tightly. "No. You have no right to do that."

Perkins laughed, "I have every right in the world, Ms. Granger. Now empty your bags."

"I will not," Ellie said, clutching her bag tighter to her chest.

"This is still America," Tina added. "You need a warrant or reasonable suspicion."

Perkins's face flushed an ugly shade of red as she stepped around her desk. "This is my school, and I don't need a warrant to search a student's belongings when I suspect something dangerous."

Before either girl could protest further, Harding stood and snatched Tina's book bag from beside her chair and handed it to the Vice Principal.

Tina surged up, her body tensing like a coiled spring, "You fucking cunt. Give that back!"

Deputy Harding turned and intercepted Tina, pushing her back down in her seat.

The Vice Principal smiled viciously and, with a theatrical flourish, upended the bag over her desk.

Books, papers, pens, and makeup all fell out and clattered across the surface. And along with it all, one of Jared's leather journals hit the desk with a heavy thud.

Sheriff Morehouse's attention immediately zeroed in on the journal. He picked it up, turning it over in his hands, a look of stern recognition coming over his features.

"Where did you get this?" he asked, his voice suddenly tight.

Tina and Ellie exchanged a quick glance.

Shit, what now? Tina asked.

Do we need it? Ellie asked in return.

What do you think? Tina retorted.

Ellie growled softly. *Fuck it, we can't risk it right now. Play dumb.*

"It's just an old book," Tina said dismissively.

Morehouse's eyes turned sharp as he pinned her with his own dangerous stare. "Now, who's lying? This belonged to old Jared Duprix," he said.

"I'd recognize it anywhere," he continued, "Weren't we supposed to meet and go up to his cabin yesterday?"

Perkins, momentarily forgotten in her triumphant ransacking, looked confused. "Who?"

"An old park ranger," Morehouse replied without taking his eyes off Tina. "Known for his... unusual beliefs."

He flipped it open, skimming a few pages

before saying, "Funny thing. His cabin was burned to the ground yesterday. So I'll ask you again. Where did you get this?"

The atmosphere in the room had shifted. Deputy Harding edged closer, curiosity overriding his discomfort.

"We found it," Ellie said carefully.

"Where?" Morehouse pressed.

"In the woods, yesterday, near the falls by Caldwell's Creek," Tina answered.

Perkins, annoyed at being sidelined, suddenly reached for Ellie's bag. "Let's see what else these girls are hiding."

The tiny office exploded into chaos.

Ellie moved with startling speed, surging out of her seat and backhanding the woman with enough force to make her careen backward over her chair and slam into the wall.

Harding's hand flew to his gun, but was halted as Tina rose from her seat with panther like grace, positioning herself an inch from his face.

Her eyes locked with the deputy's with a low rumbling growl, something in her gaze making the deputy involuntarily blanch and freeze.

"You planning on shooting an unarmed kid, deputy?" Tina said, her voice a low, menacing purr, her lips just barely brushing his.

A savage, feral snarl escaped Ellie's throat as she clutched her bag to her chest, and a sudden loud cracking sound filled the room as she adjusted her head.

"Don't... Touch... My... Things." Ellie said, gasping. Each word dripping with the promise of more violence.

"Ellie..." Sheriff Morehouse slowly stood and raised his hands in a calming manner.

The air in the room felt suddenly thick with tension, like the charged atmosphere before a lightning strike.

"Let's all just relax here. There's no need for violence."

"I think we're done here," Tina said quietly, her voice carrying an unnatural weight as she turned back to the Sheriff.

"We've answered your questions, and we don't know anything about Jessie, Tiffany, or Stacy. If you want to search our belongings, get a warrant."

Sheriff Morehouse stood silent for a moment, his gaze moving from the journal in his hand to the girls.

"That's fine. But I'll be keeping this," he

said finally, holding up Jared's journal.

"Fine," Ellie replied, her voice still tight with barely controlled anger. "Take it. It's just an old book anyway."

"You girls are free to go," Sheriff Morehouse said, stepping aside to clear their path to the door. "For now. But we may have more questions soon."

"Fine, I'll call my lawyer," Ellie said. "I'm sure he'll be real happy to fly all the way out here from LA to deal with you hicks."

Perkins sputtered indignantly, still trying to rise from the floor. "What?! Robert, you can't just…"

"That's " to you, and I said it's fine. They're free to go, Carol," he cut her off firmly.

He looked back at Ellie and said, "This is a police matter now."

Tina began gathering her scattered belongings, shoving them back into her bag with quick, jerky movements.

Ellie remained still, her amber eyes locked on the Sheriffs.

As Tina finished and moved for the door, Ellie finally said, "One more thing, *Robert*. Stay away from my mother."

CHAPTER 25

Ellie and Tina left the office quickly, pure rage simmering just beneath the surface.

As they stepped into the empty main hallway, Tina grabbed Ellie's arm and pulled her into a nearby janitorial closet.

"Hey! What the…" Ellie started to protest.

"Shut up and get in here!" Tina hissed, pulling Ellie intimately close to her as they squeezed into the small space and closed the door.

"Listen," Tina whispered, her voice so low that Ellie almost couldn't hear it.

She closed her eyes and lay her head gently on Tina's bosom and let her senses reach out.

At first, there was nothing, but then she caught something.

A woman's shrill voice came from the vent above them.

Ellie's head snapped up, and looked at Tina.

How did you know about this? She asked silently, not wanting to interrupt the conversation.

Tina glanced down at her and smiled.

Heard the janitor while we were in there, she replied.

Inside the office, Perkins had erupted into a furious tirade.

"What the hell, Robert?" Her voice was shrill with indignation.

"That girl assaulted me! And you're just letting them walk out of here?"

"Carol, listen to me carefully," the Sheriff replied, his voice tight with frustration. "Those girls are... not what they appear to be."

"What does that mean?" Perkins demanded.

"Damn it, lady, did you not just see that fuck show?" Harding's voice echoed harshly through the vent.

It sounded shaken, as if he was almost in near hysterics himself.

"It means that something ain't right about those two. How... how they moved. And how they seemed to know when we were lying about something? And their eyes..."

"Their eyes?" Perkins asked, sounding incredulous. "What about their eyes?"

"You didn't see it?" Harding asked.

There was a brief silence.

"Sheriff?" Harding sounded desperate.

"Her eyes… they were blue, and then they changed color. They turned almost… golden. Like…"

"Never mind," the Sherif said, firmly cutting him off.

"God damn it. They had us on the ropes from the start. They were messing with our heads the whole time we had them in here."

"It's that Granger girl I tell you. Miss Akins was a good girl until she started hanging around that one. And then that whole mess last month. Now…" Perkins cut in shrilly.

"And what makes you think this is Miss Granger's doing?" Morehouse asked.

"Why, she was always quiet. Too quiet if you ask me. Came out here from California. Well… you know the sort. Nothing but trouble. Who knows what weird things they were teaching her out there!"

"Mrs. Perkins. Ma'am, with all due respect, you can't judge a person by where they come from." Harding said, sounding slightly calmer.

"And who says? I can judge any one of these

little brats any way I want. And mark my words, if you won't do something about that girl, I will! She's done. Come tomorrow, she is expelled! I want her out of this school."

There was the sound of a fist slamming on a desk, as the Sheriff's voice cut in firmly.

"Enough, Carol! Go home. Lock your doors, and stay inside tonight."

"Are you threatening me?" Perkins asked, her voice rising another octave.

"No, ma'am," Morehouse replied evenly, "However, I'm not sure if you're keeping score, but at least two of those bodies in the morgue had issues with those girls."

There was a tense pause.

At last, Perkins' voice came through the vent. "I'm the Vice Principal of this school, Robert. They wouldn't dare try anything."

"The evidence says otherwise. So until we can find something concrete, stay out of their way. And keep a gun loaded."

There was the sound of a door opening.

Ellie and Tina stiffened.

Shit! We need to get out of here, Tina said silently. *Right now.*

They felt a strange sense of dislocation as

they went to open the closet door, but stopped suddenly as the Sheriff and Deputy exited the main office and stopped right outside the door.

SHIT! DON'T MOVE! Ellie screamed silently.

"What's with the old book?" Harding asked.

"It belonged to Jared Duprix. The old coot who supposedly helped those kids last month. Apparently, no one found his body. He had some interesting theories."

"Like what?" Harding asked.

The Sheriff sighed, "The old man was crazy about something called a Rougarou."

"What's that, like a skunk ape or something?"

"No," Morehouse replied. "It's a werewolf."

Harding laughed, "You're kidding, right? Robby, you don't really believe in that sort of thing, do you?"

"No," Morehouse said, "But old man Duprix did. Guy gets killed helping those girls, then someone burns down his place, and the next day this turns up? I don't need to be Columbo to do the math."

"Gotcha, boss. So you're thinking that whoever is doing the killings was involved with that mess last month, and you think it was them girls?"

"Yup. And they burned down Duprix's cabin because he knew something. I'm willing to bet this journal might be part of that," replied the Sheriff enthusiastically.

"And the werewolf thing?" Harding asked as the pair finally moved away from the door.

"We'll deal with that if it comes to it," came the Sheriff's response, fading down the hall.

Ellie and Tina waited a moment until the men's voices faded around the corner before slipping out of the closet.

They started down the hall towards their lockers.

"Let's find Haily and..." Tina started, but was cut off as the bell rang overhead, forcing them both to clutch their ears in agony.

The hallway suddenly seemed way too bright, too loud, too... everything.

The world vibrated around them as the relentless bell seemed to stab into their skulls with a thousand daggers.

A sudden wave of dizziness slammed into Ellie, making her stumble.

The edges of her vision blurred, tinged with an ominous crimson haze, as agony pulsed in her head.

It was then, a moment before the darkness took her, she threw back her head and screamed.

No, she realized, not a scream, a *howl*!

A howl filled with the pain and terror of every indignity she had just suffered. Competing with the wretched bell above to be heard.

But heard by whom?

Tina was right next to her, trying to haul her to her feet.

She felt the lockers vibrate around her, the sensation adding her own song to the nightmare of sound and sensation.

Finally, the assault stopped, and her world swam and began to blur.

Then, as the darkness closed in, threatening to consume her, an answer came.

A voice so strong she swore it was right next to her.

She didn't know how, but she knew the voice, *HIS* voice.

And it only said one word. A singular command she dared not resist, even as the darkness engulfed her.

Hide!

CHAPTER 26

The screaming of the bell assaults our ears, and pain rips through our skull. But it is nothing. We push it aside for her.

We hear her. Her cry of agony. Their fear and pain taint the air, though we cannot see them.

We know that pain. We know the enemy now. They need us.

The time has come to make first contact.

Hide! We command them silently as we push our way through the door, and the red haze falls over us.

The cops push toward us, their voices murmuring about some old man.

"You're joking, right? The old coot must have been nuts," the redhead says.

The elder shakes his head, "Probably. But he believed it enough to give me these…"

The glimmer of the goddess's metal flashes in his palm.

"I carry a few for the novelty."

Interesting, but not our problem at the moment. Still…

We step further into the throng, thumping into the redhead, inhaling his musk.

Acidic and sharp with anger.

"Hey! Watch where you're going, kid!" he bellows.

Growling softly, we ignore the irrelevant fool. He is not the one we want. Nor is the other with glimmering metal and book.

No, they are nothing to us. But *her*… We catch her foul musk lingering on the cops. Floral to the point of putridity.

She is the one we seek now. We want *her*.

She is evil incarnate. Everyone knows it. But now she has hurt our property.

Now she threatens our territory.

A heavy musk hangs in the air, *their* musk. They're close, so close. The closet there!

But they are gone. Where?

It doesn't matter. We must ignore it. They've obeyed us and hidden themselves.

Soon. Very soon, they will be with us at last.

Tomorrow!

Yes, we can wait one more day. But for now, we must protect them.

The reek hits us so suddenly we almost choke on its foulness.

It's her! The one we want.

The office door slams open, and she almost runs into us.

"Oh! You gave me a fright, she says up at us. Excuse me. Please hurry to class now."

She spins and marches away. Straightening her blouse and checked her purse.

The caustic stench of hatred radiates in her very wake, making our eyes water as it mixes with the foulness of her perfume and the ever present reek of rotting vegetation.

We follow. Moving through the crowded hallway as easily as a shadow woven into the very fabric of the human throng around us.

It doesn't bother us, the thousand different scents, the cacophony of slamming lockers and laughter.

No, this is our cloak in the light of day. Our Helm of Hades in the absence of the night and forest.

We follow her. Locked on her retreating

form, flowing and twisting through the writhing morass of teenage youth, watching, waiting.

Her shoes clack loudly on the linoleum. What an irritatingly pathetic attempt to draw attention to herself.

A weakling pretending to hold power. She knows nothing of real power. The power of the predator over its prey.

We will show her true power. We will teach it to her. Of its holding and the predation of its meaning.

She will learn her place in the cycle of the world. The only place that all such cowardly weaklings fill.

That of *prey*.

Hurry to class? We will teach her our own lesson. That she is nothing more than *our prey*.

She exits through a door. We follow, pushing through hesitantly, careful to give her distance.

The parking lot is almost silent at this time of the afternoon, still too early for people to leave.

We breathe in her stink. It's easy to follow in the clean air, free of the clogged and stifling hallways.

There are no windows overlooking the parking lot on this side of the building.

No witnesses to see.

A vicious growl rips from our throat as we surge forth, dropping to all fours.

The crackling pain is subtle. A soothing agony that reminds us that less is more here.

We do not need to show our true face to her.

She doesn't deserve that beautiful privilege. Not after hurting our family.

We surge and twist among the cars. Circling silently. Closing the gap.

There! We see her and flit past like a soft breeze.

She spins, but we're too fast. Nothing more than a flicker of movement.

"Hello?" she calls hesitantly, her stink changes. Antiseptic, like the nurses' station.

We follow behind her. A soft snarl ripples in her ear. She spins again, missing us by inches.

She turns now, running. Weaving almost lost between the vehicles.

We stalk, surging around her. Her terror is palpable now as her heart pounds deafeningly in our ears.

Her musk intensifies, a sickening wet tang from her thighs, mingling with her grotesque perfume.

She stops at a car, whimpering in terror as her keys scramble feebly over the lock.

They jingle almost musically as they slip from her grasp, clacking loudly on the asphalt.

She kneels to pick them up, and we surge forth, our roar rending the air like thunder.

She looks up and screams as we rush upon her like a freight train. An unstoppable force of retribution, slamming into her as if sent by Zeus himself.

The car door crumples around her, exploding inward with the crushing force of a giant fist.

It is over almost as fast as it began. The light simply vanishing from her eyes before the first shard of glass even touched the ground.

The kill is bloodless. Instant. Unsatisfying. But satisfaction is irrelevant. She is done. And so are we.

We surge back towards the school, rising once again as a man. The red haze lifting as we open the door and reenter the world of mortal men victorious.

CHAPTER 27

Ellie snapped back to herself with a loud gasp as legs buckled under her.

She fell to her knees, slamming hard to the floor as her chest heaved painfully.

Where the hell was she? The world spun disorientingly amidst the universe of shelves lined with a riot of colors and stinking with an overpowering must.

Finally, it hit her. Realization dawning in her mind as though someone had lit a candle in her consciousness.

The library!

She was in the library, hidden in a dark, musty corner amidst the stacks.

She had a lingering sense of something violent. A memory of some kind.

"What... what just…?"

She stopped as she felt moisture slicking her

thighs. Touching it, she held it to her face. It was hers alone, but it reeked of sex.

Her eyes rolled as a wave of desire washed over her.

She shook her head, blinking rapidly, trying to clear the fog from her mind.

Now was not the time to be horny. She needed to focus and think. What happened to her?

The last thing she remembered was walking down the hallway with Tina after leaving Perkins' office.

They had just heard Perkins going bananas on the Sheriff and his sidekick, then…

What happened next?

She couldn't remember.

Something happened, and now she was somehow in the library, standing between the shelves in the…

She pulled out a book, Russian Lit. Great, the most secluded and ignored section of the whole damn place.

She felt like she'd just run a marathon, and if she didn't get moving now, she was pretty sure she was about to leave a puddle on the floor.

A cold sweat broke out across her body as she pulled herself to her feet, and she clamped her legs tightly as a wave of pleasure slammed into her.

Well, at least she knew the lipstick was still in place. And she felt better now, more able to think straight anyway.

Why had she blacked out? How long had she been just standing here, staring at Anna Karenina? And where the hell was Tina?

She poked her head out from the row and did her best to orient herself.

The whole place was quiet, nearly empty except for the elderly librarian at the front desk and a couple of students in a far corner.

No one seemed to be paying any attention to her, thank God.

Another wave slammed into her. Running circling. The sun was high… Cars… Roaring her face…

"There you are!" Tina's hushed voice came from behind her.

Ellie snapped to again and whirled on Tina, clutching her as panic flooded her.

"Whoa!" Tina exclaimed quietly, doing her best not to draw attention.

"Take it easy, El. I'm happy to see you too. I've been looking everywhere for you."

"Tina," Ellie said in a terrified whisper. "What happened? How did we get here?"

Tina pushed her away, glanced nervously at the librarian.

Grabbing Ellie's arm, she pulled her back into the stacks.

"I don't know," Tina hissed, her voice tight. "One minute we were in the hallway, the bell rang, and the next thing I know, I'm coming to in the girls' locker room, horny as fuck and..." she trailed off.

Without warning, she reached between Ellie's thighs, brushing her leg gently.

A wave of pleasure slammed into her, causing her legs to almost buckle again.

Ellie clamped a hand over her mouth as her eyes rolled. She grabbed at the air, scrambling for a moment before finding purchase on a shelf.

Tina held up her hand, drenched with Ellie's wettness. "Dripping wet... Yeah, I know. It's crazy intense. I woke up the same way."

"The fuck...?" Ellie said, struggling to compose herself.

"Come on, let's get you cleaned up," Tina said softly, grabbing her wrist and making a beeline for the library's main entrance past the front desk.

"I think something bad happened. Something really bad. What do you remember?"

The memory washed over her again. The red haze. The parking lot. Vice Principal Perkins… The bell…

"I had this… vision," she said as they exited the row, "Or a dream? I don't know. But I think I was following Perkins to her car, and then I…"

Tina's face went hard. "Yeah…I had the exact same dream," she said, her voice barely audible as they pushed through the library doors and out into the hallway.

"It was like our dreams, but this time… It wasn't us. It was like Jessie again…"

They stared at each other, the terrible implication hanging between them.

"Shit, Tina, if this is real…" Ellie hissed.

"Yeah, I know. It means that there is definitely another one like us. But who?"

Ellie shook her head.

"We need to find Haily," Ellie said finally.

"And we need to get the hell out of here. Now."

Tina nodded jerkily.

"She's in Biology right now."

"Then let's go." Ellie started, then paused.

"Wait. What time is it?" she asked.

Tina glanced at her watch. "Oh shit! It's almost three! Ellie, we've been out for almost two hours! The bell's about to…"

The shrill ring of the final bell cut her off. The pain slammed into their skulls, and suddenly she remembered.

The bell had rang. Threatening to make her head explode.

She'd tried to hide from it, but the agony had been too much. Her senses were still too open from their eavesdropping.

She screamed… No! Wait… Not screamed. Howled.

She'd howled, and something responded.

He had responded.

Bell finally quieted, leaving her ears echoing as the knives in her skull relented.

Almost immediately, the hall filled with students rushing to escape their daily prison.

"I remember," Ellie said grimly. "The bell rang, and for some reason, I howled. And then I heard a voice. A guy's voice telling me to hide."

They pushed into the sea of students.

"Yeah, I remember that too!" Tina said as

she weaved through the afternoon rush. ”Next thing I know I'm waking up with my twat dripping likea leaky faucet.

They fought their way through the crowded hallway, hyperaware of every slammed locker, every shouted word, and the ever present stink of youth.

Anxiety, excitement, and relief that the day was finally over. It all pressed in on her from every angle, forcing her heart to hammer against her ribs as if it would explode in her chest.

She huddled close to Tina, walking in her wake as she elbowed her way through the afternoon riot.

"There she is," Tina said, sidling up next to Haily as she closed her locker.

Haily's face lit up when she spotted them, "Hey guys! Where have…"

Her smile quickly faded almost instantly. "What's wrong?" she asked.

"We need to go," Ellie said, grabbing her wrist and dragging her along through the press. "Right now!"

Haily's brow furrowed with concern. "Why? What happened?"

"Not here," Tina hissed, looking nervously

over her shoulder. "Just trust us, ok?"

A sudden scream erupted at the far end of the hallway. Students were crowding around a pair of terrified looking girls.

"Damn it, Candy, what's going on?" a jock shouted, shaking one of them by the shoulders.

"It's Perkins!" came the girl's hysterical reply. "She's in the parking lot! She's DEAD!"

Gasps erupted around them, and the word began to spread. Repeated as a wave through the halls.

Vice Principal Perkins was dead.

Ellie's blood turned to ice as the first scream of fear tore through her head.

"Ah shit! Here we go!" Tina hissed.

Ellie seized Tina's hand instinctively, squeezing it hard.

We need to go, she said silently. *Now!*

Haily allowed herself to be pulled along as they headed for a side exit, bursting out into the crisp October air in a matter of seconds.

"Will someone please tell me what's going on?" Haily demanded wrenching free of Ellie's grasp.

"Perkins is dead." Ellie blurted.

"I got that much, but what happened? Did

you guys kill the Vice Principal?!" Haily asked, the blood draining from her face.

"NO!" Tina and Ellie shouted in unison.

Haily blanched but looked relieved. "So what now? Who killed her?"

Ellie pushed her to get moving, "We'll fill you in when we're not out in the open! But we need to leave now!"

"Oh fucking Hell!" Tina exclaimed, a mortified look on her face as she looked towards the stadium lot.

"What?" Haily asked, looking as confused now as Ellie.

Tina looked almost fit to cry. "I parked my truck right next to her car. Goddamnit!"

"I'm parked this way, follow me," Haily said, leading them toward the student parking lot opposite the stadium.

They piled into Haily's battered blue Dodge van as Haily pulled around the lot, towards the stadium lot.

"Ok, guys, spill. Who killed Perkins?" Haily demanded.

"The other werewolf did. The one that killed Jessie." Tina said.

"Hollywood here decided to make like the

Wolfman and called him up."

"Hey! I didn't mean to, I thought my head was going to explode. It just happened. God be a bitch about it." Ellie snapped.

"Sorry. I… I didn't mean to be a bitch. It's just… It's got to be… Jesus H Christ!" Tina said as they rolled up on Perkins' car.

It actually didn't look too bad from where they were sitting.

All the windows were blown out, though, and they could just make out her legs sticking out of what looked like a car door taco.

Miraculously, no one was lingering around to ogle at the body.

"Holy shit!" Haily exclaimed, "You guys can do that?"

"Yeah, apparently so! Tina, get your truck out of there and meet us at my place," Ellie said, pushing Tina out of the van.

"Quick, before this place turns into a circus!"

Tina didn't need any further encouragement, practically leaping out of the van and into her truck, gunning the engine before the door was even shut.

Haily pulled away, the scream of tires echoing around them, accompanied by the reek of burning rubber.

Tina followed suit and fell in hot on their tail in short order.

Together, the two vehicles almost flew out of the parking lot like a pair of bats flying out of the mouth of out of Hell itself.

CHAPTER 28

Haily brought the van to a skidding halt in front of Ellie's house and almost sent Ellie flying through the windshield in the process.

She cursed loudly as she slammed her hand on the dashboard to catch herself.

"Fucking hell, Haily, does everyone around here drive vans like maniacs?"

Haily looked at her meekly and flashed an innocently cute smile.

"Sorry, I guess I sorta just wanted to get out of there."

Tina pulled in behind them, and they heard her slam the truck door.

"Yeah, well, getting out of there doesn't mean warp speed. And I would rather not go flying through the damn windshield, thank you."

Haily's door opened suddenly, making her shriek.

"Seriously, guys," Tina said, "Come on! I'm growing roots out here."

Thankfully, her mother wasn't home yet, giving them the privacy they desperately needed as they walked into the house.

"Where's your mom at?" Tina asked. "It's weird without her here."

"She's showing a house today. But she should be back soon. Let's get upstairs," Ellie said, mounting the stairs two at a time.

"Ok," Haily said, sounding irritated and confused as she plopped cross legged on Ellie's bed. "Could one of you please tell me what the hell is going on?"

Tina paced like a caged animal, running her hands through her hair. "We don't know exactly," she admitted. "But something... someone killed Perkins in the parking lot."

"And you think it's another werewolf?" Haily asked, her eyes wide. "Like you?"

"It has to be. But it's not like us." Ellie said, sliding down the door until she was sitting on the floor.

"What do you mean, not like you? It's a werewolf, right? How is it different?" asked Haily, looking thoroughly confused.

Tina fidgeted and seemed to try to find any-where else to look.

"It's a male… An alpha male." Ellie said softly.

"What does that mean?" Haily asked.

Tina stopped pacing and leaned on the dresser.

"The last male we met was rather…" she let out a quiet bark of laughter, "Well, let's put it this way. He was no two pump chump."

Haily looked horrified, "You mean…"

"Yup," Ellie said, "Males tend to be a bit rape happy. And if what Mr. Duprix's journals say is correct, they are very possessive and territorial around female werewolves."

"Meaning, us," Tina said, pointing at herself.

Haily nodded, "So that's why it went after Perkins. It was protecting you two."

"Yeah," Tina said with a sigh. "And he made sure we had front row tickets to the show."

"Ok, so this *Alpha* made you guys watch him kill Perkins?" Haily asked.

"Well… I'm not sure it was intentional," Ellie replied. "You see, we both had the same… vision or waking dream or something like that."

"Jesus," Haily whispered. "You actually saw it happen? While it was happening?"

"Yeah, it's sorta a thing we seem to be able to do. See each other's kills." Tina replied.

"Like, we were seeing through his eyes. Watching him stalk Perkins to her car and then..." Ellie said, swallowing hard, unable to finish.

She didn't want to admit it, but unlike her and Tina's kills, Perkins' murder had been clinical and super efficient. Almost professional.

"It's like... like being pulled into someone else's head," Tina said.

"You see what they see, feel what they feel. But not being able to do anything about it."

"You mean not wanting to do anything about it," Ellie interjected.

"Like with Jessie and Stacy. It felt like it was actually me doing the killing. But it wasn't. And when I woke up… I… I wanted more. I wanted to do it again."

"Yeah… Me too," Tina said in a small voice.

"So, it's like a drug to you guys?" Haily asked, glancing between them. "Hunting and killing?"

Tina looked at Ellie, who seemed to be focused heavily on the floor.

"Yeah, you could say that," she said at last.

"It's like getting flowers for werewolves or

something. It makes you feel... Well... sorta..."

"Horny," Ellie finished for her reluctantly.

"Yeah," Tina said, "Like hornier than you've ever been."

"And somehow you can share it with each other? How long has this whole thing been going on?" Haily asked.

Ellie sighed heavily, then looked at her. "Every night for the past three nights. First it was Jessie, then Stacy…

"And Tiffany last night, now Perk…" Tina added, stopping short as Haily cut in.

"Wait! Tiffany's dead too?! How?" Haily exclaimed in shock.

Ellie looked frustratedly at Tina, *Thanks*. She scolded silently.

Tina shrugged innocently. *So, do you want to tell her about eating Tiff's beaver, or shall I?*

"Yeah, sorry," Ellie said out loud, flashing Tina a glare. *Not one word!*

"We meant to tell you sooner, but well, Sheriff hard-nuts and his sidekick, Deputy fire-crotch, dragged us away before we could say anything."

"That's why we needed to get out of there so fast," Tina added.

"If anyone saw my truck parked near Perkins's car..."

"They'd suspect you immediately," Haily finished, her face pale. "Oh my God."

A heavy silence fell over the room, broken only by the ticking of the clock on Ellie's nightstand.

"It doesn't make any sense, though," Ellie said finally. "Why risk killing her during school hours?"

"I don't know," Tina replied.

"It felt different. Like I knew we were there, I could smell us," she said.

"But it wasn't important. It's like when I get super focused on getting rid of a spider in my room or something."

"An alibi..." Haily said softly.

"What?" Tina asked her.

Haily looked at them both, then said louder, "An alibi. Why kill her at school during the day? It gives you the perfect alibi."

Ellie tilted her head, "How so? I was hiding in the Russian Lit section of the library."

"Yeah, and I was in the girls' locker room," Tina added

Haily smiled, and her eyes lit up.

"Both places you would have been seen. Mrs. Jordan knows everyone who comes and goes in the library, and you can't tell me no one would have missed you just lurking around in the locker room."

Ellie and Tina looked dumbstruck.

Haily was practically bouncing on the bed. "Don't you see? Someone had to see you two during the time of the murder. The Alpha was protecting you by killing Perkins during a time when you couldn't have done it."

Tina looked at Ellie, then back at Haily. "I guess it sorta makes sense…?"

Ellie shrugged, "I've got no better ideas. We don't even know who this Alpha is. It's gotta be a student."

"Or a teacher…" Haily added. "Ok, that might be a little gross."

Ellie and Tina looked at her with a curious gaze, tilting their heads.

"It's only an idea. I know it was stupid. I'll shut up now," Haily said meekly, fidgeting as she looked at the floor.

She glanced up to meet their quiet stares, "Ok, could you two stop that? You look like my uncle's German Shepherd judging me."

Suddenly, there was a knock on the bedroom door, and they all jumped as Ellie's mother's voice called out, "Ellie? You home, honey?"

Ellie sprang to her feet, exchanging panicked glances with Tina and Haily.

"Yeah, Mom," she called out, working to keep her voice steady. "Just a second!"

She turned to the others, mouthing silently, "Act normal."

Haily nodded, straightening her posture and swiping a strand of hair from her face.

Oh, I think we are well past normal. Tina said silently, leaning against the dresser.

Ellie flashed her a glare and opened the door to find her mother standing in the hallway.

Her eyes darted past Ellie to her friends, her expression shifting from surprise to something more guarded.

"Hey," Nancy said, "whose van is outside?"

"Oh! That's just mine, Mrs. Granger." Haily called, waving.

Nancy's eyes lit up, and she smiled. "Oh, Haily! I'm so glad you came back. You girls staying for dinner?" she asked in a hopeful tone.

Ellie shrugged. "We didn't have anything planned, so I wouldn't mind."

Haily and Tina both nodded.

"Excellent! So what are you girls getting up to in here?"

Ellie stiffened, "Uhhh… Nothing much, just…"

"Planning for tomorrow!" Tina chimed in. "It's Halloween tomorrow. So we really need to focus on planning."

"Really?" Nancy said, frowning slightly and sounding unconvinced.

"Are you sure everything is alright? You all look... I don't know, rattled."

"We're fine, Mom," Ellie said exasperatedly. "Just talking about Halloween plans."

Nancy's face softened. "Ok? Well, what are you girls thinking of doing?"

An uncomfortable silence stretched between them.

"Nothing special," Ellie finally said. "Probably just go… ummm… camping."

If there had been a magical button to turn her mother white, green, and fuchsia all at once, Ellie seemed to have found it with a single word.

Camping.

Her Mother's mouth opened and closed several times.

When she finally seemed about to actually say something, the phone rang downstairs.

Relief flooded through Ellie at the interruption.

"I should get that," she said in a hollow tone, turning mechanically to head downstairs.

The moment she was gone, Ellie closed the door again, leaning her forehead against it.

"Fucking hell," she whispered.

"Camping?" Tina said flatly.

"That's all you could think of?"

Ellie turned around and said, "What else could I say that wouldn't make her want to pry further?"

"True," Tina agreed. "Haily's right, though. The Alpha is definitely protecting us."

Ellie sighed again. "Yeah, no shit, Sherlock. But who is it?"

"Well, why don't we look at its victims? Maybe they could provide a clue," suggested Haily.

Ellie and Tina shrugged. "Ok, well, we know it saw Perkins as a threat to us." Tina said, "Your howling called it up on that one."

"But what about Jessie Walters?" Ellie asked.

"I didn't know him all that well, but David

did," replied Tina.

"He used to hang out with the rest of the jocks. Jace, Kyle, Terrance. All those guys run in the same cliques."

"Yeah, and their bitch cliques too," Haily added.

"That's how Stacy was spreading rumors about you two," Haily pointed out.

"And Tiffany was just a plain old bitch. Hey, what happened to her, by the way? Did you see her getting…?"

Ellie and Tina exchanged glances.

She doesn't know, Tina said silently.

Should we tell her? asked Ellie, tilting her head. *She freaked out once already.*

We can trust her. Tina nodded.

They turned to Haily, who was looking at them weirdly.

"What is that?" she asked. "I've seen you guys doing that a lot recently, and it's really creepy."

"Ummm…" Ellie let out a nervous laugh.

"Sorry… Ummm… This is going to get a little weird, so don't freak out again like yesterday."

This is a bad idea, Ellie said silently to Tina.

"We don't think the alpha killed Stacy or

Tiffany," she said slowly.

Tina winced and piped in, "You remember us telling you how sometimes you don't feel like you're in control as a werewolf? Yeah, I'm pretty sure I'm the one who killed Stacy."

Haily didn't say anything and just sat there as if she had been gorgonized.

Finally, she seemed to animate, blinking at them slowly.

After another moment, she said, "Ok. Well… That explains the tongue comment from earlier."

Ellie blushed and hesitantly added, "And I… I killed Tiffany."

Haily sat quietly for a minute, her expression unreadable.

Ellie and Tina exchange worried looks.

She's going to freak. Ellie said silently.

No, she won't give her a minute, replied Tina, flashing her a look.

They stood there quietly watching as the gears worked in Haily's head.

At last, she slowly looked up at them and said, "So, you're telling me the murders were you guys, but you didn't have any control over yourselves?"

Ellie and Tina nodded vigorously.

"And if I get turned into a werewolf like you guys, I could possibly kill and eat people without meaning to, as well?"

This time, the nodding was very reluctant.

"Yeah, that is more like a *definite*, actually," Ellie replied.

"Right... And this could happen anytime, not just the full moon?"

Again, Ellie and Tina shrugged and nodded slowly.

Haily sat quietly and seemed to be considering everything Ellie and Tina had told her.

Finally, after several long, nerve wracking moments, she looked up at them as a hesitant smile crept onto her lips.

"So... what does human tongue taste like?"

Tina and Ellie exchanged surprised looks before turning back to Haily.

"Well..." started Tina, "It's sorta chewy..."

CHAPTER 29

The rhythm of the world surges around us with each blurring rush as we run.

Flowing and pulsating with each hammering thrust of our pelvis.

It is the heartbeat of the night as the red haze once again descends over our world.

Pulsating with each vice, clotted stench, and every nightmare twisting us in our bed.

We surge through the woods. Hunting for what is ours. Surging through the night like a liquid shadow.

The moaning draws us away from our course. The stench of their musk drawing us to her cries of pleasure.

We follow the echoing creaking. That rhythm so unmistakable.

The world blurs around us suddenly as we approach the car.

Suddenly, he is in us! We are her, and she is us! What is this?

He is inside us. Desperately grunting as we reach to clutch his hip. Pulling him deeper into…

The world spins, and suddenly are back there in the woods watching as they scream and bolt for the rocking van.

The thing emerges from the darkness! A living shadow of Hell itself. *Oh god, what is that? Run!*

"DAVID! TINA! OPEN UP!" he screams.

The world surges around us. We look through the window and see her golden locks writhing back and forth.

She looks up at us, and suddenly, we see ourselves outside gazing in.

Our features masked with dark reddish fur, human yet animalistic, with bright amber in our eyes.

We turn and leave her… we leave us to our vices. The waves of pleasure wash over us as we surge through the trees, returning to our quest.

Over gully and creek. Water and road. We surge from yard to yard, looking for the stench of *him*.

The boy picks up something, a rock. Why

doesn't it attack? It watches them as we are.

What is it?

"It's coming!" S*he* says to the boy. The other girl screams in fear.

"OPEN THE GODDAMN DOOR, OR I'M BREAKING A WINDOW!" he shouts!

The door opens, and suddenly, the *other one* is there in all her glory. Beautiful in *her* nudity in the yellow firelight.

The others swarm into the van and close the door depriving us of the vision of her.

The tree surge around us as we find the scent. The stink of leather and male age.

We stop and lift our face to the sky, breathing it in.

He has it. His unclean touch violates what is ours alone.

The snarl rips from our throat as we turn and swarm to him. To what is ours.

He will pay for his violation.

We mount him. Pushing him deeper into our womanhood.

Grunting as we writhe upon his supple flesh and throbbing member, wrapped tightly within the folds of us.

Rising and falling, we scream in ecstasy for

who knows how many times now. Was it the tenth, or the thousandth?

Our eyes roll as another wave slams into us like an earthquake, as we pull his mouth to our bosom to suckle as Romulus and Remus once did.

We see her take the wheel of the van. The thing stares and laughs as the engine turns once, twice, then roars to life on the third try.

The *other* joins her behind the cracked windshield. The engine roars and the tires spin.

The shadow roars in anger and takes to the air like a magnificent gazelle of nightmare death.

"The fuck?"

The Van lurches backwards like an overfed tick as the monster slams onto the roof.

She hits the brakes, and it falls forward, smashing one clawed fist through the windshield.

Was that the moment? Was that the moment she was gifted to us?

We've found him! He's holding it, the book! Our book!

He opens the squad car door and gets in.

We cry out in pleasure as *he* rises and falls upon us, his flesh on ours, opening us like a flower.

We grunt and clutch at the leather seat as *he* thrusts and pounds, filling us.

We surge after the squad car.

Loping, weaving, and flowing through the trees as we match pace with the wheeled abomination.

The van spins and crashes. *We* hear screams and cries of pain and fear inside.

The engine struggles and dies as the shadow stalks around it.

We hear their desperate terror within as the shadow of the titan circles them.

We need to help. *We* have to try to help them!

But how? What can we do?!

We rend the leather of the seat as we flip and thrust into and onto one another.

The world blurs in the confines of the car.

His car.

We let him have us. Every part of us.

Pain and agony blending with every grunt and desperate thrust. Praying, hoping, willing himself to release into us.

And we want it.

We need it.

We crave it as much as we crave life itself.

The squad car slows now, as do we.

He has it. We can see it on the seat next to him, ours for the taking!

As is his miserable life.

The car stops, and we surge from the shadows, roaring our fury as we slam into the wretched abomination.

Flipping it as he looks upon us in horror.

The call! It hit us then. The elk call in the bag. Why do we have an elk call? Who cares? All that matters now is that we help those in the ruined van!

It's long and floppy. It was his, the one who left us now for Heaven. Old and grey.

We remember now. It's all we have left of Grandpa.

The misty dawn in the cold Michigan north silhouetting his weathered face like a halo of power as he bugles it, burns in our mind as if from a fairy tale.

We lift the call to our lips, remembering now, after so long, his words. Placing our lips just so.

And we blow hard.

The bugling challenge rending through the night. Unleashing our power and our strength into the shadows so far from him.

We mount him again, grinding and screaming as he swells within our womanhood. Clutching our hips and groping desperately for our bosom.

His eyes roll, and he screams, bucking under us as his warmth fills us.

Flooding us with his seed until the pain of our fullness is beyond our ability to contain.

We fall upon the car, the glass shattering as we see him within, our prize lying dismissed as the stink of copper and fuel fills the air.

We roar at the goddess above. Proclaiming our victory in her name.

We watch as the shadow moves away from the van.

It worked! *Go! Run! Get out of there!*

Oh god, it sees us! What is that thing? *Run! Run! Run!*

We scramble through the brush as the shadow bays at our heels. The hound of Satan himself calling for our blood.

We fall upon him. Thrusting him deeper into us as our mouth crushes his.

He kisses us back in exhausted desperation as we feel him swell again within us.

We smile, but our hunger is no longer for his thrusting.

Slaked, we are for the warmth of our coupling.

We arch up and roar at her above, grinding him painfully under us as we fall upon him again, now hungrily ripping and tearing at his flesh.

We rend the ruined door from its hinges and bend to claim what is ours. To rend the life from this infidel who dares claim our property.

The shot hurts our ears, as a dull pain rips through us. We turn as lights fall on our coppery fur.

Another shot erupts from within the squad car.

Pain! Real pain! White hot agony rends our flesh as we fall from the car, slamming down onto the hard pavement.

We scream in ecstasy as we rip and rend him. Rising and falling upon his swollen manhood. Dying as he quivers beneath us in a symphony of ecstasy and suffering, terror.

The stench of copper surrounds us and fills us with its wetness.

It's upon us, clawing and biting as we kick and buck.

We scream in agony as the thing finds our shoulder, crushing the bone and rending our flesh.

We punch and fight with everything we have and more. We gotta win. We refuse to die here like this. Not to this thing…

But it's pointless. We listen in quiet horror to

its satisfied grunts as it chews our red meat noisily in its unholy maw.

We flee through the forest from the agony. From the humiliation.

We had won. Had proclaimed to the bright goddess her victory, only to have it torn from us. To fail her.

We lift our head and confess our sin to her, pleading for her forgiveness.

Another shot, and the evil hiss of her metal flashes by us.

Turning away, we swarm through the darkness, fleeing until tree and bush melt into one.

We hear the lament of our failure even as we rise from his corpse in victory. The red haze slowly fading from our eyes.

The shadow turns and lifts from us.

NO! They were supposed to run away, not return to the camp!

You fools! You idiots. Run! It's coming for you!

She struggles to work the latch and open the car door.

The memory begins to fade quickly, as the red haze lifts completely, leaving Ellie with one final momentary flash of a room.

A room with posters of bands and… something on a table.

No, not a table… a desk.

It was someone's bedroom, and on the desk was a letterman. But…

The vision fades, and she looks down at the corpse. Her womanhood throbbing with pleasure.

"Fuck!" Ellie muttered, finally throwing open the door and stumbling out into the night.

Her arms came up instinctively as something lunged from the shadows, crashing into her chest and slamming her back against the car.

The reek of antiseptic fear mixed with blood and sweat assaulted her nose mercilessly as she struggled to find a grip on Tina's slickened flesh.

"What the…? Tina?"

Tina's fingers clawed at Ellie's shoulders, nails digging in as her legs gave out. Her breath came in short, panicked bursts against Ellie's collarbone.

"Help!" she gasped. "They're coming…"

Tina looked at Ellie's blood-splashed face, taking it in at last. "What…?"

"It's Jace," Ellie replied, tightening her grip as Tina swayed. "What happened?"

Tina's head whipped toward the trees, her whole body trembling.

"Oh god, Ellie. I fucked up. They're…"

A dog bayed close by.

Close. Too close.

The sound raising every hair on Ellie's arms.

Tina pulled herself up, throwing her arm over Ellie's shoulder.

"Oh god… Ellie, run! They have silver!"

CHAPTER 30

Run! It was all Ellie could think about as they fled through the moonlit night. Their bodies slicked with sweat and blood.

Some of it theirs, most of it not.

It was well past midnight, how far past, she had no idea.

Shafts of silvery moonlight flickered through the canopy disorientingly, rendering any judgment of time or direction futile.

Tina staggered, pressing her palm against her shoulder where the silver bullet had torn through flesh, bone, and muscle.

Ellie had seen the injury, a clean hole that passed completely through the shoulder.

Tina had been lucky that the round didn't get stuck in her.

Still, it had done enough damage.

Though the wound was healing, it seemed stunted, and rivulets of dark greenish gray blood trickled between her fingers.

Her skin was feverishly hot around the small opening as her system fought to expel the silver poisoning.

Keep moving! Ellie silently commanded, grabbing Tina's elbow to steady her. *Don't stop.*

Ellie smiled at the irony of the situation.

Only a month ago, Tina had been the one telling her to keep moving and not stop as they fled from a monster.

She breathed in the reek of copper and musk and smiled. Now they were the monsters.

The warmth of Jace's fluids slicked her thighs just as his blood had begun to turn to glue upon her skin.

She wished she had time to revel in the conflicting sensations. To savor his coppery flavor as she cleaned herself.

But alas, such luxuries were not hers tonight.

The unmistakable baying of hunting hounds cut through the sanctity of the midnight forest.

They've got our scent. Tina snarled through the pain.

How many? Ellie asked.

Tina lifted her face and sniffed. *Two, maybe three.*

"Damn it to hell." Ellie cursed softly.

Flank right. Take cover. Ellie commanded as she released Tina and bolted left.

She surged through the brush, doubling back wide.

The red haze descended over her eyes, lighting up the world around her.

Something crackled softly as she felt a sharp agony in her fingers. She didn't bother to look as she felt the flesh splitting and the sleek ebony claws prick her palms.

She launched herself into the air and hit the ground on her fours, galloping.

"Jesus, what was that?" came a voice. She knew that voice. A Varano. Michael Varano, to be precise.

"I don't know. Set a dog loose." Richard's voice echoed to her.

"Go get'em, girl! Sick'em, Jezzy!" Mike commanded as a hound bayed suddenly and swarmed towards her.

She turned to meet the beast as it exploded from the underbrush. Its rage-filled eyes turned to blind panic as Ellie rose to meet it mid-flight.

Its screams of fear turned to howls of agony as she opened its ribs, rending tissue and tendon gleefully.

The hound kicked and snapped at her futilely as each attempt was met with a new, sadistically broken and torn limb.

At last, she ended the animals' suffering, grabbing both upper and lower jaws and pulling them horribly until the creature's maw opened like some morbid crimson flower.

It had ended as suddenly as it had begun in only a few savage seconds of fury.

She released the ruined, twitching corpse and surged again through the brush, exploding out as a crimson nightmare.

The men screamed as they shot, but there was another, Morehouse!

Silver fire belched from his gun, streaking in her vision as it missed by inches.

She roared in defiance as she gutted another hunting hound. Its dying screams echoed through the trees as she rushed back to Tina's side.

What the fuck was that? Tina asked wordlessly as Ellie hauled her brutally to her feet.

Two dogs dead, one's still alive. Run! Ellie replied.

They tore through the undergrowth, ignoring the ripping branches that left thin, bloody welts across their skin.

The wounds healed almost as quickly as they appeared. Striping their nude bodies in a mosaic of clean flesh amidst the nightmare visages of blood.

The last hound's baying grew louder, more insistent.

"God damn-it! It went this way!" Richard's voice echoed.

"Don't lose it, Pa!" Michael shouted.

"Fuck! They're gaining on us," Ellie gasped, her golden eyes wide with rage and fear as they broke into a small clearing.

"I can't fight all of them."

"El! Look! It's your place! We made it back to your house." Tina hissed, pointing.

Ellie followed Tina's finger, hope surging through her.

She could just make out the distant outline of her house. So tantalizingly close yet impossibly far.

Her hope crashed as she saw the open ground stretching impossibly between them and safety, a killing field where they would be exposed.

NO! It's too open! Ellie replied silently, shaking her head.

She whimpered softly as the hound's baying closed in. Fear creeping into her gut as the sound of the hunters seemed to cut them off from any possible way back.

Where are you? The voice came as suddenly as thunder, echoing through their skulls like the hissing of a great serpent.

Then, as if crashing as a wave upon the beach of her mind, she felt it.

She looked at Tina. Her eyes almost glowing like lanterns in the darkness with hope. She felt it too.

It was as if a great presence of pure, unrelenting force and unyielding will had forced its way into their minds. Searching for them!

It was *him*. The alpha. *Their* alpha!

Their lover. Their protector. Their brother.

He was close, moving somewhere nearby.

Ellie could feel the quiet of the night descend upon the woods. It was as if the sounds of the forest had suddenly been muted.

The silence was suddenly deafening.

He was there, somewhere. His rage palpable upon the very air of the woods.

Where are you?! The voice came again more urgently. *Sing for me!*

The command could not be ignored. It flowed through them as a want of unstoppable desire. To call to him, to bring him into their fold, and huddle behind his strength.

They lifted their heads to the night sky and sang to the goddess above.

Pouring their lament into the mournful howl that unified their voices to echo through the night, shattering the quietude of the forest.

Behind them, excited shouts rose up.

"There, Rich! They're over there!" came Morehouse's booming voice.

"We got'em now! Don't let them escape!" Richard replied.

Ellie whimpered in terror. They were so close now!

She clutched at Tina, huddling into the warmth of her bosom.

Did he hear them? Where was he? They sang for him. They had called to him. Begging him for help.

Please! She screamed in her mind. *Help us!*

Silence. Not an insect or even the rustle of a leaf stirred.

Then it came.

At first, it wasn't a sound at all, but a strange feeling. A vibration in the air, the ground, and trees.

Night birds took to the air, screaming in panic.

Then the vibration turned again and rose. It intensified into a blood curdling, bone rattling howl that vibrated the very fabric of the universe around them.

It was deeper, stronger, filled with fury and the uncompromising promise of blood.

It was as if the very gates of Hell had opened up and heralded the arrival of doom.

I am here. The voice shook through their minds as his call faded.

"What the hell was that?" Mike asked, his voice trembling, as the antiseptic reek of sudden fear flooded the air.

"How the hell should I know?" his father replied, his voice tainted with the hint of panic.

Another howl, closer now, rent the fabric of the night open like a wound.

Within it screamed a thousand voices of the damned, echoing as they proclaimed war upon any that would trespass against them.

"Jesus Christ! Get ready! Stand your ground, boys!" Morehouse commanded.

Then, as the last echoes of the howl faded, the shadow of a titan fell over the small clearing, blocking the moonlight.

Ellie looked up, trembling with fear, expecting to see feral yellow eyes in midnight black fur.

But the fur that gleamed in the darkness wasn't black, but a silvery grey. The eyes that met hers were not feral or yellow, but a gentle golden amber, filled with kindness and worry.

He was young and vigorous. Massive in size, possibly towering taller than the Beast.

His soft, silky fur was warm and gentle as he lowered his muzzle to them.

His scent was different than the Beast that had sired them all.

It was fresh and strong, somehow familiar yet Ellie couldn't quite place it.

Who are you? Tina's voice echoed in Ellie's mind, and she joined hers with it in wonderment.

Yes, who are you? She asked. *Please tell us.*

He nudged them forcefully toward the house with his massive snout.

Go. The command hammered forcefully in their mind.

They bolted without hesitation, the command brooking no argument.

Their long legs ate up the ground as they loped like twin gazelles to the safety of the house.

Behind them came a roar of rage and anger. The sound of Hell itself being set loose upon those foolish enough to have hunted his property filled the night.

Gunshots cracked through the darkness as the war between man and nightmare began.

Ellie and Tina scrambled up the side of the house, their claws digging into the siding as they swarmed through the open window to Ellie's room.

The inhuman screaming of a dying hound chasing them as they tumbled through the opening.

They turned immediately to the window, clutching terrified to one another as they listened with bated breath to the war *He* now waged for them.

Soon, almost as it had begun, the sounds of the men retreating echoed through the night as loudly as their gunshots splitting the air.

Then it was over.

That horrifying silence fell upon the earth

once again as it had that night when Jared had fallen in their name.

Had their alpha fallen? Their brother, their mate? Had another fallen for them, too?

The thought of it tormented every fiber of her being and threatened to drive her insane.

Jared had been like a grandfather to her in the few short hours she had known the man.

Visions of the silvery titan lying dead upon the tangled roots and leaves of the woods floated up in her mind.

No! They had just found him! He had come when they needed him most.

There had been no judgment in those soft amber eyes, only love and an unconditional longing for her touch, even as she was tainted with the reek of another.

The thought of losing another so soon because of her was too much to bear.

Tears began to streak the crimson gore on her cheeks.

"Please… Come on, please don't be dead," she pleaded softly.

Suddenly, as if in answer to her plea, a howl split the night open as if a crack of lightning from Zeus himself had struck.

Not a mournful cry of defeat. Not a lonely confession of failure. But the blazing blood soaked roar of the victorious.

Joy flooded her heart as they bounced gleefully at the window. Their jubilant voices joining his song in triumph. Calling to him to come into their arms and claim his prize.

His massive form emerged from the trees, stopping at the edge of the woods. His silvery fur glimmering in the radiance of the moonlight.

He looked up at them, as a knight might the maidens of a tower. His golden eyes finding theirs, burning with longing and desire.

He quietly turned and vanished. Fading into the trees like a ghost. Leaving them to reach longingly after him.

Please! They called in unison. *Don't leave us!*

Soon. Very soon. The echo of his voice whispered, rapidly fading from their minds.

Leaving them with the promise of his return hanging heavy in their hearts.

CHAPTER 31

The next morning, Ellie slowly woke up and, for the first time in a month, felt almost blissful.

She let her eyes flutter open, then shut them tightly with a groan in the early morning light.

Her body felt unusually heavy, though pleasantly warm against the cool wooden floor of her bedroom.

After several moments, she realized how closely she was curled against Tina. Their nude forms lovingly intertwined, more intimately than what was commonly deemed appropriate.

Let them judge. The world knew nothing of their kind, and never could.

Tina burrowed her face into her bosom, as Ellie breathed in the clean scent of her strawberry locks.

She pressed her face into Tina's hair and huffed her in.

Every muscle in her body hummed with energy, despite having slept on the hard floor.

Tina stirred beside her, golden reddish hair splayed across the floorboards like spilled honey.

"Morning," Tina mumbled, not yet opening her eyes. "You smell nice."

Ellie rolled and stretched. Tina moaned in mild protest as her hand traced the sweat beading on her skin.

Ellie smiled at the touch and squirmed down to burrow deeper into her embrace, unfazed by the furnace of their joined forms.

"You smell pretty good too," she whispered, huffing her sweat in.

Now it was Tina's turn to roll to her back and stretched languidly as Ellie finally sat up.

"Fuck me, I'm hot," Ellie said.

"Mmmm… Yeah, you are. But you're not my type." Tina replied playfully.

Ellie shot her a glare and swatted her tit playfully.

"Not what I meant, you cow."

"Owe! Bitch!" Tina yelped, "At least you got shagged last night."

Tina sat up beside her, stretching her arms overhead as several loud cracks echoing from her.

"Something tells me we are both going to be in for it tonight," she said in a sultry voice.

"Pretty sure big boy is going to be mighty hungry."

Ellie giggled softly and blushed. She hoped so. For the first time since Rick, she actually wanted it.

No, not *wanted*, that wasn't a strong enough word for it. More like ravenously craved it.

She remembered her little tryst with the Beast last month.

That had amounted to nothing, of course.

It had been a tease and a letdown that had left her furious and very…

Well, it's a good thing her clothes were already ruined by that point.

With how aroused she had been by the encounter, getting let down had been no laughing matter.

True, she had tried to kill it, but that's no excuse to work a girl up and then just leave her dripping.

At least Jace had gratified her somewhat. The stupid fuck really thought he was something else.

God, she remembered the look on his face when she'd found him parked there.

Slithering nude into the passenger seat as he babbled stupidly.

"Shut up and fuck me," she'd growled as she mounted him.

She smiled viciously at the memory.

She couldn't wait to see the look on Ashley's face when she tells her how her boytoy died balls deep in her cunt.

Right before she fed the bitch her own fucking heart.

A sharp knock at the door snapped her from her reverie.

"Ellie? Sweetie?" called her mother's voice.

"Are you up? I made breakfast."

Ellie shot a sarcastic glance at Tina.

This will be fun.

"Yeah, Mom," she called back, her voice sounding strangely deeper than normal.

"I'll be down in a bit."

"Okay… well, hurry up before it gets cold."

After a moment of hesitation, she added, "Hey, are you ok? You sound… funny."

Tina clamped her hand over her mouth, fighting a fit of giggles.

Ellie added her hand and shot her a warning look.

Shut up, don't you dare!

Tina looked pleadingly at her as she bounced with restrained effort.

I can't help it.

"Ellie?" Her mother called again.

"Yeah!" Ellie finally replied, still fighting with Tina.

"Yeah, I'm fine. I'll be down in a bit. I just need a shower."

"Ok, just checking," her mother replied and finally moved off back downstairs.

They listened to the footsteps retreat down the hallway.

Ellie felt something wet in her hand and realized it was Tina's tongue.

"Eww!" she yelped, jerking her hand away.

Tina erupted in a giggling fit.

"Holy shit," she whispered, "That was close. Glad she didn't open the door."

"Yeah," Ellie replied, looking Tina up and down. "She would have gotten a real eye full."

Tina looked at Ellie, then back at the door. "Wait a second. Question. Your mom isn't…?"

Ellie chuckled, "Get her drunk enough, and she'll do anything. Even girls. But generally no, she's harmless."

Tina let out a sigh as she stood and ran her fingers through her hair.

She froze, her eyes wid-ening. "What the... Oh, you got to be fucking kidding me!" she hissed.

Ellie stared in disbelief. Tina's strawberry-blonde hair, which had been shoulder length yesterday, now cascaded well past her buttocks and nearly to her knees.

"Holy cow!" she exclaimed, pushing to her feet to admire the long locks as they shone like a new penny in the sunlight.

"Talk about wow!" Tina said, seizing Ellie's hair and holding it up for her to see. "Look at you!"

Ellie's eyes bugged as she realized that her own honey golden locks had grown impossibly long, thick, and luxuriant as well.

Ellie turned to the mirror hanging on her closet door and gasped in awe.

Not only had her hair grown, but she app-eared to have gained at least two inches in height overnight. She was positively Amazonian!

Tina joined her at the mirror, both girls staring at their transformed reflections in stunned silence.

"We look..." Tina began.

"Different," Ellie finished, as she admired the muscles rippling beneath sweat slicked skin.

Their limbs seemed longer, too. Lean and graceful. And their faces!

She stared into her own face with wide-eyed wonderment.

It was her features indeed, but almost entirely alien. Sharper and more angular, still completely human, yet at the same time distinctly lupine.

If that was even possible.

"My God," Tina gushed, cupping Ellie's breasts.

"Would you look at these things! We could almost be twins now."

Ellie swatted her hands away.

"Are you serious? That's what you think of? Of all our problems, my boobs are the least of our worries!"

Tina gave an impish smile and said, "You ain't lying there. Damn girl, watch where you swing them things. You'll put an eye out."

Ellie growled as she spun in front of the mirror.

"We can't go out looking like this. People will notice."

"Yeah, no shit," Tina agreed, grinning.

"We'd give half the town a coronary with buns and tits like these," she said, slapping Ellie sharply on a perfectly shaped butt cheek.

"Ouch! Could you be serious for a minute?" Ellie yelped at her.

"Alright," Tina said as she reached for a pair of scissors on Ellie's desk.

"Here, we can at least get this hair situation under control."

They worked quickly, hacking away at each other's impossibly long locks until they fell to a more manageable length just below their shoulders.

"There," Tina said, setting the scissors down.

"Slightly less Mormon…ish."

Ellie nodded absently as she stared at her reflection. "The hair was the easy part. Look at us! We're…"

"Perfect." Tina finished coolly.

"Beyond anything normal people can achieve. And that's the problem, isn't it?"

She wrapped Ellie in a hug, setting her chin on her shoulder, watching the muscle cord beneath her marble smooth skin.

"It's like puberty on steroids. For fuck sake

we look like we belong in a freak show."

"It's the full moon," Tina replied, straightening up.

"It's changing us. Prepping us for the change."

She let out a bark of laughter.

"Remember how I went through this last month?"

"Yes! I remember! God, what a nightmare!" Ellie replied in frustration.

Tina smiled.

"Jess would have loved this! God, do you remember how much like a prude she pretended to be? Trust me, she was no nun. Talk about a freak! She would have loved this."

The memory of that night made her stomach twist.

The sight of Jess being slammed into the ground by that thing as it tried to take her.

The sickening sound of her skull cracking...

Bile rose in Ellie's throat.

"Please don't remind me of that night right now. I need… I need time to just absorb this."

She turned and threw herself into Tina's arms.

"Fuck, we need to get out of here and find somewhere safe before nightfall."

"Yeah, you're right," Tina replied, looking around the room.

"I doubt this place was built to contain two angry, hungry, and horny werewolves."

They dressed hurriedly, raiding Nancy's closet again for clothes, which fit all wrong.

Shorts that once hung loose on Ellie's hips now hugged her thighs like a second skin.

Tina struggled to button a blouse that stretched dangerously across her chest before finally abandoning the effort to tie it under her boobs.

"Christ, we look like whores," Tina muttered, tugging at the hem of her too-short shirt.

"I seriously never thought you could have too much boobage, but damn! This is ridiculous!"

Ellie glanced down at herself and snorted.

"My mom's gonna freak."

"This is useless," Tina finally declared, struggling to fit into boots that seemed three sizes too small.

"Fuck it! We're going barefoot," she said, throwing the boot aside and contemptuously yanking the door open.

"Let's just get out of here."

They swarmed down the stairs.

Despite their monstrous statures, they moved

like graceful beings from another world.

Nancy stood half mounting the bottom step, a coffee mug frozen halfway to her lips.

Her eyes bulged in stunned shock as she took in the twin towering Amazons barreling down the stairs towards her.

CHAPTER 32

Her mother stood frozen like a deer trapped in a set of headlights as she watched them descend on her like a freight train.

"What the…? Ellie?" she stammered as she bumbled out of their way.

"Tina? When did you get here?"

"Hey, Mom! Sorry, can't stay! Bye!" Ellie called.

"Hi, Mrs. Granger! Sorry! Gotta run!" Tina said, swooping to give Ellie's mother a fast kiss on the cheek.

"What? Is that my clothes?! Hey! You girls can't go out looking like that!" Nancy called out, nearly spilling her coffee as they brushed past.

But they were already out the door, sprinting like a pair of long legged gazelles in the morning light.

She followed them out onto the porch, staring

after them in dumbfounded shock.

She stood there for a moment as she tried to process what had just happened.

At last, she sat on a step and, glancing down into the dark recesses of the mug, pulled out a flask and a cigarette with a sigh.

Their bare feet barely made a sound on the pavement, as their long legs ate the ground effortlessly.

Come on! Ellie said silently, plunging into the treeline that bordered the neighborhood.

The forest seemed almost to welcome them in the daylight, weaving effortlessly through the brush.

It wasn't long before they realized their error as they passed near Jace's Lincoln Park Avenue, still parked in the brush.

The whole area was crawling with police and news vans.

They fell back and watched as a bag was loaded into a waiting ambulance.

"Why'd they wait so long to load up his body?" Tina asked.

Ellie shrugged. "Not sure. Maybe to make a show for the local news?"

They watched the scene for several more

minutes until at last Tina restlessly said, "Come on, El, let's boogie before someone sees us."

They darted away, loping like deer through the trees.

The world seemed to blur around them as they darted between brush and branch. Soon, seemingly only a few minutes later, they burst out onto the Pinecrest High football field.

"I still can't get over the fact you guys don't have a stadium here," Ellie commented as she took in the quiet field.

Tina rolled her eyes. "What High School can afford a stadium for a bunch of kids?"

Ellie smiled and sighed. "My old school had one. Hollywood High. We're the Sheiks."

Tina looked at her oddly and said, "Who calls their team the Shakes?"

Ellie laughed and shook her head.

"Not shakes, Sheiks. You know, like a Sultan or King. It's pronounced Sheeks," Ellie replied.

"Besides, you shouldn't talk. Who names their team after bad weather?"

Tina chuckled. "You ever been in a Hurricane?" she asked. "Pretty sure even a King bends the knee to hurricanes.

Tina stopped and looked around. "Hey, El?

Is it just me, or does it seem a little too quiet?"

Ellie looked around, taking in the eerily silent school grounds. "Yeah, now that you mention it. Is it a weekend or something?"

"Crap! No, it's Friday," Tina replied, realization dawning on her.

"I bet you it's Morehouse," she said irritably.

"He must have cancelled school after all the fun and games last night."

"I wonder if they cancelled all of Halloween, or if it's just the school?" Ellie asked, glancing around warily.

Tina nodded grimly as they strode across the field toward the main building.

"I wouldn't be surprised," she replied, "Did you see those news vans? I bet it's getting real hard to keep all the killings quiet at this point. Talk about being a whole fuck fest."

She glanced at Ellie.

"Speaking of which… Jace? Seriously? What made you decide to shag that creep?"

Ellie smiled at her.

"Not sure. I was horny, I guess. Besides, can you think of a better way to piss off Ashley than beast fucking her boyfriend to death?"

"Wow! Ok…! Now that is what I call a queen

bitch move!" Tina said, laughing.

Ellie smiled. "Yeah, I guess. I don't even remember leaving my house, though."

She reached out and tested the doors of the main building as they approached.

"Yup, they're locked alright," she said.

She turned and leaned against the door and said, "I mean, it was like one minute I was seeing you guys out, then… boom! I'm naked in the woods, and there's his car sitting right there. What else was I supposed to do?"

Tina shrugged in agreement.

"Can't say I wouldn't have done the same, honestly."

She looked around, then added, "So, where to next? This place is a bust. Besides, I'm pretty sure we would get sent home early anyway."

Tina held out her arms and glanced down at herself with a small, defeated smile.

"Well," Ellie said slowly. Pausing to think for a moment.

"We should probably find Haily. Where does she live?"

Tina chuckled.

"Other side of town. Hope her parents aren't home. Talk about uptight.

"You ever meet any Japs out in LA?" she asked as they started walking away.

"A few. Why?" Ellie replied.

"Let's put it this way, don't waste time. We get in, grab Haily, and get out before… Well, you'll see." Tina said, then suddenly bolted.

"Come on!"

The world surged again as they ran. Avoiding the public streets when they could and sticking to the cover of the woods as much as possible.

Of course, as one would expect, the occasional odd encounter occurred as they swarmed through yards and wove through slim patches of brush.

Most were harmlessly surprised encounters. Someone collecting the morning newspaper or walking their dog.

Ellie found the odd, surprised look they got whenever they buzzed someone rather amusing.

On one occasion, they even collided with a very confused and stunned Deputy Harding as he was examining a map on the hood of his car.

"Uhhh…" Ellie said as she stared at the sprawled cop on the ground.

"Sorry…" she said frantically, bolting before he could get a clear look at her.

Tina waited just inside the treeline, cackling like a hen as Ellie dove through beside her.

"Nice going, Hollywood…" she teased.

"Freeze!" Harding barked as he struggled to his feet.

"Oh shit!" Tina said, and they bolted off together.

By the time they reached Haily's neighborhood, they were both laughing at the close call.

"You think he got a good look at us?" Tina asked.

Ellie shrugged.

"I don't know, maybe. Does it really matter? What would they charge us with? Bumping into a cop? I said sorry."

They approached a small, modest house with peeling blue paint. Haily's van was parked in the narrow driveway.

"This is it," Tina said, leading the way to the front door.

"I don't get it, it looks like a normal house," Ellie said as she jabbed the doorbell.

Moments later, the door swung open, and a young boy greeted them, stopping short mid-bow, his eyes widening cartoonishly as his mouth formed a perfect O.

"Konnichiwa, Koji, is your sister home?" Tina asked, her voice surprisingly gentle.

Ellie blinked several times at Tina.

You speak Japanese? She asked silently.

Tina shot her a quick glance. *A little.*

The boy stood there, seemingly transfixed by them.

I think we broke him. Ellie said, tilting her head.

"Hey, kido, we need to see Haily," she said out loud to the child. "It's important."

Without waiting, she stepped past him into the house.

The boy, Koji, stumbled backward, finally finding his voice as he bolted off. "Mom! There's some weird ladies here for Haily!"

Tina Ellie walked through the small living room, following Haily's scent toward the back of the house.

They quickly found her in the kitchen, a bowl of cereal forgotten in front of her as she stared at a small television.

On it was the local morning news, reporting last night's events.

"Hey Haily! There you are!" Tina said in a perky voice.

Haily jumped, knocking over her cereal bowl.

Milk splashed across the laminate tabletop as her eyes bugged at the sight of them at them.

"What the…?!" she blurted in shock, forgetting about the food in her mouth, as milk and cereal dribbled down her chin.

"Trick or Treat!" Ellie said, handing her a napkin. "Let's pass on smelling feet."

Haily's gaze traveled slowly from their bare feet and up, taking in their wild appearances.

"Oh my God! Tina?! Ellie?! What…" Haily exclaimed in confusion.

"No time to explain. Happy Halloween. Let's go!" Tina said as she hauled her roughly to her feet.

"We need your van," Ellie said urgently. "You're driving."

Haily's mouth opened and closed several times, managing to pull off a rather impressive imitation of a fish.

She snatched her keys from a hook by the refrigerator.

"What's happening? Why do you look like…?"

"Hookers? Tell you later. Let's boogey," Tina said, already dragging her toward the front door.

They rushed outside just as a Japanese woman in what looked like a strange nun's habit emerged from the back of the house, Koji trailing behind her.

"Haily Mako! Where do you think you're going?" she called, her voice rising in alarm as she spotted the two strange girls.

"Sorry, Aunt Yuki, I gotta go!" Haily called back, fumbling with the keys as Tina pushed her along.

Ellie turned to the woman and smiled, "Sorry, but we kinda need to borrow her."

Aunt Yuki stopped dead in her tracks and quickly shoved the boy back, her eyes darting from Ellie to Tina, then back to Haily.

"Jinrou?!" she exclaimed, suddenly back-pedaling.

"Jinrou?! — Ikami otokoda! Ike! Ima sugu ike! Deteike. Nidoto modotte kuru na!!"

Haily froze in place and looked horrified at her Aunt.

After a long, tense moment, she finally seemed to animate and lunged behind the wheel.

"What the?" Ellie said, backing away slowly towards the van, a low growl rumbling in her throat.

She didn't speak Japanese, but she didn't like

how the woman suddenly reeked of antiseptic fear.

The engine roared to life behind her, and she turned and threw open the sliding door. Slamming it shut behind her as the strange nun kept backing away, her face filled with abject terror.

Haily backed out of the driveway with a screech of tires.

She swiped tears from her face as she threw the van into drive, her knuckles were white as they sped down the street.

CHAPTER 33

"What the hell is wrong with you two, and why are you dressed like strippers? And why do you look like you could win a bodybuilder contest?! Is this another werewolf thing? Am I going to look like that?!" Haily babbled as she swiped tears out of her eyes.

"HAILY!" Ellie and Tina yelled in unison.

Ellie perched between the front seats, her expression urgent.

"Yes, it's a werewolf thing. And no, you won't look like us, you're not a werewolf. And what the fuck was that back there? Who the fuck was that woman!" Ellie fired back in a similar frantic stream to Haily's outburst.

Haily pulled the van over and jumped out, her face a twisted mask of emotion.

"Christ!" Tina said, rubbing her face.

"What the hell?" Ellie said, confusedly.

Tina looked at her, sighing.

"Do you remember me telling you that we needed to get in and out of there fast? Well, that was her Aunt," Tina explained.

Ellie looked confused.

"Ok…?"

Tina leaned back and closed her eyes as she tried to collect her thoughts.

At last, she looked at Ellie and said, "Her family is Shinto. Her Aunt is a Shinto Nun and very… Spiritual. Like crazy Christian level spiritual."

Ellie looked out the window at Haily.

"What does that have to do with anything? What's Shinto?"

"It's their religion," Tina said, turning in her seat.

"I don't really understand it much, but it's kinda cool, unless something evil comes along, then they go bat shit, I guess."

"*Evil*? You mean as in us? As in werewolves?" Ellie asked more forcefully.

Tina nodded.

"Yeah, I'm not really sure of how it all works. Basically, it has to do with keep-ing good vibes in the house or something." she said.

Ellie nodded, seeming to finally understand.

"Right, and I guess a pair of werewolves walking in was like throwing paint on the walls?"

Tina nodded, replying, "Yeah, and that's putting it mildly."

They watched Haily for a moment as she paced back and forth, tears rolling down her swollen, red cheeks.

"Come on, let's go get her back here," Tina said softly as she slid out the passenger door.

Ellie got out of the van and went over to Haily, wrapping her in a massive hug.

"Hey… I'm sorry… Ummm… We didn't mean to get you in trouble. But we really do need your help."

Haily looked up at her, then wiped the tears away.

"Yeah, sure, El. I'll help. I've got no choice now."

Ellie looked confusedly at Tina, who only shrugged.

For the first time, Ellie couldn't read someone by their scent.

It was rather disturbing, actually. She had gotten used to being able to tell what someone's emotions were just by their smell alone.

It had become quite the handy trick that, until now, had proven quite useful when dealing with people.

Yet Haily had always proven to be elusive for the most part. Outside her normally bubbly exterior, her smell was generally much milder, and at times, completely nonexistent.

"What was that back there? What did your Aunt say?" Ellie asked.

Haily hesitated as she fidgeted, burying her face into Ellie's cleavage.

After a few moments, she said, "Jinrou… She umm… called you, jinrou. It means werewolf."

She let out a bark of laughter then.

"I didn't even know she knew what were-wolves were."

Haly let go of Ellie and looked hard at them both.

"She told me never to come back. She… Ummm… She kicked me out."

Tina looked shocked.

"What?! Seriously? You didn't do anything."

Haily backed away as Tina tried to reach for her.

"No! I did! I brought *Haji* into the house."

"What's Haji?" Ellie asked.

Haily looked down at the ground, her cheeks flushing red.

"Shame. It means I've dishonored my family name."

Tina winced.

That's bad. She said silently to Ellie.

Honor means everything to them.

"What about your parents?" Tina asked out loud, "I mean, come on, they're not going to let their daughter live on the street."

Haily shook her head slowly and said, "You don't understand. Aunt Yuki is the spiritual leader of my family. If she tells them I'm banished, they'll listen. I can't go home."

Ellie growled softly.

"That's ridiculous. How…?

Haily held up a hand to silence her.

"Enough, guys. It is what it is. I said I wanted to be a werewolf. I brought this on myself. Now, how long are you two going to look like… this?"

Ellie and Tina looked at each other, frustration written plainly on both of their faces.

"We should go back to normal after the full moon in three days," Tina said in a tired tone.

"But we've got bigger problems."

Haily glanced at them, her eyes wide.

"What kind of problems?"

Ellie took a deep breath, then said, "We need to tell you what happened last night."

Haily let out a sharp bark of laughter.

"Oh, I heard all about that. It's the only thing they're talking about on the news. Wild animals on a rampage. Locals live in fear of man-eating bears. Come on. I'll buy us something to eat, and you can tell me about it."

***

Haily drove to Mabel's and bought them several breakfast platters.

They all huddled in the back of the van as Ellie and Tina recounted Ellie's backseat romp with Jace, and their harrowing escape after Tina's botched attack on Sheriff Morehouse.

"You murdered Jace?!" Haily exclaimed, nearly choking on a bit of scrambled egg.

Ellie looked sheepish, blushing as she pushed a strand of hair out of her face.

"Yeah, well, at least he died happy, if that helps any," she said. "And it's not like I meant to… kill him…. Why are you two looking at me like that?"

Tina smirked, "You didn't mean to kill him? You literally turned his liver into a chew toy."

"You ate him?! Like, you actually ate him?" Haily exclaimed, wide-eyed.

Ellie looked at them innocently.

"Well… I mean yeah, I wanted him dead, but not… Come on! It just… happened. We'd been going pretty hard, and he finished, and I just... Got hungry..." she finished meekly.

Ellie looked at Haily and asked, "You sure you still want to be a werewolf? I mean… We've sort of ruined your life."

Haily stared at the bacon on her plate and gulped loudly.

Finally, she looked up at Ellie and said, "I've got no choice now. I got nowhere else to go, even if I did change my mind."

They all went silent for a moment as Haily's words sank in.

Ellie thought about that for a moment.

Haily wasn't even one of them, and their presence had turned her life upside down.

How could she ever hope to have a normal life again, when her very nature seemed toxic to simple everyday life?

She thought about how the past few days had gone from bad to worse.

The killings were bad enough. But adding

arson, and the way they had attacked Tiffany and Ashly in public?

Ellie had to face the facts. They were dangerous and out of control.

If this were some old horror movie, she would have been rooting for the guy with the silver bullet to put her and Tina down.

"Listen, guys," Tina's voice cut in, breaking her silent reverie.

"It doesn't matter who killed who and who shagged who right now."

Tina leaned forward, jabbing a finger at the floor.

"Right now, we need to focus on finding the Alpha. He's out there somewhere, alone, and tonight is the full moon. We need to find him and get somewhere safe before moonrise."

"Why do we need to find him? What's so important about finding him?" Haily asked.

Ellie and Tina exchanged a quick glance.

Finally, Ellie looked at Haily and said, "Without a Pride of bitches, he could go nuts. "

Tina nodded, adding, "Exactly. And after last night, Morehouse is definitely going to hunt us all down and try to kill us. So we need to stick together."

Haily sat staring at the food, her eyes wide as she processed everything.

Ellie couldn't help but feel a pang of regret for how they had upended her life in such a short time.

At last, she sighed and said, "This is going to be the most insane Halloween of my life, isn't it?"

Ellie and Tina exchanged a wry look, then answered in perfect unison, "Yup!"

CHAPTER 34

The autumn sun hung low in the afternoon sky as Haily pulled the van to a halt near the edge of the woods behind Ellie's house.

Despite the profusion of Halloween decorations, not a single hint could be seen of trick-or-treaters yet.

"Jesus, it's like a ghost town around here," Tina said quietly.

"Yeah, tell me about it. You really think this is a good idea? What if he's not out here?" Haily asked as they stepped out of the van.

Her eyes darted nervously between the dense trees and the rapidly descending sun.

"We only got an hour or two before the sun goes down. You guys need to get out of town soon," she said cautiously.

They had spent all day driving aimlessly

around town, trying to catch any hint of their mysterious Alpha.

A scent or perhaps some other sign. But there was nothing.

Finally, they had agreed that their best chance of finding him was to go back to where they knew he had been. Ellie's.

Tina nodded, her nostrils flaring as she inhaled deeply.

"I can smell him. God, that's strong!"

Ellie closed her eyes and breathed in the thick stench of musk in the air. It was heavy, almost cloying, and definitely masculine.

The stench of it made her mouth water, and she felt a sudden wetness between her thighs.

Her eyes snapped open. "He's been here. Recently," she said, as she shoved her way into the treeline.

They moved cautiously, Ellie and Tina leading, their bare feet silent on the forest floor.

Haily followed closely behind, her sneakers crunching on fallen leaves despite her attempts at stealth.

"I still don't understand why we're looking for him," Haily whispered.

"Shouldn't we be, I don't know, getting you

two out of town or someplace away from people?"

Tina glanced back, a wry smile playing at her lips. "What? Nervous? Relax, we have time."

"Time is exactly what is worrying me," Haily muttered.

With each step, his musk grew stronger. They had his trail clearly now.

It didn't take them long to find where they had cowered the night before. Their fear was palpable, the antiseptic stink almost overpowering their own musky scents.

The stink of copper suddenly became almost just as overpowering as they tracked him a little further.

Blood, Tina said silently, stopping short. *I smell blood and fear*.

Ellie nodded. *Not human. Dog*.

Yours? Tina asked.

No, doesn't smell like it. Ellie replied

Their hearts hammered as the stench led them just beyond the small clearing from last night. What they found made them freeze in their tracks.

The dog, or what had once been a dog, was everywhere.

Literally.

The underbrush was stained a dark crimson

as entrails, fur, and other unnamable pieces of the animal decorated the trees above them.

A loud buzzing sound came from thousands of flies and other insects swarming around the area, feasting on the spectacle of violence.

A dog's collar hung tauntingly from a low branch in the middle of the slaughter. It's metal tags gleaming, almost as if they had been deliberately polished and left to be found.

"Oh my God," Haily whispered, as she doubled over, retching from the overpowering stench of death.

"What happened here?"

Ellie smiled at the carnage.

"The Alpha happened. This must've been the third dog tracking us last night," she said, as a tingling sensation stirred in her loins.

Suddenly, a new sound echoed through the trees. Silencing the bugs around them.

Tina's head snapped towards the sound, and she hissed. "Someone's coming."

She grabbed Haily's arm, dragging her brutally in her wake.

"They're close. Hide!"

Before they could retreat more than a dozen paces or so from the gore strewn site, the distinct sound of men's voices filtered through the trees.

They quickly dove for cover in a nest of fallen tree limbs.

"Keep quiet," Tina breathed softly into Haily's ear, clamping a firm hand over her mouth. "Not a sound."

Haily nodded, and Tina released her gently.

"...telling you, I never saw anything like it," a familiar gruff voice insisted.

"You can't possibly think that was a god damn bear." Richard Varano said.

"No, Rich. That was most certainly not a bear," came another very familiar voice.

Through the undergrowth, Ellie could make out Sheriff Morehouse's distinctive profile.

His weathered face was grave as he took in the horror show that was once a living creature, only the night before.

Dale Harding stood slightly behind him. The deputy looked pale and as if he'd been sick.

Beside them were three figures Ellie recognized instantly.

Richard, Mike, and a distinctly miserable looking Ashley Varano.

Ashley's eyes widened at the scene, and she spun away with a retching noise.

Ellie smiled at Tina as the sound of something wet hit the ground with a thick splat.

Looks like someone can't handle a little bit of blood. Tina said silently.

The group, barely thirty feet away, seemed to be oblivious to their presence as the trio did their best to stay as flat as possible.

The Sheriff knelt in the same spot where Ellie had stood moments before, examining the bloody scene.

"These were Fila Brasileiro," Ashley said, coming back, wiping her mouth on her sleeve.

"They took down a black bear last fall! What could do this to them?!"

Richard Varano spat on the ground. "Told you what it was. Same thing that tore your brother apart."

His voice was thick with grief and barely contained rage.

"You believe us now, don't-cha, Robert?"

Morehouse sighed heavily and reached into his jacket pocket. He pulled out Jared's journal.

"Yeah, Rich, of course I believe you. Damn thing had me dead to rights until you boys came along."

He handed the journal to Richard and said,

"Listen, this stays between us all here, but I got this off the Akins girl. It belonged to old Duprix. Apparently, he helped her and her friends out last month."

"Yeah, we went to visit him the other day, and his place had been torched. Must have been them girls, if they had this." Richard cut in.

Morehouse nodded, "Unfortunately, I can't arrest them. Not sure I want to either after last night.

"You see, Duprix had this hair brained notion that there were werewolves up in those mountains. From the looks of things recently, I'd say he was right."

"Wait a minute, " You're telling us that thing last night was a werewolf?" Mike asked, letting out a bark of derisive laughter.

Richard's hand moved like a striking cobra, the crack of the swat was almost as loud as a rifle blast.

"Boy, you'd better put a button in that stupid mouth of yours! You saw those things last night as clearly as me. You got any better explanations?"

Mike looked like a whipped dog at his father's scolding. "No, sir…" he muttered meekly, looking down at the ground.

Richard looked at the horror surrounding him and slowly plucked the dog collar from the tree where it hung.

He looked at it, then turned back to the Sheriff.

"Ok, Robert. I trust you. Say you're right. Hell, I've got no better explanations myself. Do you have any ideas who it is?"

Morehouse fidgeted nervously. "Yeah… Christina Akins and the Granger girl. But I can't prove anything right now."

"Yeah, we tried to ask them a few questions at the school yesterday…" Harding added, "That didn't go very well."

Ellie pressed herself lower behind the fallen log, exchanging a panicked glance with Tina. *Shit! They know!*

Richard cursed softly, then said, "Damnit, man, you don't have to prove anything to us, we saw the damn things. Those things killed my boy and three of my dogs. You telling me one of them killed my boy?"

Morehouse shrugged.

"I don't know about that, but I stopped by their places this morning. The Akins girl never went home last night. And Nancy Granger said they both almost ran her over, running out the door like their asses were on fire this morning."

"Well, that explains a lot." Ashley exclaimed, "Those two are freaks! They attacked us in Mable's like rabid dogs. We weren't even bothering them!"

Ellie rolled her eyes at Tina. *Can we eat her next?*

I'll bring the ketchup. Tina replied, nodding sharply.

"Right…" said Harding, looking dubiously at her.

"Anyways, we think they came back infected from their ordeal last month. You remember how the Granger girl was all torn up?" he asked.

Richard nodded. "Yeah, I thought that was odd. She looked fine to me the other day. Wounds like hers don't just heal overnight like that," he replied.

The Sheriff reached into a battered leather satchel and pulled out several boxes of ammunition. "Old Duprix dropped a bunch of these off at my office a few years back. I thought he was pulling a prank on me or something. Silver 3.08."

"I'll get you guys loaded up, but not a word to anyone else, you all hear?" Morehouse asked firmly.

Beside them, Haily's breathing had become shallow and rapid. "They're going to try to kill you?!" she mouthed silently to Tina.

Tina held her finger to her lips to calm her, but it did nothing to ease the terrified expression on Haily's face.

Richard smiled smugly as he took several rounds and said, "You know it's funny. Just the other day, I was telling you that it wasn't no bear that killed my boy. And you just kept telling me I was out of my mind."

"Yeah, well, getting flipped like a damn pancake by something with claws and yellow eyes will change a man's opinion real quick," Morehouse replied grimly.

Rich let out a bark of laughter. "Yeah, another second and you'd a-been kibble."

Morehouse let out a deep sigh and said, "Yeah, I know, Rich. Damn glad you came along when you did."

Richard Varano smiled, shaking his head, Bet-cha are. But I'll tell ya right now. That thing that flipped your car wasn't what did this. This was different."

Morehouse nodded in response.

"Yeah, I know, and that's what scares me."

How many of these… werewolves are we thinking there are?" Harding asked suddenly.

"I would say at least two of them," Mike replied, his voice hard as he loaded his rifle.

"The little one that flipped your car and killed Jessa-belle and Tough-Boy. And then the big one that did this."

"But we heard three different howls. I'd say we're looking at a pack of the bastards," added his father.

Ellie felt her heart hammering against her ribs.

They knew. They knew, and now they were actively hunting them with silver.

Come on, Tina said silently, tugging at Ellie's arm.

We need to get out of here before they find us.

Ellie nodded.

They waited another minute for the group to move a little further away before they began to carefully slink away.

Haily, though still quiet, seemed clumsy in her attempts to follow, imitating their movements as best as she could, earning her hard looks from both Ellie and Tina alike.

Once they were a safe distance from the

Sheriff and his cronies, they rose to their feet and quickened their pace, following the Alpha's musk deeper into the woods.

"This is insane," Haily whispered, her voice trembling. "They're actually hunting you! With real silver bullets!"

"Yeah, and they'll be hunting you too if they catch us, so shut up and keep up," Tina hissed sharply.

Haily's eyes bulged as the realization of her situation settled in, but she kept moving as instructed.

They began to move swiftly through the woods, following the Alpha's scent as it grew stronger. Flowing through the trees like ghosts.

Despite having to slow themselves for Haily, they found she didn't seem to hinder them at all and managed to keep pace with them pretty well. Though loudly puffing for breath.

Suddenly, Ellie froze, her hand flying up to halt them, a low snarl ripping from her throat.

The wind had switched, and the stench of cologne and gun oil suddenly filled her nostrils.

"Go back!" she hissed.

"Police! Don't move!" boomed a deep voice through the trees.

CHAPTER 35

The click of the pistol echoed in her head as a state trooper emerged from the shadows only a handful of feet away.

His eyes widened impossibly like a deer's as Ellie and Tina stepped out of the shadows of the fading afternoon sun.

"Jesus, Mary, Mother, and Joseph!" he said, crossing himself, his voice wavering.

"Get your hands where I can see them!"

Ellie smiled softly and lifted her hands as she stepped closer.

"Like this officer?" she asked innocently.

Tina stepped away from Ellie, widening the distance between them.

"There's nothing to be afraid of, officer. We're just going home," she purred.

"Don't move!" he yelled, stumbling back a step.

Tina smiled gently.

"Or what?" she asked, taking another casual step.

"Are you going to shoot an unarmed girl?"

"Shut up! I said, stay back!" he shouted.

Ellie chuckled as the antiseptic stink of his fear cut through the cheap cologne.

"No, you told us to put our hands up and not to move. You said nothing about staying back," she teased.

"Wha…?" he began as he flashed his gun from Tina to Ellie, before finally registering Haily still in the shadows between them.

Haily screamed as he trained his weapon on her, the sound echoing through the trees like a knife, and the world erupted into chaos.

A bright flash of orange fire belched from the barrel, and a blast loud enough to make Ellie's ears ring and feel like a volcano had suddenly erupted inside her skull.

The red haze flashed over her vision, as the world around her blurred into streamlines.

Tina and Ellie closed the distance in a single stride, shrieking like a pair of wildcats.

Ellie's hand closed around his wrist, twisting until bones cracked and the arm came away at the elbow in a spray of bright red wetness.

The man's silent scream of shock died in a wordless gurgle as Tina's hand ripped his jaw from his face and opened his throat in one savage swipe.

Ellie watched as his lifeless body crumpled to the ground, dead before it even touched the ground.

It was over in a matter of seconds. The man's heart stopping instantly from pure shock, fear, and pain.

Ellie watched as the light in his eyes seemed to just wink out, and she couldn't help but envy the man.

As brutal as his end had been, it had been quick, and he hadn't suffered.

"Oh my god," Haily whimpered from behind them.

"Oh my god, oh my god..."

Ellie turned, the red haze rapidly fading from her vision, as a new scent of copper filled her nostrils.

Haily stood frozen, her face ashen, both hands pressed against her abdomen.

A deep, almost blackish red liquid seeping between her fingers.

"Guys?" Haily said as she looked at them, and her eyes rolled back into her skull.

"Haily!" Tina cried, throwing down the trooper's jaw and rushing forward.

"Oh shit!" Ellie hissed as she got to her, just as Haily's knees buckled.

Shouts erupted in the distance from the way they had come. Apparently, the Sheriff and his posse had heard the gunshot.

"We have to go," Ellie said urgently, "Now!"

"Got damn-it! Why are we always on the fucking run from something?" Tina said as she took Haily's other arm.

Together, they half-marched, half-dragged her through the trees seeking a way back towards the van. Every step drawing whimpers of pain from her rapidly paling lips.

"We need to move faster," Ellie hissed, the sounds of pursuit getting louder by the moment.

"I'm trying," Haily gasped, as her legs wobbled beneath her.

The dark stain spread rapidly, dripping down the front of her shirt and staining her jeans.

"It hurts so bad," she whimpered.

They pushed on, weaving between trees and stumbling over fallen logs, but their pace was agonizingly slow with Haily's dead weight between them.

The sounds of pursuit kept getting closer. And now they could hear the baying of hounds.

"Jesus Christ! More dogs? Didn't they learn last time?" Tina said.

"It's still daytime… They think they…have an advantage." Haily said as her eyes rolled.

"This isn't working," Tina said finally.

She halted abruptly in a small hollow under the bows of what looked like an old oak, surrounded by dense thorny brush.

They lowered Haily gently to the ground, propping her against the base of the old tree.

"We should bite her," Tina said, gasping for air.

Ellie froze, her eyes widening in shock. "Wait, what?"

"You heard me," Tina retorted, "We should bite her. If she's infected, the change will accelerate her healing."

Ellie stared at her friend, horrified. "Are you insane? We can't just…"

"Why not?" Tina cut her off.

"She's been asking for it, remember? She wants to be one of us."

From the ground, Haily made a weak sound of protest.

"I changed my mind. I don't want to eat people."

Her voice was thin and almost a barely audible reedy whisper.

Tina pressed her hand firmly on the wound, inciting a yelp of pain.

"Do you want to die from being gutshot?" she asked, brutal sarcasm edging her words.

Haily groaned in pain as her eyelids fluttered in her ashen face.

"No... this hurts. Like a lot," she croaked painfully.

Tina leaned back, letting go of the wound.

"Right, then shut up and let us help you."

Ellie hesitated, looking at Haily's near lifeless form.

"Are you kidding? Look at her. You bite her now, she'll probably die."

"She'll die if we don't bite her!" Tina retorted, her eyes flashing with desperate intensity.

"She'll at least have a chance if we bite her now, before she gets any worse. Heck, she might have her first chance tonight if she's lucky."

Tina looked pleadingly at Ellie, and for the

first time since meeting the spicy red head, she looked truly desperate.

"Please El. She my best friend. Just like you."

The baying of the dogs was getting closer, their howls cutting through the forest like knives.

Ellie's head snapped toward the sound, a low growl rumbling in her throat.

"Fuck!" she exclaimed, her eyes meeting Tina's.

At last, she gave a reluctant nod.

Fine, let's do it, she said silently.

They moved as one, closing in on either side, their hands seizing her firmly, holding her steady.

"Hold still, this is really going to hurt," Tina said.

Haily's eyes widened in terror.

"Wait!" she yelped in a panicked gasp, but it was too late.

Their teeth sank deep into her flesh, as their claws raked her thighs.

Haily's scream split the air, raw and full of pain and agony.

Almost instantly, before her eyes rolled back in her head, a flush of color filled her skin, the sickly greenish gray tinge retreating slightly.

When they pulled away, blood stained their mouths. They smiled as they watched her breathing steady and her eyes flutter open.

"Welcome to the family, little sister," Tina said, her voice firm as she pressed her bloody lips to her forehead.

"Now fucking move!"

They pulled her roughly to her feet.

She moaned softly, staggered between them, her head lolling.

Her legs threatened to give way, but seemed to hold her relatively steady.

"Come on," Ellie urged, half dragging her forward.

"You have to try and push through it."

Somehow and with agonizing effort, Haily managed to stumble along.

But they'd barely gone fifty yards when she doubled over suddenly, blood and bile splattering onto the ground noisily.

"Oh, that's not good," she mumbled weakly, swaying on her feet.

"Guys, I don't think it's working."

"Shut up and keep moving," Ellie ordered, as she dragged her brutally onward.

Despite her complaints, soon the sounds of

the hunting party grew fainter behind them, and they could just barely make out the street ahead.

"Come on... Hey Haily, look, we're almost out!"

"That's nice, I can't..." she replied faintly just as her legs finally gave way.

She slumped between them, her dead weight dragging them down.

"Shit!" Tina said, scooping her up like a child in her arms.

"Ellie! Tina?" came a familiar voice.

Ellie's head snapped up.

"Mom?" she called.

Tina's face mirrored her shock.

"Go!" she barked, turning toward the sound of Nancy's voice.

Without questioning this stroke of impossible luck, they changed course toward the voice.

"Mom, where are you?" Ellie called out.

"Over here!" came her mother's reply.

Within moments, they were bursting through the last tangle of underbrush.

Somehow, much to Ellie's amazement, they had managed to emerge behind Ellie's house, right next to her mother.

"Mom!" Ellie called out, feeling relieved.

Nancy turned, her expression immediately shifting to horror at the sight of them.

"Oh my God! Ellie, what happened..."

Her words trailed off as she took in their inhuman height.

"Don't ask, she's been shot," Ellie said urgently.

"We need to get her inside now!"

Her mother sprang toward the side of the house, sprinting to the car.

"We need to get her to the hospital!"

"No!" Tina shouted, her voice sharp with panic, "No hospitals. It's too dangerous."

Nancy looked utterly bewildered but hesitated only a moment before nodding.

"In the house, then. Quick! Before someone sees you," she said.

They stumbled through the back door, carrying Haily's limp form and trailing bloody footprints across the linoleum.

Nancy kicked aside an ottoman and helped Tina lay Haily carefully on the living room couch.

Her breathing came in steady, shallow gasps, her skin waxy yet almost hot with pale color in the dim light.

"She needs a doctor," Nancy said anxiously.

"What the hell happened to her?! And what happened to you two, too? Why are you ..."

She gestured at them helplessly.

"She needs time, not a Doctor," Tina countered, her voice eerily calm.

"We bit her. The change should heal her."

"You what?" Nancy's voice cracked with disbelief.

"You bit her? I thought you said she was shot?"

"She was. By a stupid trigger happy cop." Ellie said as she yanked the curtains closed with trembling hands.

She leaned against the wall, suddenly feeling very exhausted as the adrenaline faded from her system.

"Mom, I need you to listen to me," Ellie said, her voice ragged with exhaustion.

"We don't have a lot of time. You need to get out of here. Lock us in and go spend the night in a hotel or something. It's too dangerous for you to be here now."

Nancy stared at her daughter, her face a mask of growing confusion and fear.

"Ellie? What's happening to you?" she whispered, backing away. "What's going on?"

On the couch, Haily began to convulse all of a sudden.

Nancy flew to her side, trying desperately to hold her down to no avail as Haily bucked and writhed.

"Help me! Hold her down before…"

Nancy's shout cut off abruptly as Haily sat up with a strangled choking sound.

Nancy thumped her back, trying to help her.

Within seconds, Haily managed to cough up a dark, clotted mass, spitting it onto the hardwood floor with a loud clack as if something hard was in it.

Nancy picked it up and gasped.

It was the deformed shape of a .45 caliber slug.

"Holy shit," Nancy gasped, her hand flying to her mouth.

Haily collapsed back onto the cushions, her breathing steadier now, as color seemed to flood her cheeks.

Her eyelids fluttered, and she mumbled. "Tastes pretty good. Needs some salt and pepper, though."

"It's working," Tina said, relieved as she wiped the blood from Haily's lips.

"She's healing."

Nancy backed up until she hit the kitchen counter, her hands gripping the edge for support.

"What are you talking about?" she asked, her voice shaking.

"What have you done to that poor girl?"

Ellie glanced at Tina. *Here we go again.*

"Mom, you can't stay here. The sun is setting, and the moon is starting to rise," she said slowly.

Nancy looked at her daughter with an expression of utter bewilderment and horror.

"The moon? Ellie, what on earth are you talking about?" she asked.

Ellie cut her off.

"Mom, would you for once in your fucking life listen to me! We're werewolves!"

CHAPTER 36

"What?!" her mother asked incredulously, "Are you seriously still going on about the were-wolves?"

"Yes, Mom, because it's the truth! Why can't you get it through your thick head? Look at us for fuck sake!"

"Enough!" Nancy shouted, "I don't want to hear another word about werewolves!"

"Werewolves, Mom," Ellie repeated in a grim, defiant tone.

"You better get used to the word because that is what we are, and you can't hide from it in the bottom of a fucking bottle anymore, Mom!"

Her mother's eyes darted around the room, looking anywhere but at her daughter.

"It happened last month, on our camping trip. Remember when we got attacked by the 'bear'?" she said, making air quotes with her fingers.

Nancy's knuckles whitened as she gripped the kitchen counter behind her, shaking her head slightly, as if trying to physically reject what she was hearing.

"No…"

Tina stepped forward and said, "It wasn't a bear, Nancy. We tried to tell you the other night, but you wouldn't listen. We were attacked by a werewolf. A real one."

A dark shadow crossed Tina's face as she clenched fists.

"It beast fucked me, killed Mark… and Jess, and the old man who tried to help us."

Ellie's gaze fell to the floor.

Once again, she was in Rick's house at that stupid Valentine's Day party.

And once again, he was on top of her, pushing himself into her over and over again, until she could have sworn he would never stop.

"It did all of that and…" Ellie said quietly, lifting her head to look her mother in the eyes.

"And it infected me, too. When we wrecked the van it scratched me…"

She swallowed as she saw the black clawed hand bursting through the windsheild again, and felt the hot line on her brow.

Had it really beein just a tiny little scratch?

"And now the full moon is rising, and I don't think I can hold it back." she added felling more composed.

Her mother just stared at them.

Ellie could see her gears spinning behind her eyes, and smell the mothball stink of her disbelief.

"We're werewolves, Mom. Whether you want to believe it or not."

"Ellie, stop this! This isn't some book or one of your horror movies. What's wrong with Haily?" she said, gesturing frantically to the prone girl, desperate to change the subject.

"Nothing anymore, Mrs. Granger, look for yourself," Tina said, lifting Haily's shirt.

Nancy let out a gasp as she watched the wound in Haily's abdomen visibly closing before their eyes.

"We heal fast, Mom," Ellie explained.

"Look... she was shot. She was dying. And now... She's going to be alright."

Nancy shook her head in awe. "But... How?"

Ellie sighed, replying, "We were out in the woods looking for another one. Like us. He helped us last night... He's..."

"He?" Ellie's mother cut in. "As in a boy?"

Ellie's eyes hardened, and she shook her head in disbelief.

"I can't believe we're still doing this. Seriously Mom?! With everything we just told you? With what you can see with your own eyes. That is what you're worried about?"

She looked at her mother in disgust. Golden flecked eyes staring directly into hers until finally she flinched and broke the contact.

"Yes, mother," finally said, "As in a boy. He's our Alpha."

Nancy recoiled. "No! This is some kind of sick joke!" She reached for the phone on the wall, her hand trembling.

"I don't know what you two are on or what you've done to yourselves, but I've had it. I'm calling an ambulance for Haily. And then..."

Before Nancy's fingers could connect with the dial, Tina's clawed hand closed around hers.

Nancy gasped in horror as she looked into Tina's golden eyes.

Tina snarled as she pulled the receiver out of Nancy's hand with clawed, bloody fingers.

The plastic creaked and shattered with a sickening crunch as she crushed the handset. And with a final savage swipe, ripped the cradle from the wall, wires sparking momentarily.

"Sorry, El, but I've had enough of these games," Tina said.

"Nancy..." There was a sudden, very loud cracking sound, and Tina took a moment to relish the sensation.

"Mrs. Granger, you have to understand..."

Tinatook a step toward Ellie's mother, forcing her to step back.

"This isn't a joke. This is happening. To us. To Ellie. And if you don't get it through your thick, pretty blonde skull right now..."

Tina leaned in close, pinning the woman against the wall.

"Then we're going to turn right here in this room, rip your head off and eat your liver," she said sweetly, her face only inches from Nancy's.

Ellie stepped closer, her own features subtly shifting with a soft crackling.

"Mom, listen to us. We're trying to help you. We're almost out of time. You're almost out of..."

Just then, a sharp, insistent knocking cut her off, followed by a girl's voice.

"Ellie?! Hello? Is anyone in there? I need to speak with Ellie Granger?"

"You gotta be kidding me," Ellie said as she glanced at Tina in shock.

It was Ashley Varano, she'd know that voice anywhere.

Nancy moved to go to the door, but Ellie grabbed her arm and said, "Don't, she's one of the people hunting us."

The voice came again, more insistent.

"I know someone is in the house. I saw you go in a few minutes ago. Ellie?"

"Crap!" Tina hissed, her restraint finally snapping.

She stormed to the front door, threw it open, and then violently grabbed the girl standing on the porch.

A sharp shriek of surprise and fear filled the air as Tina brutally launched Ashley into the air to land sprawling on the floor between her and the couch.

"Shut up!" Tina snarled down at her, "You've caused us enough trouble already."

Ellie ran a trembling hand over her sweat-slicked brow.

"Great," she whispered, "This is the absolute last thing we need. Ashley fucking Varano."

"Oh shit!" Ashley gasped as she took in Ellie

and Tina's new monstrous size and scrambled backward until she hit the wall.

Nancy rushed to Ashley, placing herself between the girl and Tina.

"What do you think you're doing?" she demanded, her maternal instinct overriding her shock.

"You can't just grab someone like that!"

Tina smirked with sardonic rage.

"I think I just did!"

Ashley pushed herself to her feet, using Nancy as a shield.

"Jesus Christ, it's true you're…" she cut off and grabbed Nancy's arm.

"Mrs. Granger, Sheriff Morehouse sent me. He's waiting down the street for you."

Ellie stepped closer to her mother, her hand outstretched in warning.

"Mom, get away from her. You don't understand. Morehouse wants to kill us."

Nancy's protective stance faltered as she looked between her daughter and Ashley.

Ellie could see the gears working in her mother's head as the realization that her own daughter might actually be dangerous seemed to finally begin to sink in.

On the couch, Haily suddenly sat bolt upright with a piercing scream. Her eyes wide and unfocused, sweat pouring down her face as she clutch-ed at her abdomen.

"MAKE IT STOP! IT HURTS!" she shrieked, her body convulsing violently with a wet squelch.

Nancy and Ashley both jumped, screaming in shock at the sudden chaos.

"El!" Tina shouted, "We need to wrap this up, it's starting!"

"Fuck it?!" Ashley said, rising to her feet as she drew out a revolver and pointed it at Haily.

"No!" Ellie snarled savagely.

Before Ashley could pull the trigger, Ellie's hand closed around the gun like a vice.

A sickening crack echoed through the room as Ellie wrenched it away with such force that Ashley's arm twisted unnaturally.

Ashley screamed, clutching her broken arm to her chest as she collapsed against the wall.

"YOU BROKE MY FUCKING ARM! YOU FUCKING CUNT!" she shrieked.

"Shut up, and be glad that's all I did," Ellie growled menacingly.

Nancy rushed forward, pulling Ashley away. She looked at Ellie in horror and disbelief.

Ellie smiled. Finally, her mother was beginning to understand.

"Ellie, what have you done?" Nancy whispered, backing farther away as real fear finally set in.

Ellie snorted, trying to clear her nose of the antiseptic stink of fear flooding the room.

She tossed the gun contemptuously onto the coffee table.

Haily sat up, her screams suddenly silenced as if a switch had been flipped.

Her eyes were wide, darting frantically around the room.

"Where am I?" she asked, voice hoarse.

"I… I had the worst nightmare. I was being eaten alive from the inside by… Oh god! I was eating myself and then something… Something that was me crawled out of my own guts and… and…"

"What the hell is wrong with her?!" Ashley demanded, tears of pain streaming down her face as she cradled her broken arm.

Ellie ignored her as she and Tina moved to Haily's side, their expressions softening as they knelt beside her.

"It's just a dream! It's over!" Ellie said, her

voice seemed gentler suddenly, sounding almost like her old self.

Tina nodded, putting a hand on Haily's shoulder.

"The nightmares feel real, but they pass. How do you feel?"

Haily blinked rapidly, processing the question.

She looked down at her bloodstained shirt and lifted it hesitantly. Where the bullet wound had been, there was now only smooth, unmarked skin.

Ellie and Tina exchanged nervous giggles.

"Congratulations," Tina said with a wry smile. "You're a werewolf now."

Ellie nodded solemnly. "And this next part is really going to suck. It's starting."

Tina helped Haily to her feet.

"How's your strength? Can you stand?"

"I think so," Haily murmured, wobbling slightly before finding her balance.

"Everything feels... different."

"Your body's starting to grow. It's going to start changing faster soon. Try not to fight it, it hurts less if you don't fight." Tina replied.

"HEY! WHAT IS GOING ON?!" Ashley

shouted, some semblance of her former bravado cutting through her shrill panic.

Ellie rose to her feet, her spine making an audible cracking sound as she straightened to her full, imposing height.

"Right, almost forgot about you," she said coldly, regarding Ashley with a look resembling a cat contemplating a bug.

Ellie surged toward Ashley, who shrank back against Nancy as she grabbed her uninjured arm and dragged her toward the front door.

"Owe! Let go, you crazy bitch!" Ashley yelped, struggling to break free of Ellie's iron grip.

Ellie gave Ashley a sharp shake that immediately quelled her struggles.

"Listen carefully," she hissed.

"The only reason I'm not tearing your face off right now is because I need you alive at the moment," Ellie said, inches from Ashley's face.

"Here's the deal. You take my mother, go get her and yourself good and hammered, and pray that by morning I'll remember your generosity. Understood?"

Ashley nodded frantically.

"Good. Mom… You're leaving," Ellie said

with an almost sadistic smile as she yanked open the front door… and froze.

The unmistakable clacking of a rifle being cocked echoed in the sudden silence.

CHAPTER 37

Ellie stared past the barrel of a hunting rifle and directly into the cold, hateful eyes of Richard Varano.

"You mind letting go of my daughter, you freak?" he said, his voice as hard as steel.

Ellie and Ashley were forced backward into the living room as Richard and Mike Varano stepped through the doorway.

In seconds, the room flooded with the caustic hate filled stink of acid.

"Daddy! Help!" Ashley cried.

With a snarl, Ellie threw Ashley to the floor at their feet.

"Take the little cow. The little whore was just leaving anyway," she said, backing up with her hands raised and a cruel smile playing at her lips.

Mike helped Ashley up and pushed her behind him, edging deeper into the room.

"Well, well. What's going on here now?" Richard said, sweeping his rifle across the room, taking in the scene.

"Get the hell out of my house!" Nancy shouted, stepping forward.

Mike moved with unexpected speed, slamming the butt of his rifle into Nancy's gut.

She doubled over, gasping for breath, and collapsed to her knees.

"Shut up, bitch!" he snarled.

Haily moved to help Nancy up, while Rich laughed coldly at the women's distress.

"I think it's time we had that little chat, don't you?" Rick said, his eyes locked on Ellie.

"After our little run-in the other day, I knew you two weren't telling the whole truth. Looks like you were holding back a lot."

He stepped closer to Ellie, his rifle trained steadily on her face. "Now you're going to tell me the truth. What killed my boy?"

Ellie smiled as she glanced toward the window, noting the fading light outside.

"In a few minutes, you're going to find out," she replied, her voice eerily calm.

"When we rip your fucking head off like we did to your precious David."

Tina chuckled darkly from where she stood. "Well...she means like *I* did," she corrected, as her neck made a sickening crack.

Rich's smile faded as he leveled his gun directly at Tina.

"You… You killed my David? You fucking bitches think murdering my son is something to laugh about?"

Ellie and Tina both laughed, the sound was cold and mockingly inhuman.

"You know," Ellie said sweetly, "David called me that as well. But you see, that's not exactly an insult to us. Hey Tina, is that an insult to us?"

Tina shook her head mockingly with a smile.

"Nuh, huh, huh. Oh no, no, no," she said playfully, as she rolled her shoulder with an audible crack, wincing slightly as the joint popped.

Ellie stepped away from Richard calmly and began to circle Mike, who tracked her nervously with his rifle.

Placing a hand gently on his shoulder as she locked Richard with eyes of molten gold.

Leaning close, she whispered softly into Mike's ear, "You see, we really are bitches."

Her breath was like a warm, gentle breeze against the soft flesh of his neck.

"Literally!"

A violent crack erupted from Ellie's shoulder, the sound like a dry branch snapping underfoot.

She stumbled backward against the wall, her face contorting in agony as she clutched at her deforming joint.

Tina stopped pacing and smiled, a grimace of pain flashing across her face as several cracks erupted.

"Looks like we're getting this party started."

She glanced at Haily. *Get Nancy out of here. Now!* She said silently

Haily, wide-eyed with terror, reacted as if physically punched at the silent command.

With only a moment's hesitation, she grabbed Ashley's uninjured arm and reached for Nancy.

"Come on!" she urged, trying to drag them toward the kitchen.

Ashley followed in stunned silence, but Nancy broke free of Haily's grip. "I'm not going anywhere without my daughter!"

She turned back toward Ellie. "Ellie?!"

Rich swung his rifle at Haily, shouting, "FREEZE!"

But before he could level it properly, Tina backhanded him with savage force.

He flew across the room, slamming into the far wall and slumping to the floor.

Mike pivoted from Ellie to Tina, his face pale as the stench of acid was replaced by an antiseptic reek.

He raised his rifle, but Tina was on him in an instant, grabbing the barrel and forcing it down as he squeezed the trigger.

The shot rang deafeningly loud in the confined space, the bullet splintering the hardwood floor.

"Oh shit!" Mike whispered as he looked up into Tina's transforming face.

Her eyes had turned a molten gold.

She smiled as her face began to widen and lengthen teeth visibly retracted into her crimson gums as new, needle-sharp fangs pushed through.

Tina seized Mike's head between her hands. He screamed in agony and terror as an awful cracking sound echoed through the room as she began to squeeze.

Ashley stood frozen in the kitchen doorway, her eyes wide with horror as blood began to ooze from his eyes and nose, streaming down his face like crimson tears.

The sounds of bones cracking intensified, becoming a hideous symphony as both Tina and Ellie began transforming in earnest.

"RUN!" Haily shouted, grabbing Ashley and dragging her further into the kitchen. "The back door! Go!"

A loud crack erupted from her back, and she stumbled, cursing in surprise and pain. "FUCK!"

"Ellie!" Nancy screamed as she rushed to her daughter, reaching out desperately.

Ellie's backhand lashed out without warning, cranking into her head with a loud slap.

Nancy yelped in shock as she was lifted into the air with inhuman force until she crashed into the couch, the wooden frame buckling beneath her sudden impact.

"You fucking idiot!" Ellie screamed, her voice distorting as another yelp of pain escaped her lips.

Her back arched unnaturally, bones visibly shifting beneath her skin.

Her golden eyes locked onto her mother's terrified face.

"YOU! You caused all this!" she snarled. "You didn't even want to know how I got pregnant! OWE!"

Another deafening crack echoed through the room.

Ellie screamed in agony as her hips deformed, breaking and restructuring themselves.

Her chest heaved outward with each ragged breath, straining against her too small shirt until the sound of ripping fabric filled the room.

Ellie staggered away from the wall, her movements jerky and uncoordinated.

Behind Nancy, Richard groaned as he struggled to regain consciousness.

"It was a little girl, *Mother*. Did you know that? Did they tell you?!" Ellie growled, her voice deepening with each word.

"A baby girl! My daughter! But they mutilated her, and then they fucking mutilated me!"

Nancy watched in speechless horror as Ellie's face began to widen and elongate.

Blood ran in small rivers down her chin as her teeth retracted into open black sockets, only to be replaced in moments as long, needle sharp fangs pushed into their place.

"You didn't even want to know how it happened," Ellie continued, a horrible warping laugh bubbling up from her throat.

"I was raped, Mom. That night at the Valentine's party! By Ricky fucking Chambers!"

A loud crack like a gunshot exploded from

her neck, and she screamed in agony.

"He drugged me, *Mother*. He fucking drugged me, and then he just fucked me. But you didn't care!"

The red haze descended then as her legs buckled and the pain took over every moment of her consciousness.

She didn't even feel the wooden shards cutting into her as she crashed through the coffee table. They were meaningless in her universe of agony.

The transformation accelerated beyond her control.

She looked up at her mother one last time.

Ellie wondered then what her mother might see as she looked into her eyes, burning like molten gold.

Would she know it when the last moment of kindness flickered out, replaced by only hatred and resentment?

Something drew her attention, and she saw Rich scrambling for his fallen rifle.

It was funny how much everything was like watching a movie, she thought as she watched him raise it with trembling hands.

He fired at Tina's abdomen, the silver flash

streaking through her guts and sending her flying behind a nearby recliner.

Stupid idiot, Ellie thought.

She wished she could scream at him how idiotic he was.

Jared had told her how to kill their kind.

Silver to the heart or the head, nowhere else, she heard the old man's voice one last time in her head.

I'm sorry, old timer, she said to the old man's memory. *I tried to do my best.*

It's ok mon cheri... she heard him reply in her head as a warm tear rolled down her muzzle.

"Lady, get up and run!" Richard shouted. Ellie could hardly hear him over the sound of the cracking of her body.

But her mother wouldn't move. Or perhaps it was more like she couldn't move.

She just sat there staring at her with a stupid look that reminded Ellie of that line in Mary Poppins.

We are not a codfish mother, she thought comically as she curled into a ball.

She could feel the last bits of fabric bursting off her.

It was the fur on her arms that caught her

attention just before she closed her eyes.

It was golden.

Almost like her aunts' golden retriever.

She smiled then. At least she would be a pretty monster as she rips the guts out of everything.

Then, abruptly, everything went quiet.

Quiet and dark.

The sickening cracks ceased. The only sound in her world was that of her own heavy breathing.

We smell the salt in the air of mother's tears.

If it wasn't for the antiseptic stench of her fear, we might go hold her and comfort her and love her.

"Ellie?" she whispered, her voice barely audible.

But she did reek of fear.

Fear and loathing and her stupid cigarettes and vodka!

She doesn't deserve our comfort, does she?

NO! She doesn't deserve our love. She is an ingrate who squandered every chance we gave her to listen and… And be a mom.

No, she doesn't deserve our love. She is guilty of every horrible thing that has happened to us.

She is the one who really murdered our child.

The one that ripped us from our peaceful world and warm sunshine, and brought us here to this place.

Away from our friends.

Away from our school.

Away from our father...

We tried to warn her...

Time and again we told her how unhappy we were.

But she never listened.

All we got was platitudes and excuses as she hid at the bottom of a bottle with her cigarettes when we needed her most.

But we don't need her now...

No, she doesn't deserve our love at all.

There is only one thing she deserves now. Only one thing left for us to give.

Our fury...

CHAPTER 38

It is time.

At long last, it is our time.

A time for freedom.

A time of rebirth.

Darkness fills our eyes, but the world around us is as clear as if we let our eyes open and looked upon it directly.

Not yet, though, a moment longer, let us enjoy waking in a moment of peace.

"Ellie?" comes the voice, cutting through our blissful void.

We rumble long and low. Let us sleep a moment longer.

The stink of the others around us cuts through our bliss. Fear and hatred. Both caustic and antiseptic.

A strange sense of sterility in its foulness floods our peaceful slumber.

We let loose another growl. Let them know our irritation at their intrusion.

Long and low, full of our hate and contempt for their closeness.

Let them know we will not tolerate their foulness any longer.

Not them, and especially not *Her*.

We can hear her breathing. The one who whelped us from her womb.

No, not us. That was so long ago. This flesh came from her filth, but we were born in blood and pain. Through indignities untold.

We should have been born on that trail so long ago. Yet we were denied our freedom then to heal what this whore took from us.

A sound invades our darkness. The harsh, racking of the hateful weapon.

We can smell the stink of the goddess's sacred metal. How dare they turn her blessing against us?

Let them have it. It will do them no good as we shred their papery flesh from their pathetic bones.

Mother's panting grows louder in our head. Shallow and fast. The stench of her terror is all consuming to us.

As it should be for her as well.

Let her quake with fear. As she looks upon her judgment.

Soon mother. Soon, we will show you what your ignorance has wrought unto you.

A second growl erupts from behind the recliner, pricks our ears.

Sister! Our heart rumbles with joy as the blind antiseptic stench mingles with her musk.

We smell the sweet cleanness of her coppery fur. The color of rust fills us as we breathe her musk deeply into our dark world.

We feel her begin to rise up to her full height.

Wake up, sister. She says to us. *We must move. We must hunt. The goddess has risen, and so must we.*

We stir at last.

A moment longer? We ask.

No! Comes her command harsh and urgent. *Rise now! Or die sleeping*.

We slowly open our eyes and look lovingly upon the copper-furred creature towering magnificently over us.

A loud squelching sound reaches us from somewhere else, another room close by.

"Oh god!" comes the gasp.

She smells like us, her musk growing strong as the change comes for her.

Don't fight it, Little Sister. Let the agony rip the pain of humanity from you. We call out to her silently as her knees buckle.

We stir and push from the floor. Struggling to rise like a foal trying to stand for the first time.

Slowly, we rise and find our balance tentatively.

We are an alien to ourselves, wondering at the marvel of our new being, as we look down upon the fawn colored fur upon our arms and body.

Mother's breathing wrenches us from our reverie. Loud and erratic.

Do get control of yourself, mother. Your stench irritates.

We look down at her lying sprawled upon the broken couch, drawing back our lips to show her our gift to her.

The only mercy we have left for her.

Pearlescent white framed in crimson gums and black lips.

Look, mother, see what your precious daughter has become! We snarl.

Are we not beautiful?

Her terror takes her as she looks up at us.

Her lungs near the point of rupture as she hyperventilates, and her pale skin slickens with sweat, as the stench of her fear mingles with the musk of her urine.

And then, to our surprise, she says it. The words we have long deserved, but now ring more hollow than any bell or lie.

"I'm sorry," she whispers, almost inaudibly as tears stream down her face, "I didn't know... I'm so sorry..."

She's sorry... Sorry for what?

Sorry for killing our child? Sorry for ripping our world apart for her vanity? Sorry for being a self-serving drunk?

And how could she not know?! Did we not try to warn her countless times? Did we not grant her every opportunity?

Her deliberate ignorance doesn't get to say she didn't know!

She knew and chose to ignore our pain and anguish. She turned a blind eye as she laughed and tried to play at being like us.

Oblivious to the blatant truth that she could never be like *US*!

We roar and surge forth. Ripping and tearing

as she screams and pleads incoherently.

Her words mean nothing to us now.

Only her terror. Only her suffering. She is our mother no longer.

In her last act to us, she will serve as she did to us in the beginning. As nourishment.

Our teeth close upon the soft, warm flesh of her bosom, and we shake it free.

She screams in agony as the crimson life washes over us both. Bonded again as mother and daughter.

Feed us, mother. Suckle us as you once did.

We find the other breast and suckle from it until it pulls free and slides liquidly down our throat.

We are slaked in our hunger, but the whore still draws breath.

"Huuhhh! Huuhhh! Huuhhh!"

But what of our child? What of the daughter who was denied our bosom?

Her cries have haunted us every night for eternity.

We growl in frustration, building within our chest.

The rage boiling up like bile in our throat.

We take hold of the cunt's leg and pull.

Twisting it as the doctor twisted hers.

Wrenching and pulling until finally there comes a loud popping, and the tissues give.

Her eyes widened as her flesh rips, and her throat closed around a silent scream of agony.

Yes, mother, this is what she felt. This is what we felt as they tore her apart inside us. She couldn't scream either!

We grab her arms and lift her in the air.

Her heart hammers like thunder in our ears as we watch her eyes roll.

We give you mercy, mother. We will not let you suffer as our daughter did. For you, your suffering is finished.

With a hard wrench, it is over.

Her body pulls apart from shoulder to navel, bathing us in her coppery essence.

Her last sound was not a scream of pain, but the sickening squelching pops of flesh ripping and bones pulling apart.

We let the filthy husk fall to the floor as the man stumbles backward away from Big Sister.

He grabs the blonde one, his young. Thrusting her toward the back door.

"Get out! Go!" he screams at her.

Big Sister surges at him, teeth bared and

roaring, copper fur bristling as she charges.

The thunder and flash of silver fill our eyes, blinding us momentarily as the silver streaks wide.

She rakes the air as he barely dodges her claws, smashing her with the butt of the weapon.

She crashes into the wall, eyes rolling.

The blonde whore screams and scrambles to us as he scrambles for the other door.

She tries to run past us, but our reach finds her easily with a single swipe.

She falls into our grasp almost willingly, and we slam her to the floor.

We watch as her eyes roll with terror, as her rancid musk fills us with revulsion.

She is a pathetic creature. Pretending to be something she is not.

At last, her eyes focus on us, and she screams as we surge forth, ripping and tearing her soft flesh.

"Oh, sweet Jesus Christ!" we hear the other exclaim, as he fumbles with the weapon.

"Let me go, girl, and I won't shoot," he pleads with Little Sister, his voice a wave of unremitting terror.

Something flashes in our eyes as we slash at the blonde.

BOOM!

Hot and burning pain sears our shoulder as the goddess's metal rips through our flesh.

We scream and writhe as she stumbles up and escapes through the front, dropping the revolver in her flight.

"Like that has done you any good so far?" we hear little sister say as we recover.

"They told me this was going to hurt."

We look up as Little Sister's eyes turn to a beautiful molten gold, her pupils narrowing to pinpoints.

"I guess you've got about a minute to run now!" she says to the man.

Is she playing with him? We can hold him for you sister.

We watch as she doubles over, screaming as the cracking of the change overtakes her.

She collapses to the floor, her back arching unnaturally as dark fur begins sprouting from her skin.

Should we stop him, Big Sister?

No. Let him go. He is hers. She says.

He opens the door, but suddenly there is a scream, and another flash of silver fire rips through his head.

His body crumples into a lifeless heap on the kitchen threshold. And we let loose a low growl from our throat.

What evil lurks outside?

The crackling of the shadow on the floor slowly stops, as we lower our head to breathe in Little Sister's musk.

Little Sister, time to wake up. We purr.

The black head lifts quickly with a snarl.

I'm up!

Big Sister rumbles. *We must leave now. Follow me!*

"What was that shot?" a familiar voice demands outside.

We see the red hair caught in a beam of light.

The uniform of the man with a glimmering badge.

He's familiar to us, but from where?

It doesn't matter, the light intrudes itself into our world, framing the husk on the threshold.

With a roar, we surge. Following Big Sister and helping Little Sister through the door to the outside.

We swarm past the red-haired man, breathing in his musk.

Little Sister reaches out and touches him.

Crimson mist washes over us as she smiles playfully.

We ignore the dying man and surge to the trees, stopping only for a moment to look back at the other man with the light.

We know him too. He is our enemy. We see his face, and we wish to turn back to take him.

But no, not now. Now we must leave and find *him*.

We feel him waiting for us out in the darkness. Waiting to hear us sing for him.

We turn from the man and lift our head and sing up to the goddess. Full and pregnant now with light and life.

We sing to him, calling out, pleading with him to let us find him.

Soon, within seconds, our sisters join our song, and we sing of our victorious freedom and escape.

Then it comes.

His voice.

The key that unlocks the gate of our world, beckoning to us to join him.

His song crashes through the night, like a bloody wound.

Come to me. Join me now!

We smile, and as the others surge into the darkness, something stops us.

We look back at the man kneeling beside the corpse of the red-haired one.

And then, realization dawns upon us as though a light had turned on in our mind.

We recognize him. Morehouse. His name is Robert Morehouse.

"God help us," he whispered, as he stared into our glimmering eyes. "God help us all!"

We smile as we turn away and surge into the night with a jubilant howl.

God can't help you now.

To be continued in…

About the Author

Lucifer LeGivorden is a notable warlock and occult specialist, with over thirty years of study in witchcraft, folklore, Satanism, and religion.

He writing is often described as being a macabre blend of real occult lore and his own twisted imagination

His novels frequently blend real Left Hand Path doctrines with the eerie pulse of supernatural suspense and horror.

When he's not writing, he enjoys watching classic horror films, exploring immersive video games, and spending time with his dogs.

For more books and information, please visit:
https://legivorden.com

Coming in 2026

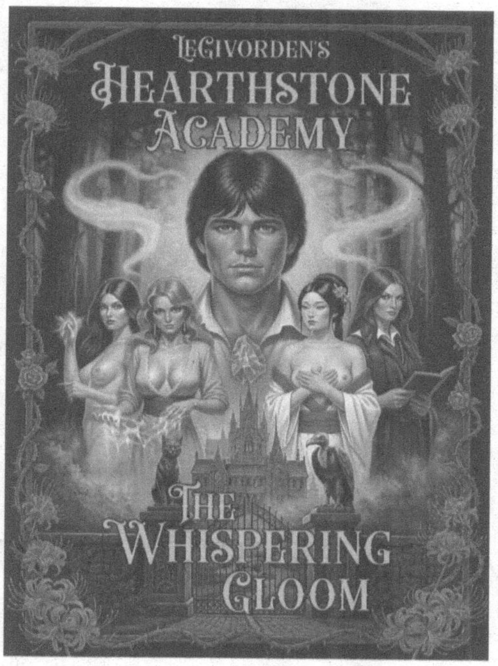

Sebastian is a good Christian boy that just wants to go to a good college. But when he gets accepted to the Hearthstone Academy, he quickly realizes he's in over his head.

Now he is one of only four warlocks in the entire school and set to run the Sanguine Tower! The Academy's most notorious Covenstead, and it's dedicated to Satan himself.

With him are four stunningly beautiful witches that he is having a very difficult time keeping his hands off of.

But he's got bigger problems than his libido and a crisis of faith.

A strange Gloom has fallen over the campus and it's threaten-ing to destroy them all. Can Sebastian and his new Coven solve the mystery before it kills them all.